The Hι

For

Wotak

by Denise Beddows

MISBOURNE PRESS

First edition

Published in 2020 by Misbourne Press

Copyright © Denise Beddows

ISBN: 978-0-244-85793-6

A CIP catalogue record for this book is available from the British Library.

Cover design by **Will Aldersley at True Story Digital.**

ACKNOWLEDGEMENTS

I should like to express my personal gratitude to those able intelligence men and women who work, anonymously and behind the scenes, to safeguard the sovereignty of our realm and to protect the citizens of this nation. They do so without recognition or fanfare, for little financial reward and often at some personal risk.

Chapter 1

Passengers queueing at Oxford Circus for the southbound Victoria Line train crowded the platform. As always at this time on a Monday morning, passenger traffic was at its height and the queues were backing up along the white-tiled corridors. Tugging down the peak of his khaki cotton baseball hat, Alex observed that the crowds were so dense one could hardly slide a sheet of paper between them. Uncomfortable and stuffy though it was, the crush suited his purpose.

The digital clock on the overhead display clicked away another minute. The illuminated warning to commuters that the next train to arrive would not be stopping at this station was reinforced by an announcement via the station's public address system. Despite this, as the distant rumble of the approaching train became audible, the crowd shuffled forward, inching towards the edge of the platform and jockeying for prime position for the stopping train that would be only three minutes behind.

This couldn't have worked out better, Alex thought, as he slid the slim stiletto blade further back into its wrist scabbard. Circumstance had just presented him with a better option. Lights now appeared in the mouth of the tunnel and the advance rush of air ahead of the train ruffled commuters' hair and whipped at summer dresses. The roar of the train grew louder and louder. Alex knew he had just seconds to act. His breathing quickened and his eyes darted rapidly between the oncoming lights and the figures in front of him.

He positioned himself immediately behind his target, a short man with greying hair and a bald patch. He rested the edge of his newspaper up against the back of the man's neck and placed his knuckles against the man's shoulder blades. Uncomfortable, yet unsuspecting at this contact from a stranger, the man shuffled even further forward towards the platform's edge. Edging up behind him, Alex now had a close-up view of the man's bald patch. He had followed that bald patch all the way from East Acton. His instructions were that the man must not be allowed to reach Victoria. The information the man carried in his balding head must not reach its destination. As the train rattled out of the tunnel and the noise and air displacement reached its height, Alex simply extended his hands quickly beneath the newspaper and gave the target a sharp shove.

The result wasn't quite what he had anticipated. He had expected there would be blood and flesh splattered all over the tracks, and people screaming as they were splashed with gore. However, it didn't happen like that. Hardly anyone realised a man had been hit by a train. The impact had flung the man ahead of the train and had launched him at speed into the darkness of the tunnel, where a large flash indicated he had landed on the live rail. There were no screams or shouts, only the intense screeching of the brakes and wheels as the train, which was not intended to stop, now did so.

The few people who actually noticed what had happened were doubtless struck dumb with shock. Of course, Alex reasoned, the driver of the train, at least, would be all too aware he had hit someone. As realisation of the tragic incident quickly spread in whispers back along the platform, those commuters who anticipated how it would affect their morning commute began to retreat from the platform's edge and head for the exits or for alternative routes. Alex joined them. As he stepped slowly away, he imagined the sequence of events that would follow. The shaken driver would probably be sent home. An ambulance would be summoned, but would take an age to make its way through the morning's rush hour traffic. It would be a pointless journey anyway. The man in the tunnel would be dead. Some poor wretches would have to gather up his broken remains and stretcher them back along the tracks to the cleared platform.

2

Doubtless, a search through the contents of the man's pockets would quickly identify him.

As he headed along the tunnel signposted to the Central Line, Alex ditched the baseball hat and smiled at the thought that the incident would almost certainly be written off as a suicide. After all, there were several such suicides a year on London's transport. He surmised that the station would be closed for hours; services on the three lines which passed through the station would be disrupted; many commuters would be inconvenienced; the coroner would be informed and, then, very gradually, everything would return to normal. The incident might not make that evening's edition of *The Standard* but should appear in the following morning's *Metro*.

A death in transit would appear suspicious to no-one, except possibly the Security Service, who, in any case, would not make their interest known. The target had been on his way to a meeting with members of the service in an anonymous looking house in Victoria. He would not now arrive.

Once seated on the Central Line train, Alex silently congratulated himself. This was a good method of despatching a target. It was less messy than a stabbing, surer than smearing a nerve agent on a door handle, and easier to arrange than dropping a dose of polonium into a target's tea. There was no need to smuggle in a banned substance or to risk being caught carrying a blood-stained weapon. Alex assured himself that, unlike those dolts who had messed up in Salisbury, he would not incur the wrath of his masters.

He was sure there would be nothing to connect him with the incident. Even if someone monitoring the station's CCTV spotted Alex's face beneath the brim of his cap, and if they thought it an odd choice of headwear for a man in a business suit, or, indeed, if they noticed the sudden movement of his hands beneath the newspaper in the split second prior to the incident, it was unlikely they would identify him. Even if they did manage to connect the incident with the hatless man who passed their cameras a little further along the corridors, who would think a respectable businessman would have any reason to push a fellow commuter under a train?

As he emerged into the sunlight at Bond Street, he felt quite elated. It was a lovely August morning and it promised to be an equally lovely day. There were blue skies over London and he had successfully completed another mission. The Colonel would be pleased with him. As the customary surge of adrenalin pumping through his veins slowly began to subside, he now felt hungry. He always did, afterwards. He glanced at his wrist watch. He had ample time to stop off for breakfast at his usual café and to compose himself before heading into the office.

Chapter 2

It was just after ten o'clock that morning when Harry Edwards returned to his desk at Thames House and placed the wrapped sandwiches on top of his in-tray. Prising the lid from the takeaway cup, he took a sip of the freshly brewed Americano. Next, he flipped open his desk diary to the start of the new week. He sighed. It was only Monday, and the entire working week still lay ahead of him. He swept back unruly strands of blond hair from his eyes then unlocked his desk drawer and removed some of the more pressing files from it. Settling into his chair, he decided to finish his coffee before getting stuck into his reports.

Lorna Bayliss now emerged from the office kitchen carrying a steaming china cup of Earl Grey tea. Smiling at him, she headed for her own desk.

'What did you get me?' she asked.

'Smoked salmon and cream cheese bagel.'

'From Mario's?'

'Of course.'

'Lovely.'

Mario's was their favourite little Italian sandwich shop. There were other sandwich shops nearer to Thames House, but it was worth walking an extra block for Mario's made-to-order rolls and baguettes. The ingredients were always fresh and Mario and his staff were impossibly cheerful first thing in the morning.

Another customarily cheerful face appeared around the door of the counter-espionage section. Fifty-two-year old Johnston Freeman worked in the mail room and was an inveterate whistler. He breezed in and deposited a small pile of envelopes on Lorna's desk.

'Anything for me?' Harry asked.

'Nope, it's all for Miss Bayliss this morning,' Johnston grinned broadly at Lorna.

'You seem even more cheerful than normal this morning, Johnston. You won the lottery or something?'

'No, Miss. Just waiting for Saturday to come around. Then I'm off to Kingston to visit family.'

'I take it you don't mean Kingston-upon-Thames?' Lorna teased.

'No, indeed. Kingston Jamaica. This time next week, I'll be lying on a beach, sippin' rum and roastin' me toes.'

'You lucky sod!' Harry said. 'Don't give a thought to us back here, roasting in the city.'

Johnston's response was to burst into song. As he headed back out into the corridor, he treated Harry and Lorna to a snatch of 'Jamaica Farewell':

'Down the bay where the nights are gay and the sun shines daily on the mountain top …' and then he was gone.

'I wish we were going to Kingston on Saturday,' Harry lamented.

'We're going to my mother's on Saturday,' Lorna reminded him.

'Oh. So we are.'

Harry consoled himself with the thought that at least their office had air conditioning. It offered a welcome refuge from the heat out of doors. It was probably as hot in London this summer as it was in Jamaica, he thought, but without the blissful sea breezes. Lorna, too, looked more comfortable now that she was in the comparative cool of the office. She had pinned up her long, dark hair that morning for their journey to work on the stifling underground but she now reached up and removed a few hair clips, allowing her tresses to cascade about her shoulders.

Harry watched her admiringly as he sat back sipping his coffee. He loved her hair. He loved her brown eyes, too, and the tilt of her nose. In fact, he loved every damned inch of her. He had probably loved her from the moment they had first met. That had been on his first day with the Security Service. He hadn't been able to take his eyes off her. He still couldn't. Some days, he couldn't believe his luck, since the lovely Lorna loved him, too. He reflected that they had been a couple for almost five years now and, even though they shared an office as well as an apartment, he still loved her as he had never loved anyone else.

The sudden ringing of the desk phone in front of him disturbed Harry's reverie. Lifting the receiver, he found himself speaking to a Special Branch officer. Harry jotted down the information, thanked the caller and hung up. Frowning, he dialled his boss's mobile. He was soon connected.

'Adrian Curtis.'

Harry could tell from Adrian's breathing that he was walking.

'Adrian, it's Harry. Where are you?'

'Just got off the train at Victoria.'

'Special Branch just rang. They had a call from British Transport Police regarding Pavel Stasevich.'

'I'm on my way to meet Stasevich now.'

'No point, Adrian. He's dead.'

'Shit!'

Chapter 3

It had been an exceptionally hot August so far. Those who had been summoned to Thames House the following Wednesday were pleased to make their way there in the relative cool of early morning, avoiding the rush hour. They filed into the building where they collected their passes from security. Given the collective importance of the visitors, the early duty custodian was on his feet to process them briskly but with due deference to their rank.

In the air-conditioned conference room with its tones of muted brown and burnt orange, the Art Deco burr maple table had manila conference folders neatly arranged around it, and a large basket of freshly baked croissants had been placed in the centre. The welcoming aroma of coffee invited the delegates to help themselves from a side table.

The head of the Joint Intelligence Committee, the silver-haired and softly-spoken Sir Stuart Bridgeman, was the first to take his seat and the others quickly followed suit.

'Good morning gentlemen ... and lady,' he nodded deferentially to the only woman member of the otherwise all male JIC. Helena Fairbrother was not the first woman to have been appointed Director General of the Security Service but, at forty-eight, she was the youngest female to have held that position. Her magenta-coloured linen jacket added a splash of colour to the mainly grey-suited assembly. Helena's preferred combination of flattering black dresses or separates, offset by brightly coloured jackets, had become something of a trademark. Her short brown hair was, as always, neatly coiffed and business-like.

'Thank you all for coming,' Sir Stewart continued, 'and for attending so early and at such short notice. Breakfast meetings are so much more productive, and I think each of us will have an especially busy day ahead of us today, so let's get straight to the issue in hand. As you are all too aware, Britain has been experiencing regular cyber-attacks over the past few years. Most have been sporadic and, we suspect, have emanated from one or more sources or states. Over the past twelve months, however, the attacks have become more frequent and more sophisticated and, potentially, more devastating. Helena, do you wish to remind us?'

'Thank you, Sir Stuart. Firstly, we had attacks on the IT systems of the National Health Service. These caused enormous inconvenience. Surgical operations were cancelled and staff were unable to access patients' records. Last summer, and again this summer, the systems of a couple of UK airlines were hit, causing widespread travel chaos and major backlogs at airports, both nationally and overseas. Next to be targeted were several high street banks. Computer-controlled timer mechanisms on their vaults were hacked, causing the vaults to open automatically at midnight; alarm systems failed and front doors unlocked themselves. Mercifully, only one branch of one of those banks was robbed and the amount stolen was only in the low hundreds of thousands'

'It was still a significant financial loss for one of our members, not to mention the loss of public trust,' chipped in Glaswegian James McLean, intelligence representative of CIFAS, the cross-sector fraud prevention group.

'Indeed,' Helena continued, 'though it could have been a great deal worse. More recently, we had the attack on the national grid, leading to major loss of power in large sectors all across England. Public disquiet was assuaged by statements attributing all of these incidents to computer failures. And now … well, now, there has been a rather sinister development.'

Helena turned to Adrian Curtis, the fifty-year old head of her counter-espionage section, 'Adrian, please expand.'

Adrian cleared his throat.

'Nine days ago, Ronan Rogers, editor of *The Times*, received a letter, copies of which you will find in your folders.'

Adrian waited for the paper shuffling to subside and for all the assembled visitors to read the missive. The first to react was Sir Robert Vanbrugge, the perma-tanned Director General of The Secret Intelligence Service. Vanbrugge appeared the epitome of a Savile Row patron, in his well-cut charcoal grey suit and gold cufflinks. The man had an impressive presence. Even his expensive cologne vied for attention with the aroma of coffee in the small meeting room.

'Good God! You've had this for nine days before bringing it to our attention?'

'Not I, Sir Robert.'

Adrian's voice remained calm. He was sufficiently senior and experienced not to appear cowed in the presence of those who outranked him.

'Ronan didn't think it was genuine. Yesterday, however, he received a second letter, seemingly from the same source, and, in the light of recent events, he decided it should be taken seriously. He brought the letters to me at my home last night.'

'Why to you?' Sir Robert asked.

'We're near neighbours and members of the same golf club. As you can see, the author of the first letter claims responsibility for all the recent cyber-attacks, and for a few incidents we hadn't even realised were attacks – such as the points failure and derailment of two trains last month. He's demanding a ransom, in return for which he will cease his activities. Now, please look at the second letter in your files.'

The awed silence that followed was broken by the impressively uniformed Lieutenant General John Hooper, Chief of Defence Intelligence. Even seated, he appeared taller than everyone else in the room. His generous moustache bristled.

'Christ Almighty! Oh, begging your pardon Ms Fairbrother, but the bugger's owning up to Monday's twitter hoax, too.'

'Not exactly, Sir,' Adrian corrected him, 'for, if you look at the postmark on the attached copy of the envelope, you'll see that the second letter was posted last Thursday. The faked tweet from Buckingham Palace, announcing the sudden death of Her Majesty, only appeared yesterday morning. He's not owning up to it in the letter but is predicting it. As you see, the writer states that some imminent news regarding the monarch would have thousands of people flocking to the palace gates and would bring the city to a standstill, which it did.'

'It also took the cricket off the air,' grumbled Sir Henry Mortimer, the pin-striped Cabinet Office Permanent Secretary.

'Quite,' Adrian continued, 'so I think it is safe to assume the writer, who cryptically signs himself WOTAK, was also the author of the hoax tweet. He must have hacked into the Palace staff's twitter account. Whether he's also responsible for the major cyber-attacks, as he claims, we don't know.'

Several voices responded at once. The loudest of them was that of Sir Arnold Mayhew, Director General of GCHQ. Mayhew had come to his elevated position from army intelligence and many supposed he might have developed his lung power from bellowing at his men. It was, perhaps, somewhat ironic that the booming Sir Arnold should be in charge of discreet communications.

'Good grief! Our people have taken down an inordinate number of hackers recently, but this seems to be a new one. Who the devil is WOTAK, or *what* is it? Is it an individual or an organisation?'

'We don't yet know, sir. We have our best analyst working on it and have come up with some possibilities, but no hard evidence as yet.'

Smoothing down his tie, Adrian continued, trying to make his reassurance sound less hollow than it actually was:

'We're following up a few leads. It's perhaps a bit too sophisticated to be the work of a lone individual. It could be the

11

Chinese, the North Koreans, the Russians, the Iranians, or one of the new breed of *hacktivists.*'

'Or simply organised crime,' Sir Arnold interjected. 'Russian organised crime, perhaps.'

'Has anyone just googled 'WOTAK'?' Sir Henry demanded.

Adrian checked an urge to respond *'Oh, no, we didn't think of that,'* and, instead, reassured the Cabinet Office man as tactfully as possible.

'We actually have some rather more sophisticated research capabilities than the basic internet search engines, Sir Henry, and, apart from a Welsh occupational therapy company and a Chinese air conditioning manufacturer, both known as 'Wotac' spelled with a 'c', we have found no company or individual listed as WOTAK with a 'k'. '

'Where were the letters posted? That might give us a clue,' Sir Henry asked.

Clearly, the presence in his folder of photocopies of the envelopes with their London postmarks had escaped his heavily bespectacled eye. Sir Henry had a net of red thread veins across his nose, which always mesmerised Adrian. No-one knew whether the weight of his substantial spectacle lenses was the cause of the veins or whether he might simply like his brandy a little too much. Adrian would forgive him that little peccadillo, though, as Sir Henry, whose remit also ran to being head of the civil service, had a reputation for being a fair and honest man. Trying not to be distracted by the Permanent Secretary's nose, Adrian answered tactfully.

'The first was posted in the pillar box just outside here, at the corner of Millgate. The second near Vauxhall Bridge – the nearest post box to *your* offices, Sir Robert. Perhaps he's trying to let us know that he knows where we all live, so to speak. And, before anyone asks, the letters were printed on a standard office printer using basic printer ink and the usual mid-priced printer paper manufactured by Britain's biggest wholesale and retail stationers. Fingerprints and DNA traces were found, but I'll wager these will turn out to belong to staff at *The Times*. Anyone with the ability to create such carefully planned mayhem will certainly have the nowse not to lick the envelope and stamp.'

A further thoughtful silence ensued, broken eventually by Helena Fairbrother.

'Well, gentlemen, we need to decide what we are going to do about it – collectively and separately. As a starting point, we should set all of our best analysts to work on identifying WOTAK and, in the meantime, Adrian will liaise with his counterparts at Vauxhall Cross, Cheltenham and Corsham to organise a joint tactical response. Ellis, I imagine your centre will take the lead on analysis?'

Ellis Graham, the fifty-four-year old head of the National Cyber Security Centre, was pleased to be asked for his input. Though his department was the most junior of all the intelligence agencies represented around the table, clearly it was the most appropriate one to lead what would be a Level One operation. His relatively newly formed offshoot of GCHQ had been tackling almost a hundred cyber breaches a month since its inception, but this would be its first Level One tasking. Ellis seemed excited at the prospect.

'Absolutely.'

Sir Henry, however, looked worried. He pushed his heavy spectacles further up the bridge of his nose.

'This couldn't have occurred at a worse time, what with the US President and other heads of state in London for the G8 summit.'

Sir Robert Vanbrugge had a sudden thought:

'You don't suppose it's more than coincidence, do you? I mean, Putin being in town for the summit, along with his dubious heavies and hangers-on?'

'I thought the Russians had been kicked out of the G8. Is it not the G7 now?' McLean, the CIFAS man, queried.

13

'They were indeed excluded following their annexation of the Crimea,' Adrian explained, 'but the most powerful man in the group, the US President, insisted we forgive them and invite them back to the table. Still, so long as they're inside the tent, we've a better chance of seeing which way they're pissing out – to misquote an overused cliché.'

Helena smiled at the allusion and agreed.

'Adrian is my Russia specialist. Neither he nor I think the SVR or GRU would try anything like that, not with the boss in town. They certainly don't need to be here physically in order to carry out a cyber-attack. And, as for posting anonymous letters, they have enough sleepers and assets around the place to do that.'

Sir Arnold Mayhew agreed, 'yes, and in any case, the Russian delegation members are under twenty-four-hour surveillance.'

As the meeting broke up, Helena motioned to Adrian to remain behind. Closing the door after the last of the senior JIC members had left, she re-filled her own and Adrian's coffee cups and sat back down.

'What Sir Arnold didn't say,' she confided, 'is that *all* the delegates to the summit are under physical and electronic surveillance.'

Chapter 4

The following day, over at 'The Doughnut', GCHQ's ring-shaped headquarters on the outskirts of Cheltenham, Sir Arnold Mayhew was holding his own breakfast meeting with his own heads of department. Unusually, the meeting also included one relatively low ranking-member of staff. Fifty-two-year old Colin Holder was a former field officer from the Secret Intelligence Service, now seconded to GCHQ as part of an on-going and largely successful series of temporary exchanges of personnel. 'Cross-fertilisation' was the term which had been used to sell the scheme to the main intelligence agencies and it had been running for some years already. It was also hoped it would obviate potentially dangerous rivalry between the agencies.

Although, in terms of his appearance and personal habits, Holder was unprepossessing, to say the least, his exceptional IT skills had made him easy to 'loan' to GCHQ. As his current line manager within GCHQ had explained to Sir Arnold when suggesting Holder be included in the meeting, their SIS secondee had an instinctive flair for interpreting and interrogating computer programmes and fathoming complex IT systems. He was highly adept at conducting forensic examination of computers, as well as accessing other organisations' systems. He was, as they say in the cyber intelligence game, 'the hacker's hacker', and he had demonstrated his worth to the cyber intelligence world in a number of successful operations. In addition, he also had some useful language skills. His laundry skills, his manager would occasionally point out, were sadly lacking but might, perhaps, be overlooked in view of his other abilities.

Holder was clearly enjoying the breakfast meeting, not just for the croissants and coffee, but also because his manager had told him he would be playing his part in the hunt for WOTAK.

Sir Arnold loudly declared to those assembled that the task would be one of the section's biggest challenges yet. He described the mysterious WOTAK as a skilled and formidable foe. However, he assured them, WOTAK would find that the GCHQ staff were skilled and formidable, too.

Sir Arnold further advised the meeting that Colin Holder was to join an inter-agency team which would be charged with identifying and tracking down WOTAK. He was to clear or hand over his current workload immediately and then contact the NCSC's Warren Daley over at Corsham.

The last to leave the room when the meeting broke up, Holder casually stuffed another croissant into his mouth and a couple more into the pockets of his corduroy jacket. He hurried back to his desk where he had a few important loose ends to tidy up before he ceded responsibility for the surveillance of the G8 dignitaries and their delegation members.

Holder sat at a corner table in the staff cafeteria to consume his lunch of meat pie, chips and gravy. He usually lunched alone and it seemed to his colleagues that he preferred it that way. At least, no-one usually sought out his company. The meals on offer included some healthy options but, in the main, they reflected the heartier sort of stodge served up at the public schools which had turned out many of his co-workers. Although Holder had been a grammar school boy, it was apparent that he shared his colleagues' love of comfort food. Today, he had some thinking and planning to do. Over the syrup pudding and custard, his expression of intense concentration slowly turned to one of resolution and he nodded to himself.

Back at his desk, he donned his headphones and played, for the tenth time, the recordings of the phone calls made from room 312 of London's exclusive Gorelands Hotel. He heard the mature and urgent tones of Hans Peter von Schellenberg, the German Finance Minister, and, by turns, the soft and throaty laughter of the minister's Personal Assistant, Erika Stratmann. It didn't need a fluent German speaker like Holder to interpret the nature of the conversation on which he was eavesdropping. It was clear from that conversation that the middle-aged Minister and his young assistant enjoyed phone sex as much as they regularly enjoyed real thing, and it was obvious to Holder that they were planning to engage in the real thing the moment von Schellenberg returned to the hotel from his meeting.

Holder now had a sufficient number of recordings and even a couple of covert photos he had taken of the couple entering and leaving room 312. The recordings of the intercepted phone calls were sufficiently explicit for his purpose. Saving the recordings onto his mini flash drive, he popped the flash drive into his wallet and, signing himself out early, he headed off to the station to catch the 4.10 to London.

Holder spotted the middle-aged Minister and his assistant as soon as he entered the Gorelands' sumptuously appointed restaurant. Flushed from their post conference coupling, the pair were now enjoying some juicy steaks and an expensive looking bottle of red wine. Holder's envious gaze rose from the steaks to the generous bosom of the Minister's Junoesque, blonde companion. The couple looked up uncomprehendingly at the shabby stranger who seemed so out of place standing by their table. Holder drew up a chair, sat down and, without a word of explanation, he produced the mini recorder from his pocket and pressed 'play'. The origin of the laughter and suggestive comment emanating from the recorder was instantly recognised by the Germans. The Minister at once grasped the implication. The blood drained from his face.

'What is it you want?' he asked.

'I imagine you are good for twenty-five thousand euros.'

'I don't exactly have it in my pocket,' the Minister was sweating now.

'Call your bank first thing in the morning – I believe your savings account is with the Spaarkasse at 13 Bahnhofstrasse in Hannover – and have them transfer that sum to this account.'

Holder handed over a piece of paper with account details printed on it.

'You can't hope to get away with this,' the German spluttered.

Holder smiled.

'The money will bounce multiple times around the world in a clever illegal banking system before it eventually reaches my offshore account. I'm untraceable and the money will be too. If the money does not reach this account by the last morning of the summit, then all the other delegates, your president, your family, your cabinet colleagues, your friends on social media and the German press will all receive copies of this recording.'

The blonde tried to snatch the recorder from Holder but was not quick enough. Holder laughed, ejected the flash drive and handed it to her.

'Take it as a souvenir. I have numerous copies.'

He rose and walked away. Strolling back to the station, he spotted a Turkish kebab house and called in to pick up a takeaway for his supper.

Chapter 5

Harry awoke with the alarm. Extending one reluctant arm from beneath the duvet, he smacked the clock into silence. His arm now swept the other side of the bed for Lorna but she wasn't there. Lifting his head, he heard the sound of running water. She was already in the shower. Harry's tousled blond hair obscured his view of the clock and his eyes were still blurred with sleep. He stared at the clock until the time it displayed eventually registered with him.

'Shit!'

He leapt out of bed and began pulling underpants and socks from the chest of drawers and a clean shirt from the wardrobe. Lorna came into the bedroom. She was wrapped in a bath towel and was dabbing a hand towel around her long wet, hair. Noticing the fact that he was half in and half out of a shirt, she frowned.

'Not having a shower? Harry Edwards! Shame on you!'

'Haven't the time. Why didn't you wake me earlier?'

'I tried. I re-set the alarm for you.'

Towelling her hair gently, she picked up the hairdryer. Before she could switch it on, there was a loud buzzing noise.

'Mine or yours?' she asked.

'Both, I think,' Harry grabbed his mobile from the bedside cabinet.

Lorna put down the hairdryer, tripped around to her side of the bed to retrieve her mobile, too. They both quickly scrolled through the text.

'You know Wiltshire better than me. How long will it take us to get to Corsham? Is it anywhere near your Mum's?' Harry asked.

'I'm not sure. I don't think it's as far west as Marlborough. They want us there by eleven o'clock latest. It says to bring overnight things and a few changes of clothes.'

Harry threw off his shirt and climbed back into bed.

'We can relax for another quarter of an hour or so, then.'

He reached out, grasped the edge of her towel, and gradually pulled it to him, drawing her towards the bed. She leaned forward and slid her hand slowly up his muscular arm. His skin was invitingly warm to the touch, whilst hers was still damp and beginning to cool down after her shower.

'A quarter of an hour?' she said, stepping out of the towel and sliding into bed alongside him, 'is that all I'm worth?'

'Lorna Bayliss,' he chided, 'shame on you!'

A couple of hours later, the green vintage Morgan was swinging effortlessly around the winding Wiltshire lanes. Harry was pleased he had cleaned up the points at the weekend. It was so good to be heading out of London in an open-top vehicle on such a warm morning and the old girl was running well. Seated beside him, his other favourite girl did not seem to be enjoying the experience to quite the same degree. It was too hot to be wearing a headscarf but Lorna's long, dark hair would be in tatters if she didn't.

'You'll miss all this, you know,' Harry said.

'Why? Are we emigrating?'

'I mean when we're married with a couple of kids.'

'Three.'

'Eh?'

'Three kids. One like you, one like me and a brainy one. That's what we'll have.'

'Oh, will we?'

'Of course I'll miss it. Maybe I should stay with the firm and you stay home and look after the kids.'

'Hmmm.'

A little way west of Corsham, they came to Basil Hill. All Harry knew about the place was that the site, once an army barracks, had encompassed an underground emergency government HQ during the Cold War, but it had recently undergone an £800 million upgrade. It was well-known in intelligence circles that, as well as housing MOD personnel and offices, Basil Hill Barracks was home to Ellis Graham's National Cyber Security Centre, and this was where Edward and Lorna would be meeting the rest of the tactical and IT operatives engaged on *Operation Skylark*.

'Wonder why they called it *Op Skylark?*' he mused.

'Ah, when I first joined the firm, I used to be in charge of allocating operational names. I got to choose acceptable names. Of course, no operational name should ever reflect the subject or target of an investigation. Some ministers are careless about carrying files around in public. If the press or public catch a glimpse of a file with the operational name emblazoned on the front, they shouldn't be able to deduce from that name what the op is about.'

'So, how did you choose the names?'

'I'd just think of a group of neutral things, say, rivers or breeds of dog, then I'd write down as many names as I could of things in that group. I'd allocate them on a first-come-first-served basis. Looks like they're using birds at the moment, and, so far, we're down to the letter 's'.'

'What was the most unusual group of names you ever came up with?'

'Well, that would be dead rock stars' surnames. I was quite proud of that one. Mind you, I had trouble with some of the chaps who wanted to call their project *Op Hendrix* when that had already been allocated, and I wanted to give them *Op Joplin*. They didn't want a girl's name. Well, tough. It was a case of take it or leave it.'

21

'So, Adrian or Helena wouldn't have chosen *Skylark* for this operation, then?'

'No. But, here, did you know, Adrian and Helena used to be an item?'

Harry hadn't known. This surprised him.

'You're kidding? The boss and his boss?'

'Seriously. It was before you joined the firm, and before my time, too. And before Helena became DG, naturally.'

'So, what happened. I presume they're no longer in relationship?'

'I dunno what went wrong. It can't have helped that she got promoted over him. He married someone else eventually. They seem to work together amicably enough, though.'

'Dear oh dear. I don't approve of office romances. Never know where they'll lead.'

Lorna blew a raspberry in his direction, though the effect of it was lost in the breeze.

Arriving at the security barrier at the bottom of the driveway to the site, they produced their IDs.

'Harry Edwards and Lorna Bayliss. Thames House,' Harry informed the security guard, who ticked them off on his clipboard and raised the barrier.

They followed the direction in which the guard pointed and soon parked up in front of the accommodation block. Checking in, they admired the bright new surroundings as they made their way to their respective single rooms. It seemed that the staff accommodation was strictly single occupancy. Harry had heard there were some first-class sports facilities on site. He would have liked to have used them but didn't think Lorna would appreciate it if he deserted her during the evenings as well as overnight, so he returned his sports holdall to the car.

Once they had settled in, they made their way across to the NCSC's smart new offices to be introduced to the other

22

members of the *Op Skylark* team. There were a few familiar faces assembled, including their own covert technical operations man, Kirpal Kohli. Like Harry and Lorna, Kirpal was in his early thirties and, although he was a practising Sikh, he eschewed the turban, was clean-shaven and kept his hair cut short. As a highly-skilled software engineer, his work was mainly office-based and there was very little he didn't know about computers and electronics in general. However, he was also called upon from time to time to join field operations and undertake surveillance.

Harry had once asked him why it was that some Sikhs didn't wear turbans. Kirpal had said he couldn't answer for all his co-religionists and could only say why he didn't. He explained that he had heeded his surveillance trainer's recommendation that one should maintain an unobtrusive appearance when surveilling people or premises. Accordingly, he had decided that wearing a turban would make him appear too distinctive.

'God will recognise me, even without my turban,' he had said.

Kirpal's technical skills were valued by his colleagues and he never seemed to take offence whenever Harry referred to him as 'top nerd'. A keen squash player, Kirpal, too, had brought along his sports bag in anticipation of using the sports facilities.

'Did you bring your squash racket?' he asked Harry.

'Er, no,' Harry fibbed, 'but maybe you could get a game out of your oppo from GCHQ.'

Harry nodded towards Colin Holder, who sat alone in a corner.

'What, Wurzel Gummidge over there? You're kidding.'

Lorna glanced across at the grubby bright green socks visible between Holder's brown suede shoes and his wrinkled trousers and she raised a hand to her face to discreetly conceal her amusement. Holder had also noticed Lorna and clearly liked what he saw. He flashed her the forced rictus which customarily passed for a smile. Lorna spotted it and quickly looked away.

She took hold of Harry's hand and this seemed to send Holder an appropriately discouraging signal. Harry had not noticed Holder's attentive stare at Lorna and he was surprised at her touch. They usually endeavoured not to broadcast the fact that they were a couple. However, he guessed she had good reason.

Another familiar face soon joined them. Forty-two-year old Corey Hart was based at the US Embassy and worked for the National Security Agency, America's principal intelligence service. He was Harry's regular point of contact at the NSA. As always, the affable Oklahoman was well dressed. Harry guessed the NSA paid much better wages than the Security Service.

Harry felt Corey was an able ambassador for the UKUSA alliance, as the agreement between the allied nations was called. The UKUSA agreement, which also included Australia, Canada and New Zealand – but nobody could come up with a clever combination of all those initials – ensured multi-lateral co-operation on intelligence exchanges. It was also referred to as 'Five Eyes', since five pairs of eyes were better than two when it came to the allies' intelligence gathering capabilities. The alliance was more important now than ever before, especially since the UK had quit the European Union and, consequently, had been denied direct access to Europol's intelligence database.

'Who's minding the shop, then?' Harry greeted Corey.

'Nobody. They're all up in town babysitting the President. I'm the only one who could be spared to join this operation.'

'Confirms what I've always known, Corey, you're not indispensable.'

'Sticks and stones, Harry boy, sticks and stones. As you know, though, it takes a whole team to guard the President – two to watch his back and four to watch his mouth. Never know what the 'stable genius' is gonna say next.'

An attractive young woman had joined the assembly immediately behind Corey. Fair-haired Rosie Leyton was Harry and Lorna's point of contact at the UK's Secret Intelligence Service.

'I guess you both know Rosie from Vauxhall Cross?' Corey asked.

'Of course we do,' Lorna stepped forward to kiss Rosie on both cheeks.

'Rosie and I are chums. We actually have much in common. We were both army brats, you know. We spent our childhoods in Germany, didn't we, Hon?'

'*Ja, das ist wahr,*' Rosie agreed.

Glancing over Rosie's shoulder, Lorna noticed that Holder was surreptitiously using one of the office phones. She nodded in his direction to draw Rosie's attention to him. The way his hand curled around the mouthpiece suggested it was a private call. From what they could overhear, he seemed to be asking someone to pop in and feed his cat. Rosie leaned in to whisper to Lorna and Harry.

'Holder there is a man of limitless imagination. You'll never guess what he named his precious cat.'

Lorna shook her head.

'Catto!'

'He certainly looks the part; an old-style GCHQ computer nerd,' Lorna said.

'Actually, he's probably the best nerd in the game, but he's not one of theirs, he works for us. He's just on loan to Cheltenham.'

'Why would you lend them your best IT man?'

Rosie hesitated for a second, clearly considering the wisdom of sharing a confidence. She and Lorna trusted each other, however, so she steered her friend to one side.

'Strictly *entre nous*, he's under a bit of a cloud at the moment. He's been seconded to GCHQ temporarily as a disciplinary move.'

'Why? What did he do?'

'Well, I'm not sure whether it was during his last posting to Warsaw, or the one before that to Berlin, maybe both, but he was running ghost agents.'

'Running what?' Lorna hadn't heard the term before.

'He told his desk officers back in London that he'd recruited a number of 'assets' – you know, locals paid to act as agents to gather intel for him. It's a standard strategy. Locals can go where we can't. Except Holder's agents didn't actually exist. He was pocketing the regular sums sent out for him to pay them.'

'Didn't he have to prove they existed, like the police do with their informants?'

'No. You can't exactly have your 'assets' sign receipts for the cash. A paper trail could compromise their anonymity and their safety. Of course, Holder isn't the first SIS man to have made a packet out of that type of fraud, and he probably won't be the last. His attachment to GCHQ is intended to keep him on ice whilst SIS decide what to do with him.'

'Crumbs! Do GCHQ know?'

'I very much doubt it. Bit of a dilemma, really. We can hardly have him prosecuted. You can see the newspaper headlines – *'007 caught with hand in the till'*. And he's too useful to be sacked.'

'I suppose, the trouble is, it's what we're paid to do, isn't it?' Lorna theorised. 'Lies and deception, I mean. We do it on a daily basis for HMG. There's always going to be the temptation to do it for ourselves.'

'Tell me about it!'

Lorna's face fell. It was clear she was regretting not having considered her words before she spoke them.

'Oh God, I'm sorry, Hon. I didn't mean …like … your Chris.'

'Not *my* Chris any more. No. He can have his bits on the side for all I care. For me, fidelity is everything. You've bagged a good one in Harry. Anyway, I've moved on now. I'm seeing someone else. So far, he seems to be a good 'un.'

'I'm glad to hear that. You deserve better. Is he with the firm?'

'Not our firm. Someone else's. Another country's firm, I mean.'

'Well, I hope he's NATO. Remember our training mantra – *if you're going to sleep around, sleep NATO*?'

'He is. He's a bit older than me. A nice, steady sort. I'll fill you in when I know whether it's going anywhere.'

'Do. We should have a night out and a bit of a catch-up. It's been ages.'

'Yes, let's make it soon. But look, don't let on I told you about Holder, will you? Hopefully, he's behaving himself over at Cheltenham, but, whilst we're here, just don't leave your handbag lying about when Noddy's around.'

'Noddy?'

'Yeah. Well, he shares a surname with the seventies' Glam Rocker, Noddy Holder. The nickname was inevitable, wasn't it?'

The morning's briefing kicked off at eleven-thirty and the colleagues soon learned that the National Cyber Security Centre had around a hundred highly trained and experienced staff, including IT operatives, analysts and investigators and many of them had useful background experience in computer science, commerce and academe. It seemed that a large chunk of the centre's staff, as well as their state-of-the-art facilities, were at the disposal of the *Skylark* team.

A half dozen of their staff were sitting in on the pre-lunch briefing called by Warren Daley, Ellis Graham's man who had been appointed to lead the operation. Since all the members of the team were already fully up to speed on the subject of the operation, Warren began the briefing with a brain-storming exercise and, in a soft, Northern Irish accent, he invited all those present to volunteer their thoughts on WOTAK.

'Okay, so yous have all seen the WOTAK letters. What might we deduce from those? C'mon, give it your best shot.'

One of the Corsham analysts kicked off:

'If he really has carried out all the attacks he claims, then WOTAK has access to highly sophisticated and expensive kit and software, so, probably, we are looking at a major state or a big organisation with big funding.'

'Or maybe he's simply a very skilled individual working alone – someone who really knows how to use technology,' Holder suggested.

'Hmm, a lone hacker with special skills,' Lorna pondered, 'perhaps a bit of a loner, maybe even someone with autism?'

'Not necessarily autistic,' Holder flashed her his seedy smile again, 'just very adept, highly intelligent.'

'But not smart enough to ask for a decent sum,' Harry interjected, 'after all, a million pounds is small potatoes when you are holding a wealthy western nation to ransom. He could have demanded a great deal more. I know I would.'

Holder didn't seem too impressed with Harry contradicting him. Another of the Corsham analysts ventured a view.

'Perhaps that suggests it's a major state-run attack, since a wealthy country or a big organisation wouldn't need the money. Maybe it's just a token ransom. Maybe seeking any ransom at all is intended to focus our attention away from a hostile state.'

It was a thoughtful Rosie who spoke next:

'A token ransom might still point the other way, to WOTAK being a lone wolf. Maybe he's not doing it solely for the money, but mainly to show how clever he is. Perhaps he's using this scam to showcase his talents.'

'Yes, he could be a narcissist, or maybe even a psychopath,' Harry added.

Warren Daly now chipped in. His accent was easy on the ear, Harry felt.

'Well, whatever the case, the UK won't be paying any ransom. We do not fund terrorism, and these cyber-attacks are just that – acts of terrorism. Terrorism doesn't just manifest itself in bombs and barricades. Believe me, I have experience of both. So, we'll have a great deal to discuss today and tomorrow, and mebbe the day after that as well. I feel we've already got off to a good start. So, people, let's see how many more ideas we can come up with before lunch.'

The two and a half days Harry and Lorna spent at Corsham were intensive but useful. As they climbed into the Morgan after lunch on day three, they were pleased to be heading home, not least because it meant they'd be back in their own bed again – together.

It took a few tries for Harry to get the engine started as his 'old girl' had been sitting idle for a few days. Eventually, however, the car roared into life. As they were moving off down the long driveway, Lorna noticed Rosie emerge from the building followed by Corey Hart. Glancing back over her shoulder, she spotted Rosie climbing into the passenger seat of Corey's BMW. She smiled approvingly.

Chapter 6

Piercing alarms suddenly sounded in the control tower at RAF Coningsby, startling Duty Officer Will Cummings into action and causing him to knock his coffee over his half-completed crossword. Moments later, two Typhoon jets were scrambled and were heading out over the flat Lincolnshire landscape. Just a few miles out over the sea, they spotted the two Russian TU-142 'Bear' bombers and soon caught up with the intruders, forcing them to wheel back around to the east.

At Lossiemouth, the UK's other Quick Reaction Alert station, three of the recently acquired Boeing MRA-1 aircraft were also taking to the sky, following an alert that another two Russian military aircraft had been spotted heading south down over the Irish Sea. These, too, were promptly located and firmly escorted out of UK airspace.

Cummings had attended all the briefings warning that Russian incursions into the UK's airspace were on the increase. He'd seen the confidential circulars advising that, of the fifty-two incidents reported over the previous five years, thirty-nine of them had occurred in the past twelve months. He had read in the press that the UK's territorial waters, too, had seen an increase in Russian activity. It was generally known in both the RAF and the Royal Navy that the Russians' latest Novorossiysk B-261 submarines were prowling the sea around Faslane, the home base of Britain's Vanguard class ships. Of course, it was no secret that, from Faslane, ships armed with Trident nuclear weapons patrolled and protected the British coast, and it was not just the 'senior service', but also the 'Brylcreme boys' who kept surveillance on the Russian subs that frequently shadowed those ships.

Official briefing notices made available to all Britain's armed services had warned that the Russians' latest submarines were

30

virtually silent and therefore very difficult to track. The reason for their presence in UK waters was known. They were trying to obtain the Vanguard ships' 'acoustic fingerprint' – a sort of electronic signature, which would enable the Russians to track and even sink the ships wherever they might encounter them. It was all part of the Russians' strategy of assessing the UK forces' response times and, thereby testing the nation's preparedness for war.

There were cheers in the control room at Coningsby when their pilots radioed back that they had seen off the interlopers and were returning to base. Cummings was just about to log the incident on his desktop computer when, quite abruptly, his screen went completely blank. He tried to re-boot the system but realised there was no power getting through to his console. He flicked his desk lamp on and off just to confirm there was no electricity at all at his work station. Glancing around the control room, he saw that it wasn't just his station that was affected. His colleagues, too, were looking at blank screens. Looking out across the runway, he saw that the runway lights had also failed. He snatched his phone receiver with the intention of dialling his technical section, but there was no dialling tone. The internal telephones, too, were powered by the base's electricity sub-station.

His attention was again drawn to the airfield where an armed response team was driving swiftly across the runway in the direction of the sub-station. A few minutes later, he saw them slowly returning. His main priority, however, was the two Typhoons still in the air. They had radio communications on board but the comms equipment here in the control room had shut down. He dashed across to the charger unit where, mercifully, half a dozen hand-held radios were fully charged, as a back-up means of communication held in readiness for any emergency. At least he could maintain contact with the pilots and give them clearance to land. As soon as the handset crackled into life, Cummings heard the familiar voice and designation of the pilot.

'Lost contact with you for a bit there, Control.'

'Yes, apologies, Mike. We've got a power outage here. Someone's gone to find a coin for the meter.'

'I thought the power supply was all computer-controlled now?'

'So did I, mate. So did I.'

Chapter 7

Three days later, at Thames House, Harry, Lorna and Kirpal had their heads together, discussing possible lines to follow in the *Op Skylark* investigation, when Johnston Freeman entered the office brandishing their mail.

Lorna was surprised to see him. He wasn't whistling as he normally did.

'Hey, Johnston, I thought you were in the Caribbean?'

'I didn't get no further than Gatwick, Miss. Them drone things was on the runway so the planes couldn't take off. My flight got put back a week.'

'Oh no,' Lorna sympathised, 'I hope you can re-book your leave.'

As a dejected Johnston left the room, Lorna looked genuinely disappointed for him.

'Poor Johnston,' she lamented, 'did you know he has a seriously handicapped son. The complicated arrangements he must have made for that trip …'

Her comments tailed off as Adrian breezed in with James McLean, the CIFAS man, in tow. Adrian summoned his team, including Carole Murray, his fifty-year old senior analyst, into the small briefing room. Adrian had a new development to report.

'We've had another letter from WOTAK. There's a photocopy here for each of you. This time, it was posted on Wednesday evening at a post office on Westwells Road at Basil Hill, just outside Corsham.'

'Basil Hill's where *we* were on Wednesday,' Harry said, 'that can't be a coincidence. Does the post office have CCTV?'

Adrian shook his head.

'It was posted in the external post box. Their internal security camera doesn't cover that box. And you're right, it can't be coincidence. I mean, WOTAK couldn't have known that the team investigating him was actually in Corsham that day, but he could easily have known of the existence of the Cyber Security Centre. Details of its construction were in all the papers when they were tendering for contractors. It could just be an educated guess on WOTAK's part that they would be the lead agency on the case. He's either showing how smart he is or he's trying to make monkeys of us. Maybe both.'

Adrian's team perused their copies of the letter. WOTAK had revised his ransom demand. He now wanted five million pounds and this time he provided details of the account into which the money was to be paid. Failure to pay up within seven days would, he promised, lead to a more serious attack.

'Can we trace him via this account?' Lorna asked.

Adrian turned to McLean to answered her question.

'No. He's using the Hawala banking system. In case you're not familiar with it, this is an age-old system of borrowing and debt repayment which, for a few decades now, has been used by crooks and terrorists as a means of money laundering.'

McLean went on to explain how the system worked, that there were no direct cash transfers involved. Electronic transfers flashed back and forth between unrelated accounts in a large number of locations across the Middle East and Africa, the sum transferred being used as payments of loans and debts for a large number of unconnected individuals and corporations. The end result was that the sum deducted from the payee's account ended up in the final recipient's account but with no paper trail and by a lengthy and circuitous route which would be impossible to track.

'Of course, we don't intend to pay him a penny,' Adrian said, 'but how are we getting on with identifying him?'

Carole Murray spoke first. Her curly black hair was lightly streaked with silver and she swept one wayward lock behind her ear before spreading out on the desk her copies of the WOTAK letters.

'Okay, so, we've got our psychologists looking at the wording of the letters. Though the text is brief, it's just possible they may come up with some sort of profile. We're wondering if this character might also be connected with an incident which occurred a few days ago at RAF Coningsby. Whilst a couple of their jets were engaged in intercepting Russian bombers violating UK airspace – yet again – the base suffered a total power outage. It shouldn't have happened since their electricity supply, powering the buildings, security gates and alarms, is computer-controlled.'

Kirpal also had something to say about the incident.

'I'm working with the RAF's IT people in trying to establish whether their systems were hacked. If they were, we'll see if we can identify what sort of malware might have been used. If we find the same malware was used in previous incidents, such as that business with the banks, that will confirm whether the incidents are linked.'

Adrian smoothed his tie between his thumb and fingers, something he often did when thinking.

'It seems an unlikely coincidence that the power cut should happen during a critical operation to counter a Russian incursion. This suggests to me that the Russians are behind these cyber-attacks,' he added.

'Meanwhile, we've still not found any individual or organisation named WOTAK,' Carole said, 'lots of Wotans, but no WOTAKs. Our linguistics specialists are considering what language or race it suggests. They're liaising with SOAS.'

Aware of a couple of blank faces, Carole explained:

'That's London University's School of Oriental and African Studies. We're also considering whether the WOTAK letters might stand for something. Just as we have JTAC, the Joint Terrorism Analysis Centre, WOTAK might also stand for

35

something 'tactical', say, 'Western Operations Tactical ... Attack Coordination', or something similar. It's all speculation, though. We really don't have a clue.'

'I'll go through our Russia files again,' Harry said, 'but I've never come across any branch of their military or intelligence with those initials.'

Lorna, too, had something to add.

'You, know, apart from the fake tweet about the Queen, WOTAK hasn't really predicted anything. Mostly, he's claiming responsibility for incidents which have already occurred, and he's promising more of the same. Maybe he's little more than an opportunistic extortionist.'

Adrian closed his manila folder and glanced at his watch.

'Well, there's another meeting of the JIC this afternoon and I have to attend. I wish I had something more positive to give them. At least the G8 summit is over and the delegates have all left. Now, we can all concentrate on the cyber-attacks. We've warned all government departments they may be targeted in his next attack. Hopefully, everyone will be tightening up their own IT security. Seems we'll just have to wait and see what this WOTAK does next.'

Chapter 8

A pleasingly unexpected vista of rolling, sunny meadows stretched out as far as the eye could see, as the grey saloon emerged through the Stokenchurch Gap on the M40. Alex turned off at junction seven and navigated the network of leafy Oxfordshire lanes. It was a warm afternoon and the beech trees were all in full leaf. Everywhere there was birdsong and the woody scent of hawthorn hedgerows. Soon, the car slowed to a crawl as the large gated mansion came into view.

Parking up in a quiet back lane just beyond the mansion, Alex removed the golf bag from the back seat and threw the strap of the bag over his left shoulder. Glancing up and down the lane, he satisfied himself there was no-one around and he walked towards the property. It was the perfect time of day, early afternoon – too early for mothers and *Au Pairs* to be heading out on the school run and much too early for anyone to be returning home from work. He glanced casually through the gates as he walked past the house. He saw the Minister's Daimler parked at the top of the carriage driveway just outside the entrance to the house.

He maintained his casual stroll and, glancing around to reassure himself there was still no-one else about, he disappeared into the wooded area which skirted the Minister's walled grounds. The woodland rose up ahead of him to a steep incline. The sharp gradient took him to the top of what was an ancient barrow, a scheduled monument nowadays. From the top of the barrow, he had a clear view down onto the Minister's manicured back lawn and extensive terrace. The Minister's swimming pool was very blue and very inviting on such a hot afternoon. He guessed the Minister would think so, too.

Alex put down the golf bag and withdrew from it the gun case. Removing the SVLK sniper rifle, he lowered its bipod and set it upon the ground before lowering himself down alongside it. Shuffling comfortably on his belly, he adjusted the sights until he had the Minister and his female companion in sharp focus. Of course, the SVLK wasn't the newest model available to a Russian sniper. The latest model, the Chukavin or SVC, was more powerful, but Alex had declined the Colonel's offer of one of these. Alex was used to his trusty SVLK and was very comfortable with it. It had served him well in the past.

Of course, it was risky transporting out of the city such a high-powered weapon, and one which would, if he were caught, betray his connections with the Russian military, yet he had no choice. This particular target never travelled by tube or rail but was usually chauffeured everywhere. He was rarely seen out and about without his personal protection officers – rarely, but, as Alex's best informant had revealed, the Minister had lately taken to giving his minders the slip.

The ammunition used would be identified as Russian, of course, but that was the point. Putin wanted the world to know that the Russians would not be pushed around. He wanted the British to know what would happen to a politician who stood up at an international summit and ridiculed him; a Foreign Secretary who led the other powers to threaten sanctions against Russia unless they ceded the Crimea back to the Ukraine. He wanted the British government to consider that the same fate might befall their Prime Minister, Ivan Thompson, the privileged clown whom he so detested.

The Minister was up on his feet now and was removing his white towelling robe. In a moment or two he would be in the pool. The time was now. Alex's heart rate began to increase as the adrenalin kicked in. He held his breath and began to close his index finger gently around the trigger. Suddenly, however, from the corner of his eye, he spotted a movement below him. He took his eye away from the rifle sight and glanced down towards the perimeter of the estate. To his annoyance, he saw there was someone else there. Squinting down the hill through the fairly dense foliage, he could just make out a figure. He released his grip on the weapon and raised himself up onto his knees to have a better look.

Unbelievably, there was a man standing on the roof of a parked car and peering over the wall into the Minister's garden. A bloody peeping Tom! What the hell? Alex now saw that the shabby little man held a camera with a telephoto lens. A *paparazzo*, perhaps? The sight made Alex shake with anger. He had rehearsed this job several times over the past few days and had even been out with shears, cutting back a discreet circle of foliage to ensure he got a clear view into the garden without being seen. All this preparation and, now, some joker, a newspaper hack seemingly, was going to spoil it for him.

For a moment, he trained his sight on the 'Pap', but he did not shoot. That could alert his true target and cause him to run for cover. He had missed the shot now anyway, and the Minister was in the pool. He could wait for the *paparazzo* to leave and for the Minister to climb out, but that could take too long. In any case, he couldn't risk being seen by the *paparazzo* who could jump into his car and get away long before Alex could clamber down the hill and get into his own vehicle. It wouldn't do for Alex to appear in any of his photos, either. Disappointed, he began to pack away his weapon.

Driving back along the M4, Alex took out his mobile phone, hit one of his speed dial numbers and put the phone on hands-free. Soon, he was connected.

'Colonel? It's me.'

'Is it done?'

'Not yet. I was at the house, but there was someone else there, probably a paparazzo taking covert photos of the Minister. I couldn't risk it.'

'*Nevezeniye.*'

'Yes, my bad luck.'

'What will you do?'

'If the reporter publishes his photos, the Minister will be on the alert. The opportunity to catch him off guard might not come again. A creature of predictable habit he may be, but, if those photos are published, he is unlikely to be cavorting in his pool again with his teenaged mistress. I will deal first with this idiot with the camera. The target can wait another twenty-four hours or so.'

'*Udachi!* But do it soon, Alex. Moscow wants it done yesterday.'

Chapter 9

The following afternoon was a real scorcher. The summer heat showed no signs of abating, and nor did the challenges faced by the Security Service. Adrian Curtis found himself reporting once more to the JIC.

'Yet another letter from WOTAK has been received. Copies are before you. Posted in Cheltenham town centre the evening before last, it is as brief and to the point as the others. He, or they, are claiming responsibility for the latest series of computer and power failures and there is clear impatience that we haven't responded to his ransom demand. The profilers couldn't get a handle on him, since there isn't enough in the letters to go on, but there is some good news.'

'Thank God!' Sir Henry Mortimer, the red-nosed Cabinet Office Minister, gave an exasperated sigh. Adrian chose to ignore it and continued.

'We have identified the nature of the spyware and malware which was used to hack into the MOD's and others' IT systems. It appears to have been recently developed by a London software firm – part of the Luxembourg-based Lurman Corporation. My officers are meeting with their CEO tomorrow morning to find out how widely this software was distributed and what its capabilities are.'

'I trust you've got your best IT people working on this?' the GCHQ Director General boomed, 'that Holder fellow, for example?'

'Yes, Sir Arnold, we're right on it. However, Colin Holder e-mailed in sick last night. Now, analysis of the pattern of incidents shows us …'

Adrian halted as a knock at the door heralded the entry of a messenger, who went immediately to Sir Stuart Bridgeman and whispered urgently in the Chairman's ear. The JIC members all seemed surprised and a little annoyed that the messenger should consider whatever news he had might be of sufficient importance to warrant interrupting such an urgent meeting. However, a flicker of intense alarm immediately spread across the Chairman's face.

'Gentlemen, I shall have to suspend this meeting. I'm afraid something very serious has occurred. Just this lunchtime, the Foreign Secretary, Geoffrey Bowker, has been murdered!'

That evening, the rush hour was well under way as thousands of weary commuters poured steadily into the city's tube stations, many of the passengers bemoaning the lack of effective air conditioning in London's ageing underground system. The rail stations, too, saw the usual build-up of weary workers eager to escape the heat of the city. As the crowds reached maximum capacity on the platforms at Waterloo Station, suddenly, all the train display boards started going haywire. The digital displays started to blink on and off and the wording turned to gibberish. At first, the commuters found it an amusing diversion and there was some laughter. However, when the display boards went completely blank, they stopped laughing.

Alan Blake, the station controller picked up the phone to dial the engineering centre, but found the line was dead. Glancing at his console, he also saw that, if the live train movements display was correct, all the incoming trains had suddenly halted on the tracks at varying distances outside the station. Cursing loudly, he pressed the button on his public address system, intending to make a bland but apologetic announcement to reassure the baffled commuters. However, the expected red light did not come on. This wasn't working either. It seemed there had been some sort of power failure. Cursing again, he ran to his cupboard, grabbed a megaphone and headed down to the public concourse.

The station had quickly become dangerously over crowded as commuters continued to pour in and tried to board the empty trains which would not be going anywhere, since the power supply to the rails had failed. Using his mobile phone, Blake called the police and requested the attendance of as many officers as possible to effect crowd control until barriers could be erected and the station could be officially closed. However, he was advised that Kings Cross station had also been hit by a serious power outage and so most available officers had already been sent there. Some officers would be diverted to Waterloo, but not immediately.

As the evening wore on, numerous trains with passengers trapped on board were still halted out on the tracks. The commuters remained stuck on board for several hours in stifling heat until Blake was able to rally sufficient rail staff to get to each train in turn, release the passengers from the carriages and walk them back along the tracks to the station. A number of passengers had collapsed in the heat of the crowded carriages and ambulances were summoned but they took some time to negotiate the rush hour traffic. First aiders gave what assistance they could, and staff at some of the station's cafés handed out free bottles of chilled water to the passengers, though supplies quickly ran out.

Lorna had managed to miss all the travel chaos and, indeed, seemed blissfully unaware of it, as she walked along the side of the Thames to the wine bar. Rosie was already there when she arrived. Making her way over to the table, she saw Rosie had a bottle of Sauvignon Blanc nestling invitingly in an ice bucket. Rosie greeted her friend with a kiss on each cheek. Lorna sank into a seat and gratefully accepted the glass of wine Rosie poured.

'Sorry I'm a bit late, Hon.'

'Long day?'

'Oh yes. How about you?'

'Every day's a long day, these days?'

'And, um, how about the nights?'

'Scuse me?'

'How's Corey?'

Rosie blushed.

'How did you know?'

'Female intuition and observation. Can't blame you, though. I mean, I would.'

'Hands off! You've got your man.'

'Is it serious, then?'

'Too soon to tell. But it's going well. Very well.'

'I can just picture you, sitting on a swing seat on a veranda outside a little wooden house in Oklahoma, knitting for your five kids.'

'Maryland. He's *from* Oklahoma but he's based at Fort Meade, Maryland. That's when he's in the US. Over here, he spends some of the time at their London embassy and the rest with the NSA unit up at RAF Menwith in Yorkshire. It's lovely up there, Harrogate especially. We've had a couple of lovely weekends there. Anyway, never mind us. How about you and Harry? Have *you* got plans for five kids and a serious knitting habit?'

'I dunno. Maybe. I mean, we'd like to get married and start a family. My mum would like that, too. She's the family knitter. It's all she's thought about since we lost my dad. It's just a tough decision giving up the career. Can't envisage raising a family *and* staying with the firm. That wouldn't work.'

'Yeah,' Rosie agreed, 'a tough decision. More wine?'

She topped up their glasses and immediately heard a text ping in on her mobile. Scrolling through the message, she seemed surprised.

'Speak of the devil. It's from Corey, Seems there's major chaos at Waterloo and King's Cross. Both stations are closed. It's backed up to the tube stations, too.'

'Not again! It'll be a nightmare getting home.'

'Tell you what, Rosie beamed, 'why don't we just sit out the chaos here and finish this and then get a taxi back to my flat? I've got another bottle chilling in the 'fridge. I'll do us some supper and you can stay over at mine tonight. I can lend you some pyjamas.'

'That would be fun. I'll text Harry. Here, though, I've just had a thought – Rosie Hart. That has a really cutesy ring to it.'

'Shut your face, Bayliss!'

It was almost eleven o'clock that night, before things quietened down at Waterloo and Alan Blake was able to head wearily back upstairs to the office tearoom. He made himself a cup of strong black coffee and flopped down in one of the rather battered easy chairs. He was both mentally and physical exhausted and his feet hurt. Absent-mindedly, he picked up a well-thumbed newspaper which was lying on the tearoom's coffee table. Ironically, it was open at the 'Situations Vacant' page. He spent the next half hour scrutinising the page to see if any of the available jobs on offer promised a less stressful career. Soon, however, he was asleep in his chair.

Chapter 10

The power at both Waterloo and King's Cross was back on within twenty-four hours but the shutdowns would lead to days of chaos and confusion, since many trains were stranded in the wrong place. Timetables fell by the wayside; transport chiefs were grilled by the media, and public anger grew. The press headlines demanded to know if Britain was falling apart, and suggested greater investment in all infrastructures was needed urgently.

The Minister who held the post of Secretary of State for Digital, Culture, Media and Sport, Mark Tredarran, urged the British press and television news desks not to exaggerate the situation in their reporting. The Government's wish, he explained, was to play down the crises and, at all costs, to avoid responding to hysterical accusations of outside interference by a hostile state. Public disquiet was alarming enough these days, he explained, without introducing the spectre of disruption controlled by a malevolent foreign power.

Harry and Kirpal noticed a greater police presence on London's streets the morning after the rail stations' shutdowns. Having reached their homes very late the previous evening, owing to the problems on public transport, they had not switched on the television news but had fallen wearily into their respective beds. It was only when they picked up copies of the *Metro* on the tube that they learned of the assassination of a senior government minister the previous afternoon on the doorstep of his Oxfordshire Mansion. In fact, everyone seated or strap-hanging on the tube was engrossed in reading the reports of the incident.

The brief official statement released to the press by Downing Street was that a young female member of Geoffrey Bowker's office staff – it was claimed she had been at the house to take some urgent correspondence – had heard but not seen the assassin arrive. Allegedly, it was common knowledge at Thames House that Bowker had several times been castigated by the Prime Minister for giving his SO1 protection officers the slip. The press reports confirmed that, so far as his minders had known, he was still at his official residence in London's Carlton Gardens. However, during the lunchtime handover of responsibility for his safety, he had again slipped out and had jumped into the Daimler and driven himself and his assistant to his Oxfordshire home.

They had only been in the house for an hour or so when the doorbell had rung. The Minister's household staff having been given the afternoon off, it was the Minister himself who had answered the door. Seemingly, the young woman assistant had not realised anything was amiss until she had entered the hall and found the Minister lying dead, apparently shot, and the front door wide open. She had heard a car engine departing but had seen nothing. The Foreign Secretary's wife, who had been visiting their daughter in Scotland for a few days, was reported to be in deep shock but was making arrangements to return home.

St Christopher's Place was very smart, if a little difficult to find. Accessed by a narrow alleyway leading off the brash and bustling Oxford Street, the area was home to various upmarket shops and eateries and had an air of quiet calm, almost a village atmosphere in the heart of London. The software company occupied four of the upper storeys in one of the many tall, redbrick terraces which ranged around the square. The ground floor was occupied by a smart French patisserie and coffee shop, and the two sets of premises had adjacent but separate front doors. Climbing the steep, thickly-carpeted Georgian staircases – buildings of this age rarely had lifts – the colleagues were greeted firstly by the aroma of coffee and then by the company's CEO, Edmund Gray – a Canadian, Harry judged by his accent.

Passing through the small but elegant reception area, Harry and Kirpal were guided into Gray's much larger and impressively appointed office and were soon seated in very comfortable rosewood and leather armchairs. Harry noticed that they were iconic Eames chairs. The paintings on the wall looked equally expensive. The receptionist followed them in and poured out their coffee into stylish 1960's reproduction coffee cups, or perhaps they were genuinely vintage, Harry speculated. Kirpal appeared less impressed by the décor and china than by the little tissue-wrapped Italian almond biscuits she slipped onto their saucers.

'So, gentlemen, what can I do for you?' Gray asked, sinking back into his own sumptuously stuffed executive chair.

Harry presented their freshly printed business cards, suggesting they were Ministry of Defence security employees. He explained that spyware used to hack into the IT systems at an RAF base recently was believed to have been developed by Gray's firm and he would appreciate any co-operation Gray could give regarding the nature of that software and its distribution. Gray said he was surprised and dismayed to hear this. He assured his visitors that Lurman Corporation did not produce that sort of software.

Handing them his business card and a series of expensive, glossy brochures, Gray outlined the company's products and services, which comprised mainly high definition graphic design software as well as the delivery of training in its use. He explained that he handled the business and publicity side of the London branch. He would introduce them to his technical manager, based back down on the second floor, who interfaced with their software development arm and who was more *au fait* with the corporation's software generally. He assured them that his colleague, a Mr Goodenough, would be much more knowledgeable about the company's products than he.

When they had finished their coffee, and Kirpal had crunched his way through his and Harry's biscuits, Gray gave them a guided tour of the office premises. Passing down the stairs to the two lower floors, Gray showed them several training suites where smartly-dressed men and women were seated at computers whilst some very competent-looking trainers were clearly delivering instruction.

'We train a fair few civil servants here, as well as people from commerce and industry,' Gray explained, 'and our graphic software products are ideal for staff who themselves are involved in designing training programmes. As you can see, none of our clients looks like a dangerous hacker.'

The set-up all looked perfectly genuine to Harry and Kirpal. Down on the first floor, Gray left them in the care of his more technically aware colleague. Goodenough ushered them into his office, which might have been equally as smart as that of the CEO, if one could but see beyond the range of large desktop screens and other equipment that dominated the room. Harry explained the reason for their visit and Goodenough reiterated Gray's denial that Lurman were in any way interested in developing spyware or malware.

'As you can see, we have a thriving commercial enterprise here. We not only offer our software products for sale but we train the end users in how to make the best of them. Our training courses are fully booked up to the end of next year. We're market-leaders in the field of graphic design programmes. Edmund is the business wizard and I'm the one with the technical understanding of our products. I personally train our trainers, all of whom are very capable individuals. My skills are such that I'm also paid a retainer to act as a consultant to a large internet service provider here in the city. But, if I may ask, what makes you think *our* company is responsible for this malware?'

Kirpal launched into an explanation regarding the parity of electronic signatures of the malware and some of the Lurman products. The technical discussion which ensued went over Harry's head but he was content to sit back and weigh up the man himself. For a fifty-something desk-jockey, Goodenough looked fairly fit physically. No wedding ring, Harry noticed, so he probably spent his free time at the gym, trying to stave off the effects of both middle-age and his sedentary occupation. There was something about him, though, which Harry felt didn't fit. Was it his closely-shorn blond hair and his intense steely-grey eyes? Perhaps it was the way his gaze darted back and forth from Kirpal to Harry, as if he were scrutinising them every bit as earnestly as they were trying to get the measure of him.

Harry reckoned that Gray, the CEO, had pure commerce flowing through his veins. He had no technical expertise. He probably wouldn't know a RAM from a ewe. Goodenough was obviously the technical brains of the outfit. There was something Harry didn't like about Goodenough, though, something he couldn't exactly put his finger on, and Harry knew he should trust his own instincts.

Kirpal and Goodenough had now run out of technical discourse. The meeting was at an end and they all rose to their feet and exchanged business cards. Harry shook Goodenough's hand and thanked him for his time. The man had an uncomfortably firm grip, Harry thought. Holding onto Goodenough's large hand for a second longer than necessary, Harry looked him in the eye and smiled genially.

'Goodenough – that's a Scottish name, if I'm not mistaken?'

'Yes, I believe it was, originally. I always think, if it was good enough for my ancestors, it's good enough for me!'

Harry forced a laugh, just to be polite.

'What did you make of Goodenough?' he asked when they were seated outside the nearby Lamb and Flag, having a pub lunch.

'He certainly knows his stuff. With his depth of knowledge, though, I'm surprised he isn't working at the company's main development arm. Seems like he's wasted here. Anyway, he believes someone may have copied their software, or so he says, but I'm not persuaded that's what's happened. Bit of a cold fish, wasn't he? Probably more at ease with computers than people. What made you ask him about his surname, though?'

'My old school headmaster was called Goodenough. He once told us the name was of Norman origin, and he came from Cumbria.'

Chapter 11

It was after midnight when Alex returned to the basement apartment in Cheltenham. He had no trouble securing entry once more. He'd had a busy couple of days, driving between Cheltenham and Oxfordshire and back again, and he had needed more time to finish what he had started here two nights before. The unopened mail lying on the doormat reassured him that no-one had been in since his last visit. He picked up the letters and took them into the lounge.

Holder still sat where Alex had left him, cold and dead in the armchair. The blood had congealed around the small hole in his temple and his fingers were still curled around the gun. Everything was just as Alex had left it. There was no knowing when Holder's corpse would be found. All the signs were that Holder was not used to having visitors. The state of the place testified to that. A sticky whisky glass and a plate bearing stale cake crumbs sat on the coffee table and, in the small kitchen, dirty dishes festered in the sink and on the drainer. The kitchen bin overflowed with empty foil take-away containers, polystyrene burger boxes and plastic carrier bags.

Alex moved around the apartment. The smell of dirty laundry, grubby bed sheets and cat litter assailed his senses. Two nights ago, after he had despatched Holder, accessed Holder's e mail account and e-mailed Holder's line manager at GCHQ claiming illness, he had remembered to open the curtains in the apartment so the neighbours would not think anything was amiss. Now he closed them again.

Seating himself at the L-shaped desk which, with its impressive array of computer monitors, dominated that corner of the apartment's only bedroom, he switched on the desk lamp and the computer processor unit. The monitor blinked into life. He lifted the wireless keyboard and took it into the next room.

Taking care not to disturb the body or the gun, he angled the keyboard beneath the dead man's hand and pressed a stiff, cold index finger down onto the user recognition key. Taking the keyboard back into the bedroom, he was able to resume his interrogation of Holder's electronic files.

If he had wondered how Holder could have afforded such sophisticated technology, then the covert images, sound files, e mails and other evidence of widespread blackmail provided the answer. As he trawled through the programmes, he observed the way in which Holder had modified some of the software for his own nefarious purposes. Holder may have been a slob, but the signs were that he was also a computer genius. Alex coolly began transferring everything onto the remote hard-drive he had brought with him. When he was finished, he disconnected the hard-drive and slipped it into his computer bag. After a few seconds' deliberation, however, he decided to take the computer's slim processor unit as well and he slipped that into his bag, too.

The still livid scratches on the back of his hands reminded him about the cat. He returned to the kitchen where he retrieved the strangled feline corpse. Still lying where he had left it two nights before, it was now as stiff as its deceased owner. Stuffing it into a used plastic carrier bag from the kitchen bin, he switched off all the lights and opened the curtains again before exiting the apartment. He walked to the spot, three streets away, where his car was parked and, pausing only to tip the cat into a darkened front garden, he climbed into the car, placed his computer bag in the footwell beside him, started the engine and headed back to London.

Chapter 12

The furore over the shooting of the Foreign Secretary rose to a fever pitch over the next two weeks. There was much speculation in the press as to who was behind it. After all, leaving aside the historic shooting of Prime Minister Spencer Percival, the assassination of a British cabinet minister was wholly unprecedented. Naturally, fingers were pointed at the Russians, particularly in view of Bowker's recent unfettered criticism of their invasion of the Crimea. Then again, the Russians had not been the sole targets of his outspoken ire.

Adrian held a briefing for his *Skylark* team. Although the murder of Geoffrey Bowker was being looked at by Thames House's counter-terrorism section, Adrian explained that the possible Russian connection meant Adrian's staff needed to be up to speed on the incident. He related how, unusually for a Foreign Secretary, Bowker had actually served with the Foreign and Commonwealth Office. He had been ambassador to several African nations. In that capacity, he had, on several occasions, acted as the mouthpiece for the British government's rebuke of a foreign regime, whilst making it appear that his views were entirely his own. This had earned him a not entirely deserved reputation as a rogue ambassador. Whenever his comments had embarrassed his host nation, he had been hastily withdrawn from post, only to be immediately and conspicuously granted a new, more prestigious post.

Having become comfortable with the principle that the pursuit of diplomatic goals did not always mean one must be diplomatic or exercise tact, and having formerly enjoyed the protection of diplomatic immunity, once he had entered politics and secured a cabinet position, he had continued to express his views freely. He had done so, regardless of the effect his candour might have on international relations. In short, Adrian said, Bowker had made numerous enemies.

Adrian advised the team that SO15 had been asked to suppress, for the time being, the fact of Russian-made bullets having been used to murder Bowker. This fact, in itself, did not constitute irrefutable proof that the Russians were behind the killing. Indeed, any aggrieved party might have obtained such ammunition. However, pointing an accusing finger right now might well undermine the ongoing dialogue which other, less outspoken diplomatists were holding with the Russians over a ceasefire. The possible long-term restoration of peace in the Crimea was the most desirable goal. Whilst many people suspected the Russians would have been behind the assassination, Adrian explained, Mark Tredarran, the Minister with responsibility for Media relations, had persuaded the Home Secretary that there should be no official accusations at present.

Over the coming days, public outrage was gradually diverted by other events on the world stage, such as the ongoing impeachment process against the highly unpopular US President, as well as incidents nearer to home, including the death in an Iranian prison of a British aid worker, arrested on trumped-up spying charges. The storming of the US embassy in Baghdad, followed by reprisals including the assassination of a senior Iranian military man in the capital by US forces, led to threats of an all-out war in the middle east. All of this dominated the news and pushed domestic incidents firmly into to the background.

The funeral of the Foreign Secretary was very well attended. Bowker hadn't been a popular man but such events always brought out those self-serving and publicity-seeking politicians, to whom being seen to attend was important. Even those of Bowker's cabinet colleagues who didn't like him, and the Foreign Office senior diplomats who condemned his bullish stance on Syria, the Crimea and Iran, all turned out to pay their respects.

The little Oxfordshire village was gridlocked with diplomatic Daimlers and unmarked police Jaguar XFs, and the little parish church was soon filled to capacity. The Prime Minister, Home Secretary and most of the Cabinet were there. Ambassadors from several of the foreign embassies were in attendance, too, and many of the villagers, even though they had never met him, felt compelled to stand outside during the service, if only out of curiosity. As if to make up for their failure to protect Bowker, SO1 protection officers were present in force. As for the deceased Foreign Secretary himself, it was the first time he had ever entered his local church.

On Adrian Curtis's instruction, Harry and Lorna attended, too. They and Rosie Leyton had travelled out in the same car – not in Harry's open-top Morgan this time, but in a more discreet official vehicle. Adrian had no proof that the killing of the Foreign Secretary was the work of WOTAK, but he was pretty sure the Russians would have had something to do with it, and his working theory was that WOTAK *was* the Russians. The views of the JIC, however, were more mixed. GCHQ's Sir Arnold had declared it was more likely that Islamic ideological terrorists would be behind it, whilst Sir Robert Vanbrugge suggested that SIS's money was on the Iranians. He had sent Rosie to the funeral for the same reason Curtis had sent his own *Operation Skylark* officers. They sat in the rear pews, glancing around discreetly from time to time to see which, if any, of the mourners might look as if they didn't belong.

Discreetly armed plain-clothed police mingled with the mourners and an armed response unit waited in a quiet lane less than a quarter of a mile away. Some killers derive a perverse pleasure from returning to see the aftermath of their handiwork, so there was always a chance the assassin might be present. Also, the presence of so many members of the government in such a confined space might attract an attack from just about any hostile faction.

In the event, the funeral passed off without incident, or almost. The Prime Minister gave a speech and he stuck to the script he had been given, or at least, mostly he did. His only departure from the carefully worded eulogy was to comment that Bowker was the first MP to have been assassinated since Airey Neave. The reference to the 1979 murder by the IRA of the Conservative Shadow Northern Ireland Secretary caused the Irish Ambassador's cheek to tighten and the acting Foreign Secretary to wince.

'The PM couldn't get through it without making a gaffe, could he?' Harry remarked as he, Lorna and Rosie tucked into their lunch at the Fox and Pheasant. They had decided to break their journey back to London by stopping off for 'refs' at one of Harry and Lorna's favourite country pubs, just off the M40.

'Didn't he get the memo about being nice to the Irish?' Rosie joked, 'they're the only friends we've got left in Europe now. And their economy is propping up ours. I thought the deal was that we don't mention the troubles and they don't mention the famine.'

'Didn't see anyone who looked like they might be WOTAK, though,' Lorna lamented.

'Trouble is, at funerals, nobody wears name badges,' Rosie said. 'Goodness, this roast lamb is good.'

'They also do an orgasmic apple crumble and custard,' Harry enthused.'

Lorna put down her knife and fork. The huge portion of beer-battered cod and chips, tasty though it was, had defeated her.

'Really, though, haven't you wondered what he does look like?'

Rosie put her index fingers to her temples and pulled her eyelids into a squint.

'Charlie Chan, an inscrutable foe in a pointy hat.'

'I see him as a big bear of a Russian, with an astrakhan tea cosy on his head,' Harry grinned.

'I'm wondering if he might even be a group of individuals,' Lorna added. 'Some of them will be techie geeks, hacking away day and night; others are carefully composing the next letter from WOTAK, and there'll be a couple of messengers in nondescript cars, tootling around the place posting them. He just might be part of a team.'

Chapter 13

In early September, a gas-fuelled power station in central England suddenly failed, cutting power to hundreds of thousands of homes. Harry and Lorna were grateful that the areas affected did not include Greater London. They watched an uncomfortable director in charge of the National Grid apologising live on television and reassuring the public that the power shortages would be short-lived.

'The failure is simply a fluke,' he promised. 'It will soon be resolved and power will be restored.'

As he spoke, however, a red 'breaking news' banner appeared beneath his image, announcing that an off-shore wind farm had suddenly shut down as well. The total number of homes now without power exceeded one million. The reporter bombarded his interviewee with accusations regarding the UK's failing infrastructure and lack of investment in essential services. The director's discomfort was hard to watch. No official source seemed willing to even suggest the hand of an outside agency in all of this disruption.

The press would describe the incident as Britain's worst ever power outage. As suddenly and shockingly as the incident had occurred, however, equally suddenly and inexplicably it resolved itself. The restoration of power to so many homes did nothing, though, to restore public confidence. The incident influenced the thinking of the *Op Skylark* team at Thames House.

'I'm beginning to think WOTAK might not be a person but an agency – a group of individuals,' Adrian Curtis said to his contingent of the *Op Skylark* team who were seated around a conference table at Thames House. 'Carole will explain why.'

Harry turned to Lorna and nodded to acknowledge the fact that Curtis shared her theory. Adrian glanced across at Carole, who held up her copy of the latest letter and addressed the team.

'More than two weeks have passed since the last missive was sent. That's the longest gap we've had between letters. And now this one has arrived. We've detected some significant differences between this letter and the previous ones, though. The paper and envelope used are different. They're from a different manufacturer, sold by another nationwide supplier but not the same one as before. The chemical composition of the printer ink is slightly different, too. The ink used previously was a cheaper, dye-based one which mixes several colours to achieve black, whereas this one is a more expensive, pigment-based, pure black kind. That suggests different printers were used, or at least that WOTAK splashed out on some better ink – pun intended. Harry, you and Kirpal checked out that IT company up the West End, didn't you?'

'We did,' Harry confirmed. 'It seems perfectly legit, but we're doing background checks on their employees.'

'Well, going back to the letters, there are also some slight linguistic and stylistic differences.'

Carole took from her folder photocopies of the previous letters and spread them out on the conference table.

'Firstly, in one of the earlier letters, the writer says to pay up, 'unless you'd *rather* I caused more of the same chaos ….', but, in the current one, he says 'perhaps you'd *sooner* have me give you another demonstration …' etc., etc. 'You would rather' is more usual than 'you would sooner', but what is unusual, in my opinion, is for someone to use both phrases.'

Harry nodded in agreement. Carole continued:

'Also, all the earlier letters were addressed to *'The Editor, The Times Newspaper',* and on each envelope the address was fully punctuated, which is a little old-fashioned these days. The current letter, however, addressed a little differently, to *'The*

Times Editor ', is unpunctuated, as per the modern business style. There are differences in the line and word spacing used, too.'

'So,' Adrian sat back in his chair, 'what do we make of that?'

'More than one person is drafting the letters?' Lorna volunteered.

'Or one individual is drafting them but wants us to *think* he is part of large organisation with serious capabilities,' Harry suggested, 'and maybe he's just an ordinary Joe who has two printers and uses different styles to throw us off the scent.'

Carole leaned forward and rested her elbows on the table to indicate she had something of importance to impart. She swept her shoulder-length, gypsy-like hair back from her face, as if to add a little drama to her hypothesis.

'I think the main indicating factor is the format, especially on the envelopes. Two different styles of address definitely suggest to me two different authors. The writer of the earlier letters may have learned his or her keyboard skills in England but a long time ago, possibly before the late 'eighties or early 'nineties.' The author of the latest letter, however, is using the more modern international business correspondence format.'

The thoughtful silence which followed suggested Carole's view was gaining acceptance.

'Before I trained as an analyst,' she continued, 'I was a PA. I learned my typing skills a few years before office computers and word processing came into general use. At secretarial college, it was drilled into us that a full stop should always be followed by two spaces before we began typing the next sentence. Punctuation, too, was formulaic. With the advent of the word processor, however, new protocols came into usage. Only one space now follows a full stop. The indented paragraph has given way to the blocked style, and so on.'

'So, what does that tell us?' Adrian asked.

'My feeling is that the first author learned to type a long time ago, but the second one learned to type on a word processor, so more recently perhaps. It may be that the second author is younger than the first, or, alternatively, he could have gained his keyboard skills later in life. He doesn't seem to have picked up any old-fashioned British typing and drafting habits like the first author has, so, if he is an older individual, he could even be foreign.'

As everyone took in what she had said, Carole indulged in a little trumpet-blowing.

'Having a bit of experience beyond these walls is an advantage.'

'Being middle-aged is an advantage, too,' Kirpal joked.

Carole cast him a half-serious withering look.

'Thank you, Carole, that's most helpful,' Adrian smiled.

Carole looked suitably pleased.

'My pleasure. I'm glad you value my opinion. It would be good to have a little more respect around here – looking at you, Kirpal – and a little more help with the analysis work would be nice, too. Anyone know when Noddy's coming back to work?'

'I'll check with Rosie Leyton,' Lorna promised.

Adrian called the impromptu meeting to a close and Lorna went off to phone Rosie, whilst Carole headed off to make herself a coffee.

'You were treading on thin ice,' Harry joked with Kirpal as they headed back to their desks. 'You should never mention a lady's age, especially once they're over forty.'

'Oh, Carole knows I was only joking. She's actually quite attractive – for her age, that is!'

Chapter 14

By the time Harry, Lorna and Kirpal arrived at the basement flat in Cheltenham, the body had been removed and the SOCOs had completed their examination of the crime scene. By prior arrangement, the Senior Investigating Officer, DCI Dave Lloyd, was at the scene to meet them. He introduced himself to the three people he had been told were from the Ministry of Defence. He assured them the body was no longer there and confessed he was relieved about that. His pale blue eyes reflected that relief as he explained he'd been a policeman for thirty of his forty-eight years, and had been a murder detective for the past twenty-five years, but that hadn't made him immune to the revulsion he always felt at the sight of a dead body. Running a weary hand through his dark wavy hair, he quickly got down to details.

'One shot to the right temple. The weapon used was in his right hand. No sign of forced entry or burglary. Unfortunately, as you can probably tell from the … er … aroma, he wasn't discovered for the best part of a week. Given the warm weather and with all the windows closed, the body wasn't in a good condition. The post mortem should tell us more.'

'Was it suicide then?' Lorna asked.

'It has the appearance of a suicide,' Lloyd said, 'but it wasn't.'

The three colleagues looked at him quizzically.

'It's been staged to look like a suicide. The deceased had gunshot residue on the hand in which the gun was found, and, if his shopping list in the kitchen is anything to go by, he *was* right-handed. Our forensics people are working on the gun and ammo. However, the residue on his hand wasn't the usual spotting pattern, but was smeared. Also, SOCOs found a small trace of gunshot residue on a single key on his computer keyboard.'

'Could that residue have been propelled across the room onto the keyboard when the gun went off?' Harry asked.

'It could've, if the keyboard had been in this room, but it wasn't. It was next door in the bedroom. GSR doesn't travel through solid walls. And the deceased could hardly have shot himself fatally in the head then gone next door and switched on his computer before coming back, sitting down, taking up the gun again and expiring.'

This guy's pretty astute,' Harry thought.

'Which key had the residue on it?' Kirpal asked.

'The one that scans the user's fingerprint to access the computer.'

'So, the killer accessed Noddy's computer *after* he shot him,' Kirpal thought aloud.

Lloyd's serious expression gave way to one of amusement. 'Noddy?'

'His name is ... was Colin Holder. Naturally, his work colleagues called him Noddy,' Harry explained, 'but is there anything else you can tell us that might be helpful?'

'Yes. I suspect the killer was a professional. It's my belief that he wasn't let in. I suspect he gained entry via the front door, leaving few signs of a break-in, just some faint, tell-tale scrapes around the Yale lock. And he did all the right things to make it look like suicide, right up to the point where he accessed the computer. Then, presumably, something he found on the computer made him decide to steal, not just the information, but also the computer's processor unit.'

Harry continued to be impressed by Dave Lloyd's assessment of the situation. The detective went on:

'He could have just uploaded what he wanted, and maybe he did, but clearly, he didn't want anyone else to see what was on the computer. There don't seem to be any other hard drives or memory sticks around, either. The killer would know that the missing hard drive would make it look less like a suicide, but

64

whatever he found on the computer must have been important enough for him to take that risk. Would you know what was on his computer?'

Harry said they didn't know. He explained that Holder had been working on something very important for GCHQ. He couldn't say what that was, but he thought it most unlikely Holder would or could have brought his work home with him. It should only have been personal information on his home computer.

'Was he not missed when he didn't turn up for work all week?' the detective asked.

'He'd e-mailed in sick,' Lorna explained, 'or, at least, somebody had, using his e mail address.'

'If it was the killer who e mailed, and if he did it using Holder's computer, then he must have wiped the keys clean of his own prints. The only print found on the keyboard, was Holder's, and that was just on the access key. Well, I expect you people would like to have a look around for yourselves,' Dave suggested. 'I guess you won't need the key to the front door. We got it from the upstairs neighbour who held it for the deceased. She won't need it back now. I'll return it to the letting agent in due course. Here's my card. You know where to find me if you need to ask anything.'

'We do,' Harry smiled as Dave Lloyd departed.

Harry and Lorna began their search of the apartment. Harry started looking through the drawers in the living room whilst Lorna checked the kitchen from top to bottom and Kirpal went to the bedroom to see what was left of Holder's IT and what the bedside cabinet and wardrobe might reveal.

'This place has been thoroughly searched already,' Harry said, when he had finished, 'firstly by the killer, I should imagine, and then by the police. Not much left for us to find. Anything come to light in the bedroom, Kirpal?'

'Nothing evidential, but he has some pretty expensive kit in there – top quality monitors, some impressive digital cameras with long range lenses, miniature recording equipment and stuff. It's the sort of kit used for covert surveillance rather than for birdwatching. It would be interesting to know what he was snapping and recording. However, as the DCI said, there's not a single memory card in the place. The killer may have taken those, too. If he'd been just a common burglar, though, he'd have taken the cameras.'

Lorna emerged from the kitchen.

'You know, for someone who hadn't lived here all that long, he'd let this flat get into a right state. GCHQ wouldn't have rented it for him in this condition. What a slob. And didn't Rosie say he had a cat? There's a litter tray but no cat flap, so I wonder what happened to the cat. Maybe he'd put it out just before he died and it couldn't get back in. But you'd expect to find it sitting on the doorstep.'

'Can't imagine the killer would have left the cameras and stolen the cat,' Kirpal added, 'so maybe a neighbour has taken it in.'

Lorna returned to the kitchen and was back a few moments later with a cat's feeding bowl. It was encrusted with dried cat food. The rancid smell made her hold it at arm's length.

'What did Rosie say Holder's cat was called?'

'Um, 'Catto', wasn't it?' Harry remembered.

'He had a funny way of spelling it,' she said, turning the bowl around to show them the side which had the cat's name printed on it.'

'Katow,' Harry read aloud, 'is that Polish for cat?'

'Or Chinese?' Kirpal suggested.

'I don't know,' Lorna said, 'but what I do know is what it spells backwards.'

'WOTAK!' Harry and Kirpal chorused in unison.

66

Chapter 15

'It doesn't seem possible.' Adrian Curtis reacted in the presence of the JIC members at Thames House the following day. 'I can't imagine Colin Holder could have been WOTAK. For one thing, he couldn't possibly have had the resources to cause all of those cyber-attacks.'

'Actually, I think he could have been behind some of them,' Sir Arnold Mayhew looked grave, 'since he had a very high level of computer skills. He had access to some of our most sophisticated IT at GCHQ and he had proven himself an ace hacker in the pursuance of some of our legitimate operations. If anyone could hack into organisations whose IT security was anything less than our own, it would be him.'

'But what motive would he have had?' Adrian asked.

He glanced across at Harry, who was a little overawed by having been invited to sit in on this impromptu meeting of some of the principal members of the JIC. The meeting had been called urgently, specifically to discuss the apparent murder of a member of the *Operation Skylark* team. The DGs of SIS, whose officer Holder was, and GCHQ, to which agency he had been attached at the time of his death, both had an interest in Holder's murder, and so did Adrian's DG, Helena Fairbrother.

'Money?' Harry ventured. 'There seems to be an exceptionally large amount of money in his current account. It is possible that, with his know-how, he had other accounts somewhere, too – offshore, perhaps. He may have dressed badly and lived like a hermit, but it looks like he had spent a lot of money on acquiring a state-of-the-art computer system at home, and some other high value electronic items.'

'But, don't forget,' Adrian continued, 'according to the pathologist, Holder died *before* the most recent letter from

67

WOTAK was posted. And it's a bit of a stretch making such an accusation based on a cat's bowl.'

'Then we have to wonder *why* he was murdered,' Helena Fairbrother chipped in.

'Do we know anything adverse about him?' Sir Arnold asked, looking across at Sir Robert Vanbrugge, 'surely, there wasn't any reason to doubt his integrity?'

Sir Robert fiddled with his gold cufflinks. He seemed a little uneasy.

'Well, there was a little bit of financial irregularity a while back, but nothing to suggest he would hold the country to ransom for millions of pounds.'

'What sort of financial irregularity? Fiddling the petty cash?' Sir Arnold bellowed.

'More or less,' Sir Robert squirmed uncomfortably in his Savile Row suit.

The GCHQ Director General's eyes narrowed as sudden realisation sank in.

'You sent him to us on a disciplinary, didn't you? He was on *jankers*, wasn't he?'

'Not at all, Arnold. His management … just thought an attachment would … let him see how things were done in other agencies and would broaden his experience. He'd just got bit jaded, that's all. And we thought you would appreciate his extremely good IT skills.'

The assurances did nothing to allay Sir Arnold's suspicion. He continued to glower at his SIS counterpart until Helena made a diplomatic intervention.

'Well, gentlemen, I'm not sure exactly what it is we are accusing Holder of here. Even if he did write the WOTAK letters, or at least some of them, he couldn't have been behind the cyber-attacks, or at least not all of them. He could easily have hacked into Buckingham Palace's twitter account and we're certain that whoever is WOTAK did so. But do we really think he was responsible for the death of the Foreign Secretary? And what about the Russian air and sea incursions? He could hardly have masterminded those.'

'Maybe he was working *for* the Russians,' Sir Arnold suggested, 'or the Chinese, or the Iranians, or God knows who. Maybe he was just one of several WOTAKs.'

'That's very possible,' Harry suggested, 'but, what we need to know is what was on his computer and who killed him to get it.'

Adrian flashed Harry a look that plainly said *'get on with it.'*

Chapter 16

'DCI David Lloyd, to see DCI Peter Webb, please.'

Taking a seat in the reception area, Dave Lloyd accepted the glossy brochure the young civilian receptionist gave him to peruse whilst he waited. He hadn't been in the new Police HQ at Curtis Green before, though, as a young policeman, he had once visited the previous building, also known as New Scotland Yard, with a group of other trainee constables.

'Do you know about our Black Museum?' the receptionist asked as she put down the internal phone.

'Oh yes. I visited some years ago – when it was in your old building. To be honest, I can't shake off the memory of those amputated arms they've got in a glass case. Have you seen them yourself?'

The receptionist shook her head.

'Seems they'd belonged to some perp who had murdered his mother then fled to Germany where he killed himself, probably out of remorse. Anyway, some copper with schoolboy German was instructed to compose a letter for the German police requesting them to forward the dead man's fingerprints, so's they could confirm his identity. There must have been some error in translation, though. Instead of fingerprints arriving by return post, what turned up was a large jar of formaldehyde with the perp's forelimbs floating in it.'

'Oh, yuk!' the receptionist squirmed.

'The other constables I came with thought it was quite funny. I didn't. Still haven't been able to get the image of those severed arms out of my head.'

'How horrible.'

'And they've got Dennis Nielsen's cooker – the one he used to boil up the dismembered bits of his victims.'

'No!'

'Straight up. All sealed in a big Perspex case, it is. There was a big, enamelled cooking pot on the hob with strands of uncooked spaghetti poking out from under the pot lid. Some wag had put in a few strands of what was supposed to be human hair. It was gruesome. I mean, I'm a murder detective and I see enough death during my working week. Didn't need to see more on my days off.'

'So, you wouldn't recommend me to visit, then?' the wide-eyed young woman asked.

'Not within an hour of eating, Love.'

He opened the glossy brochure to take his mind off the horrors of the 'Black Museum'. The leaflet explained that Curtis Green was the third Metropolitan Police building to be known as 'Scotland Yard'. The name 'Scotland Yard' was, the brochure informed, a metonym for the Metropolitan Police HQ, just as 'Wall Street' was a metonym for New York's financial district. Each time the police headquarters had moved, they had taken the name 'Scotland Yard' with them. This wasn't news to Dave, of course. He was well aware of the history. He hadn't come across the term 'metonym' before, though. Maybe he'd be able to work that word into one of his reports. That would impress his Super.

The loud 'ping' which announced the arrival of the lift disturbed his reading. A smiling DCI Webb stepped out and came to shake his hand.

'Hello, Dave. I'm Peter. Thank you for coming all the way over from Gloucestershire. Let's head upstairs and we'll get you a coffee, pronto.'

'No, cheers. I had a strong one on the way over here. If I have any more, I'll be awake all afternoon,' Dave joked.

On exiting the lift, Lloyd's attention was taken by the panoramic views visible from the corridor windows and he almost missed the 'SO15' sign on the office door as he was ushered into Webb's department.

71

'Christ!' he thought, *'this is the Counter-terrorism Command!'*

'I'm glad you were able to come over here at such short notice,' Webb began, 'I e-mailed you in response to the bulletin you put out, asking if any other police districts had recently encountered shootings in which a Russian-made gun and ammo were used. May I ask why you wanted to know that?'

Lloyd felt relieved once the reason for the summons was explained to him. He'd been wondering if he'd dropped a clanger and was there for a bollicking, or 'a pep talk' as his Super would describe it.

'Yes, of course. We've had a murder in Cheltenham. Middle-aged bachelor; an IT specialist at GCHQ. One shot to the head and the scene made to look, initially at least, like a suicide; a carefully forced entry; gun in the victim's hand; gunshot residue smeared onto that hand, presumably by his killer. The lab identified the bullet as being nine by eighteen mil, Russian-made. The semi-automatic pistol was a Makarov, also Russian-made.'

'Ah, the Makarov. Bit old now. Post-war Soviet-issue hand gun. Lots of them still about, though. The Russian military and security forces still like them. Fairly compact, easily concealed and very accurate. In short, a good assassin's weapon. Good for the single kill-shot at close range. So, any idea why your man was assassinated?'

'None. You'd have to ask the Security Service. They'll probably tell you more than they'd tell me. Three of their number came to the crime scene. Allegedly they were MOD, but I know a spook when I meet one. Is there anything else you can tell me – for instance, what *your* interest might be?'

Webb smiled enigmatically.

'Since you've guessed which agencies might be involved, you can probably guess more than I'm allowed to tell you. What you'll already have surmised is that we're looking at a high-profile victim murdered with Russian ammo. Our people will liaise with your lab about the ballistics, but I'd like to hear more about your victim and the crime scene.'

Settling into an empty carriage for the two-hour train ride back to Cheltenham, a weary Dave Lloyd took out his mobile and called his superintendent.

'It's Dave Lloyd, Sir. On my way back now. Well, they weren't giving away much but, if Webb's victim is who I think it is, then I suspect the Holder case may be taken off us and given to SO15.'

Chapter 17

It was raining lightly that Saturday morning, which made it even more surprising to Lorna that Harry should suggest a visit to her mother's. Usually, he had to be cajoled into going. He didn't dislike Mrs Bayliss, and nor did he feel that she disapproved of him. It was just that he felt she was a bit too controlling of Lorna. She worried that Lorna's work might be dangerous or that she might be travelling around London on her own late at night. She even worried that Lorna wasn't dressing warmly enough in winter. Perhaps, though, that was how mothers should be around their adult children. He didn't know, for he didn't have many memories of his own mother.

Also, he and Mrs Bayliss were poles apart politically. She was a dyed-in-the-wool Tory, one of the 'hang 'em and flog 'em' persuasion, and any discussion on current affairs would usually descend into a disagreement. She considered Harry to be a trendy liberal, if not 'a leftie'. More often than not, therefore, Harry would have a lie-in on a Saturday morning, then he would wander down the High Road to do some grocery shopping, whilst Lorna went to her mother's alone. Today, however, with the top up on the Morgan, they set off down the M40.

'Why are we turning off here?' Lorna asked as Harry flipped on his indicator.

'I thought, since we're out this way anyway, we'd have a quick look at the village where the Foreign Sec was killed. You don't mind, do you? We'll get to Marlborough in plenty of time to take Mum out for lunch.'

'Oh, I see. I thought you'd have an ulterior motive. Lunch'll be on you, then?'

'Yes. My treat.'

Harry parked up a little way along the lane from the late Minister's front gates. He knew the area would have been swept

74

by the best SOCOs in the business, and, in any case, this morning's rain would probably have removed any clues that might have been missed, but he wanted to see the area for himself; to get the feel of the place. Naturally, he hadn't thought it appropriate to go poking around the village on the day of the funeral.

The lane in front of the house seemed fairly pristine, so he and Lorna walked around the perimeter of the estate. The lofty flint walls rose up alongside them. The killer hadn't needed to scale the walls. He'd just strolled in through the front gates which were not locked. Harry reasoned that the killer or killers must have been observing the Minister and his movements beforehand. He didn't really expect to find anything relevant immediately around the outside of the estate. He glanced up at the nearby hillside with its dense cloak of deciduous woods and wondered why the killer hadn't taken advantage of the hill. He would probably have had a clear view down into the house and garden from there. Maybe he *had* been up there, though. Maybe he had used the hill to reconnoitre the estate.

'Let's climb that hill,' he suggested.

'What, in these shoes?' Lona protested, 'My feet'll get soaked. You climb the hill. I'll wait back in the car.'

Harry reached the top of the hill and wandered around. There would indeed have been a good view down into the Minister's back garden had it not been for the tangled foliage. However, Bowker had been shot dead on his front doorstep, which was not visible from this part of the hill. After a few moments, however, Harry spotted the rough circle which had been cut through some of the ivy and cascading birch fronds. Squatting down as low as he could without getting his clothing wet, he angled his head downwards and realised the gap in the foliage did indeed afford him a good view into the Minister's grounds. The curled brown edges of the leaves suggested the gap was not a natural one but one which had been cut deliberately and quite recently. He almost felt the killer's presence. At some point, the assassin must have lain exactly where Harry now crouched.

As he glanced around looking in vain for anything the killer might have dropped, he decided a gunman who had made such careful preparations would have been too professional to leave anything behind. Since he had apparently been up here, though, and had seemingly prepared the spot, Harry wondered why he hadn't carried out the execution from here. Did he only have a hand gun with him and was the distance too great? No, a professional would have worked out the distances and brought an appropriate weapon with him.

Perhaps the Minister hadn't been visible on the day? Maybe he hadn't ventured out of doors? But the entire month so far had been an extremely hot one, and Harry could see a swimming pool in the Minister's back garden. Bowker must have spent some of the hot summer out of doors, either in or by the pool. So why did the killer not fire from here? Surely, no-one in the house could have seen him up here. Nevertheless, perhaps he had been disturbed. Walkers might have come up the hill and put him off, or maybe he had decided a direct attack at the front door, and a fast getaway using a car parked in the lane, would be less risky.

Still mulling over the many possibilities, Harry headed down the steep hill and back to the car.

'Found anything interesting?' Lorna asked him.

'Not really.'

'Well I have,' she unfolded her handkerchief and showed him a small black plastic object concealed within it.

'Where did you find that?'

'It was leaning against the wall down by the side of the house. It's quite thin and it was lying on its edge so it could've easily been missed in a search. It's the cap from a camera lens, isn't it? There wasn't any other rubbish lying around so, rather than having been dumped there, it must have been dropped. Why do you suppose someone would be using a camera by the side of an eight-foot wall? It's not as though there's any kind of a view from down there. No, don't touch. It might have prints on it.'

'That camera at Holder's place – the one with the big telephoto lens attached. Did it have a lens cap on?'

'I don't recall. But we can check with Dave Lloyd. A photographer would have to remove a lens cap in order to screw on a telephoto lens, though, wouldn't he? But Holder was killed before the Minister was. So, surely, it can't be Holder's lens cap.'

'Depends when it was dropped. Someone's been cutting back foliage up on the barrow to get a better view down here. I suspect Bowker's killer might have made more than one visit here, maybe to recce the place. And maybe, for some reason, Holder was here, too.'

'You definitely owe me a decent lunch now,' Lorna grinned, 'and I might just manage the apple crumble, as well.'

Chapter 18

Unlike New Scotland Yard, Thames House was somewhere Dave Lloyd *had* visited previously. It was a good few years ago when he had attended a one-day security course there. The training had been fairly basic stuff, but a day away from his local nick and a convivial evening out on the town with fellow police officers had been a welcome change from routine. This morning, having again spent two hours on the train up from Cheltenham, he welcomed the chance to stretch his legs as he strolled along Millbank.

The coffee they'd laid out in the Security Service's small conference room was good. He toyed idly with the visitor' security pass on the lanyard around his neck whilst he sipped his coffee and waited for Harry. His Super had said it was a good sign that he had been invited to the imposing Portland stone building which served as The Security Service HQ. The fact that he had been invited up to Thames House suggested he wasn't being side-lined. The Holder case hadn't been taken off him, at least not yet.

Harry breezed in.

'Hello again, Dave. Many thanks for coming.'

'Goodness, you MOD people get around,' Lloyd's sarcasm was jocular in tone.

'Yes. Sorry. Need-to-know, and all that. Still, now you do know and I appreciate your taking the time to come and see me.'

'I'm happy to help. Thanks for the lens cap, by the way. You were right. It's the same make as Holder's camera and is a good fit. Although there was only a partial print on it, it was Holder's print.'

'Yes. It's lucky it was lying in the lee of the wall so the rain didn't get at it.'

'So, what's your theory on how it came to be where you found it?'

'We're still trying to work that one out, Dave. Clearly, Holder couldn't have killed the Foreign Sec. He was already dead himself by then. But maybe the Minister's killer is responsible for killing Holder, too. It's unlikely the assassin would have taken Holder's lens cap with him to the Minister's house, especially as he hadn't stolen his camera. But it looks like they may both have been in close proximity to the house at the same time, sometime before Holder was killed, obviously. Maybe they went there together to reccy the place. So, either they were working together or Holder was there for some other reason when the assassin spotted him and decided to kill him to keep him quiet.'

'But why kill him in Cheltenham? Why not kill him right where he encountered him? It would have been risky letting him go home, when he could easily have dropped him on the spot.'

'Maybe he didn't want to alert the Minister or his staff. He'd probably have had a silencer with him but he'd have had to move Holder's body. If they'd found a dead body anywhere near the Minister's house, they'd have increased his personal security. That would have made it harder for the killer to get close enough to Bowker to kill him. I can't immediately think of any other explanation, can you?'

'Well, Holder could have been the killer's accomplice, but, clearly, his killer wanted whatever was on Holder's computer. Either he wanted it for himself, or he didn't want anyone else to have it. If they were in it together, though, why would he need to kill Holder to get it? He could have simply visited or broken in when Holder was out and uploaded whatever he wanted.'

'That's true.'

'And what would have taken Holder to the Minister's house in the first place, and why take a long lens camera? Why would he be taking covert photos of the Foreign Secretary? Perhaps the killer was after those photos. Maybe Holder *didn't* see the killer reccying the house but maybe the killer saw him taking photos and, for some reason, he wanted them. Maybe he thought he might have been captured on one of Holder's photos.'

Harry smiled. He liked Lloyd's reasoning. Lloyd continued:

'Harry, do we know what the Minister might have been doing that Holder would have wanted to photograph.'

'Well, it might not have been *what* he was doing, so much as *who*. On the day he was killed he was home alone with a young female assistant. He'd dodged his bodyguard, and not for the first time. His wife was away and his domestic staff had all been given the afternoon off. Bowker had left himself very vulnerable. He paid a high price for his bit on the side.'

'Could Holder have been intending to blackmail him, do you think?'

'That's possible. Quite possible.'

'Shame we can't access the memory on his home computer,' Lloyd pondered, 'but has anyone thought to check out the computer terminals he might have used at work? He might also have saved the images there for safekeeping. You see, I keep a spare set of house keys in my locker at the nick. Police stations rarely get robbed, and I imagine the same goes for GCHQ.'

Harry was impressed.

'Can't imagine why we didn't think of that. Look, why don't I drive you back to Cheltenham? I'll bring Kirpal, too, and he and I will go to GCHQ. We'll ask if we can have a look at Holder's work station. If there's anything on his work computer, Kirpal will find it.'

Dave nodded, but he was still thinking.

'You know, I'm just wondering how Holder actually *got* to the Minister's house. He held a driving licence but he didn't own a car. If he didn't go there with the killer, he may have rented a vehicle. I'll get onto that as soon as I get back to the nick. If we can track down the car, and if they haven't valeted it yet, there might just be something interesting in it.'

Chapter 19

Dave Lloyd sat back comfortably in his business class seat, sipped his cold beer and gazed out at the clouds over the channel.

'You been to Germany before, Dave?' Harry asked.

'No, never. It was pretty decent of you to insist I came with you. If I'd had to arrange this through police channels, it would have taken forever, if they agreed to it at all. And I'd have been booked into economy class. You guys must have a bigger budget than Gloucestershire Constabulary's.'

The German Bundestag was in recession so they had arranged to interview the Minister at his home in Hannover. They were met on arrival at Langenhagen Airport by Hauptkommissar Paul Tischler of the German Federal Police. Tischler greeted them warmly. He told them the Minister was expecting them and had agreed to co-operate fully, but he asked them to be as diplomatic as possible with their questions. They agreed they would be. Tischler conducted them to where an unmarked car and police driver waited, immediately outside the airport entrance, to take the three of them to the Minister's house.

The von Schellenberg house was an impressive stone-built mansion of some antiquity set in a very pleasant, tree-lined suburb. The Minister was awaiting them in his oak panelled study when the maid showed them in. Trepidation was etched on his forehead, Harry thought. Harry and the detectives quickly made their introductions, declined the offer of coffee and got straight down to business. The Minister spoke perfect English, a fact for which Harry was grateful, since he had no German. Harry explained that some compromising recordings had been found on the office computer of a man who, subsequently, had been murdered. Also on the computer were details of the Minister and his PA and of the hotel rooms they had occupied during their recent stay in London for the summit.

'We believe the voices on those recordings to be yours and your assistant's,' Harry said, trying to be as tactful as the circumstances would permit, 'and the nature of the conversation you had leads us to believe the murdered man may have intended to blackmail you.'

The Minister nodded. He had guessed the visit by the police might be connected with the blackmailer and he decided to come clean.

'Yes, gentlemen. I do hope I may rely upon your discretion in this matter. He approached us in the hotel restaurant and he demanded twenty-five thousand euros. The next day, I paid it into what he said was some sort of money-laundering account. He said you wouldn't be able to trace the final recipient of the money. I was relieved that he never contacted me again to ask for more. I fully expected him to do so. It didn't occur to me that he might be dead.'

The Minister handed over the scrap of paper he had been given with Holder's bank account details on it, and he produced his own desk diary to show he had been in Berlin at a number of high-level meetings at the time Holder had been murdered. He expressed the earnest hope that he was not a suspect in the murder. Harry reassured him and asked him to describe the blackmailer. He described the distinctive Colin Holder perfectly, even down to the bright green socks he often wore.

'There's a good chance you'll get your money back,' Harry told the Minister.

Harry glanced at the framed photograph on the large oak desk. The photo portrayed a nice-looking woman in her sixties. She wore evening dress and was linking arms with the tuxedoed Minister. Both were smiling. Harry guessed she was the Minister's wife. The Minister noticed him looking at the photograph and gave a rueful smile.

'What is it that you English say? No fool like an old fool.'

That evening, as they tucked into some hearty Saxon cuisine and quaffed large tankards of foaming beer in Paul Tischler's favourite *Stube*, Harry reassured the German policeman that they had no further interest in the Minister. He explained that the Minister was not the only victim of Holder's extortion activities, merely the most recent one. Having interrogated the blackmailer's work computer, they now had hours of recordings to listen to, files full of photographs to peruse and numerous other suspects to interview. Tischler wished them the best of British luck.

On the last flight of the evening back into Heathrow, Harry tucked the duty-free shop's carrier bag into his large briefcase and stowed it in the overhead locker. It contained a bottle of schnapps – a peace offering for his mother-in-law, to atone for their late arrival at her house the previous Saturday lunchtime, and also a multi-pack of Lorna's favourite German spiced gingerbread, the brand she had liked ever since her childhood years spent on a British Army base on the Rhine.

'Are we back at square one, then?' Lloyd asked him when he had settled into his seat.

'Well, I'm not so sure we're going to find our killer amongst the victims of Holder's extortion racket. We'll have to check them all out as best we can anyway, but my hunch is the man we're looking for is a professional assassin. Holder's scheme targeted people he had legitimate cause to put under surveillance; people whose dirty little secrets he chanced upon in the course of his work. Most of them were old men with a penchant for younger women. I don't think we'll find the killer of Holder and Bowker amongst them.'

'You believe both were killed by the same person, though?'

'Yes, I do.'

Chapter 20

'I think we may have had a bit of a breakthrough,' Kirpal advised the *Op Skylark* team. Warren Daley had summoned all the team members to a progress briefing at Corsham. His face was suffused with relief at Kirpal's announcement.

'Good man yourself, Mr Kohli. Please make my day and get the JIC off my back.'

Kirpal took a deep breath.

'Well now, we weren't getting very far looking at the people in the images and recordings on Holder's office computer – that is, the people he was blackmailing. So, I started looking at *how* he had actually made the images and what he had done with them. Loading your own software onto the computers at GCHQ is a hanging offence, naturally, and Holder would have known better than to do that. I suspected, though, that some of the images weren't as compromising as he'd have liked, so he used software to manipulate them before e-mailing the images to his work account for safekeeping.'

'So, he was photoshopping the images?' Daley asked.

'Yes, to enhance them. So, I had a look at the software he had used. You can tell what it is by checking out the properties of the images. I found a familiar software signature – one that we have seen before. So, next, I got SIS to give me details of Holder's service record, in particular the contents of his training file. Prior to starting his attachment to GCHQ, he undertook some IT training. I don't imagine he needed any further tuition. He was an expert in the field himself. But, as you know, we all have to take those ten compulsory training days a year, and he decided to opt for a course in graphic design, as part of a 'training for trainers' objective in his work plan.'

Harry sat bolt upright.

'Don't tell me. He went to …'

'Yep. St Christopher's Place. SIS paid for him and a few others to take a commercial course with Lurman Corporation.'

Back at Thames House, Harry rifled through his desk drawers and fished out the two business cards. Just then Lorna appeared with two cups of coffee and a plate of German gingerbread.

'I need your help, Love,' he said.

'Anything for the man who buys me my favourite *Lebkuchen*,' she smiled.

'I need to run urgent checks on two businessmen. Would you do one of them for me?'

'Of course. What do you want, full background, credit status?'

'Anything and everything you can get, Love. You're an angel.'

'Just waiting for my wings.'

Harry started out with DVLA records to confirm Edmund Gray's date of birth from his driving licence application, after which Canadian birth records found on the International Genealogical Index confirmed his birth in Manitoba. A check of company directorships filled in more of Gray's career history, then a delve into the Office of National Statistics' database brought up a marriage in Richmond, Surrey. Gray's Home Office file next revealed his permanent residence had been granted on the basis of an earlier marriage in Canada to a UK citizen. Either his first wife had died or that first marriage must have been dissolved, he reasoned. Harry requested a CRO check, in case the guy had form, and he thought it would be a good idea also to ask SIS if they had anything on Gray. Before he could pick the phone up to call Rosie Leyton, however, Lorna was back.

'Done.'

'What do you mean, 'done'? You've only been gone a few minutes.'

'Nevertheless, I'm done. The search yielded no results for anyone of that name. No birth record exists and no driving licences or passports have been issued in that name. Your Alexander Goodenough simply doesn't exist.'

Chapter 21

Lorna glanced admiringly at some of the window displays as she strolled along Oxford Street. Harry had said she might have trouble finding the place, and it didn't help that there were so many distractions along the way. Eventually, she found the little lane he had described which led through to St Christopher's place and, soon, she was in the office of the company's tech supremo, Alex Goodenough.

She handed him her business card, the one describing her as Assistant Director, Home Office Training Directorate. Taking his card in return and grasping it carefully by the edges only, she slipped it surreptitiously into the small plastic evidence bag within her handbag.

'So, how many Home Office staff would require our training?' he asked.

Lorna glanced into what Harry had described as Goodenough's soulless, steely eyes. They seemed to bore through her.

'Probably twenty at a time, continuously, over a period of say, two years. As well as our core training unit staff, though, we have around thirty different departments and agencies within the Home Office, such as Border Force officers, Passport Agency staff, and of course, since the Brexit process began, we have recruited lots of new counter-terrorism staff.'

There was a perceptible raising of Goodenough's eyebrows at the mention of counter-terrorism staff coming to the training school.

'I'd see this as an ongoing commitment,' she continued,' so perhaps I could take some of your brochures and price lists to show to my Director?'

'With such a large take-up of our courses, we would, of course, give a generous discount and we would tailor make the courses to your specific requirements. Perhaps I could meet up with your counter-terrorism staff to discuss what they would need,' he smiled as he handed her the literature.

She slipped the brochures into her bag with the same care she had exercised with the business card. The glossy brochures should retain a good set of prints. She rose to leave. Having shaken her gloved hand, rather firmly, Goodenough rushed across to open the office door for her. The instant he turned his back, she snatched the plastic tumbler from which he had been sipping water during his sales pitch. In a flash, she flung the last few drops of water onto the carpet and dropped the tumbler into her bag. The cup would add a bit of DNA to the investigation.

It was Corey Hart, their NSA contact over at the American Embassy, who made the identification. He wouldn't say too much on the telephone, so Harry and Lorna crossed the Thames to the new US embassy on the south bank. Having crossed the moat and entered the brand new, bomb-proofed building, they steeled themselves for the ridiculously stringent physical security checks.

Lorna had remembered to leave her handbag back in her desk. On a previous visit, an over-zealous member of the embassy's US Marine Corps had confiscated her birth control pills, 'because they are red, Ma'am,' and had also relieved her of the CD containing documents she was planning to share with Corey. The CD was denied entry to the building because 'all electronic gadgets are prohibited, Ma'am.' Her insistence that the CD was no more than a sliver of plastic had cut no ice with the bull-necked marine, until Corey had appeared and put him straight.

Corey came downstairs to meet them and took them up in the elevator to his office suite. Having passed through several code-operated security doors, they were soon seated in his well-appointed room. Corey got straight to the point.

'Yup, we got him. He'd submitted his fingerprint to get a visa and also when passing through our border-control posts a few years back. Looks like he'd got his US visa in a different name. Could be it's his real name, though we can't be sure.'

'So, who do you have him as on your system?' Harry asked.

'Alexei Godunov. A Russian citizen. Here's a photocopy of his visa application.'

Harry looked at the photocopy of the original photograph which had been submitted with the application. It was a grainy image, but it was indeed Alex Goodenough.

'That's him. Scottish my arse!'

'Say, what?' the American looked baffled.

Harry scrutinised the copied application.

'According to this application, he was a Russian army officer?'

'That's right. There was something of a brief thaw in Russo-American relations at the time and we agreed to an exchange of military personnel. Wouldn't happen nowadays, of course. And they were only allowed to visit our training facilities at Westpoint and a few other low-grade military establishments. The Ruskies are a lot more subtle nowadays. You heard about those sleepers we had a few years back? Been in the US so long they spoke perfect American.'

'We believe we have long-term sleepers here, too,' Harry confided, 'and it looks like this may be one of them.'

'Is this your WOTAK fellah?'

'Could be, or there may be more than one WOTAK. Will you keep all this to yourself for the moment, Corey? We don't want Godunov to get spooked and run. We need to find out what he's up to and who his contacts are.'

'You got it.'

Chapter 22

That same afternoon, Adrian Curtis called an urgent meeting at Thames House of as many of the *Op Skylark* team as he could get hold of at short notice. He could have included more of the team by using conference call facilities but what he had to say was best discussed within solid stone walls. Harry spotted a strange face in the briefing room. Adrian introduced the man as Detective Chief Inspector Peter Webb of SO15.

Adrian stood, leaning against his desk, to address the meeting. Harry had noticed that Adrian always liked to deliver significant news whilst standing. It was a bit of a foible, perhaps, but it meant his people knew to listen carefully to whatever he was about to say.

'We believe we now have a better handle on this. Colin Holder had been operating a long-term extortion racket. Using information he had acquired via his normal electronic surveillance duties, he had been blackmailing a number of individuals. Looks like he then decided to up his game. We are convinced he was responsible for writing the initial WOTAK letters and, probably, for that twitter hoax, too. But it's doubtful he could have arranged some of the major power outages and other cyber-attacks. However, he knew some of the details about them which we hadn't released to the public and so it was easy for him to claim responsibility for them *after* they occurred – again with a view to extorting ransom money, but this time from HMG.'

A few people shifted uncomfortably in their seats. No-one liked to hear that a member of the intelligence community, and, moreover, someone who had been on this very team, had gone to the bad.

'Somehow, whilst attempting to take some compromising photos of the Foreign Secretary – not that we have found any such photos – Holder must have blundered across the path of the assassin who was about to carry out the execution of the Minister. We further believe that the assassin then followed Holder to his home where he killed him and stole his hard drive and flash drives containing all the evidence of his blackmail.'

Webb raised a hand to interject. Adrian nodded his assent.

'DCI Lloyd, whom I believe you know, as he's the SIO investigating Holder's murder, has traced a vehicle which Holder hired the day before Geoffrey Bowker was killed. It's almost certain he used it to travel to Bowker's home. The mileage he clocked up is about right. Just as you say, it's likely the killer saw him there. The hired vehicle had been thoroughly cleaned on its return, so it looked like there would be no way of connecting it with the murders of Holder or Bowker. However, DCI Lloyd had the presence of mind to conduct his own physical scrutiny of the car anyway and he found a pretty sophisticated tracking device concealed under a rear wheel arch – not a place the hire company would have cleaned. Holder's killer, the man we believe also killed Bowker, must have put it there.'

'I wonder why he'd have a tracker with him?' Harry said.

'I wondered that, too.' Webb said, 'and I can only surmise he may have intended to put it on the Minister's car if he found he couldn't get a clear shot up at the house. In that event, he could have killed him elsewhere, on a quiet Oxfordshire lane, perhaps.'

Adrian nodded in agreement and continued:

'Clearly, Holder wouldn't have had the capability to carry out some of the more serious cyber-attacks which have been perpetrated of late. We believe others are behind these. We also think that his killer, having interrogated Holder's computer and seen what he was up to, then decided to take over the extortion racket himself. That's the most likely reason why he decided to take the computer's CPU with him, hoping no-one would discover what Holder had been up to. The most recent WOTAK letter was probably sent by Holder's killer. Furthermore, we now believe we know who this new WOTAK might be.'

Adrian nodded to Harry to explain further.

'He's a Russian. Alexei Godunov. He's been operating under a completely fake identity as Alex Goodenough and has been working for an IT company. He also works as a consultant for one of the largest internet service providers based here in London.'

Seeing some concerned faces, Harry sought to reassure them.

'Don't worry. We've had a quiet word with the MD of the internet provider and they'll restrict whatever access he has to the more sensitive areas of their network without him realising it. He's been in the UK for at least seven years, probably longer, and speaks unaccented English, but his background is in the Russian military. Given the lack of a driving licence issued in the Goodenough ID, he's probably using other IDs as well. It's likely he acquired those alternative identities via the usual scam, using dead British infants' identities to give him 'clean skins'. That way, he could obtain British passports and driving licences in various IDs.'

DCI Webb had a question:

'We all know how easy it is to assume a genuine British identity. We saw how it was done in *The Day of the Jackal*. But why do you think Godunov would choose to use a completely fake identity when he could have used a dead infant's one with a genuine birth record to back it up?'

Harry had a theory:

'I think it was partly arrogance. He probably likes his own name and thought he was pretty clever anglicising it. Holding a driving licence in an additional ID, though, means that, if he gets pulled over for a driving offence, the police will be looking for that ID and not for Alex Goodenough. Conversely, if he only used 'clean skins', there'd be a record of where a recent copy of the infant's birth certificate was sent. And there'd be a record of

93

the address any passport or driver's licence in that ID was sent to. Also, there would always be a photo on record of the man using those documents. A totally fake ID, however, has no records to back it up but, at the same time, it leaves no trail.'

There was a short silence as everyone absorbed the information. Adrian spoke again:

'Okay, so, what I'm going to tell you all now must not be spoken of outside this room. A little while back, a Russian 'sleeper' working for GRU defected. He told us he was one of a sizeable network of sleepers who have been in the UK for up to twelve years, waiting to be tasked. The defector – we've given him the pseudonym Oleg – doesn't know the identities of the rest of the network. He believes that no member of the ring, apart from its leader, knows any of the others. Just recently, he was contacted by the head of the ring who didn't reveal his name but gave a pre-arranged code word and told him that he and the other sleepers were soon to be tasked with their missions. Oleg is awaiting his masters' further instruction. We have him and his GRU-issued mobile phone under our protection in a safe house.'

'What's his motivation in defecting?' a dubious Carole asked.

'He fears that, once he's completed his mission, they'll pull him out back to Russia and he doesn't want to go. He's made a good life here. He has a good job working with an internet company and he has a British wife, and young children at good schools. As you know, integration is always a risk the Russians take with sleepers. Also, if he were to carry out his mission, he fears arrest and probable deportation at the end of his sentence.'

'Have we any idea what his mission is likely to be?' Peter Webb asked,

'Well, given his current line of work, we could hazard a guess that it'll be something related to disrupting computerised communications or any internet-run systems,' Adrian said. 'Like Godunov, Oleg started out in the Russian military and GRU arranged for him to study computer science to a high level.'

94

'Any idea why they've decided to act now,' Webb asked.

Adrian nodded:

'Oh, Yes. Putin was as mad as hell after his agents failed to kill the Skripals. A few other Russian defectors targeted for assassination were also poisoned but have recovered. Putin's reaction is almost child-like. If you log on to the Russian Embassy website, you'll see a running banner message on the home page accusing the UK of failing to solve the poisonings. It's laughable, really. It's fooling no-one. The Russians hate losing face, though. Putin's only had one lucky break of late, when one recent defector seems to have accidentally fallen under a tube train. At least, we're presuming that was an accident. But there's no doubt Putin has been humiliated by the failures.'

'He's had a few other disasters, too,' Harry added, 'such as one of his latest 'super' missiles blowing up on the launch pad in northern Russia, and one of his expensive new spy submarines sinking off British waters. As we all know, he let his submariners suffocate rather than accept the Royal Navy's help with a rescue.'

'Indeed,' Adrian agreed, 'and he wasn't exactly pleased at how the recent G8 meeting went. He came in for a lot of criticism, not least from our own late Foreign Secretary. So, now, it seems he has decided to utilise his network of sleepers in the UK as an act of revenge.'

'Do we know who and where they are?' Carole asked.

'All we know is that Oleg and two of the other defectors worked for UK internet service providers. We suspect the Russians have infiltrated numerous such service providers right across the panoply of Openreach and fibre broadband companies. His most likely plan is to have them shut down our entire internet simultaneously at a given signal. He probably hopes it will add to all the turmoil we've experienced since the Brexit business, and that it'll destroy what's left of British trade.

95

His aim, in short, is to severely weaken us. EU or no EU, we're still viewed by Putin as a credible threat to his expansion plans.'

'Should we arrest this Godunov?' Webb asked.

'Not yet, Peter. Not until we can identify others in the network. Taking out just one of them might have little effect on their planned mission. As we speak, I have a sizeable mobile surveillance team scrambling. They'll follow him night and day and we'll start intercepting his communications.'

'Do you need our help with the surveillance?' Lorna asked, 'after all, Harry and Kirpal and I know what he looks like.'

'Absolutely not,' Adrian said, 'since he also knows what you look like. No, Lorna. I want you to go over to the safe house and meet Oleg. Find out if he's been given any more recent instruction regarding his mission and if there's anything else he can tell you which might be helpful. Ask his minders to take a discreet look at his mobile phone while he sleeps to see if he's received any calls lately that he hasn't told us about. In the meantime, we need to get a carefully-worded warning to all the internet providers. They may have saboteurs on their staff. It's possible the plan may also include mounting physical attacks on the internet exchange points. Kirpal, you need to establish where these are located and how vulnerable they might be.'

Chapter 23

Lorna parked at the top of the lane and walked to the small farmhouse. She knocked but there was no reply. She checked her watch. It was lunch time, so it was possible they were in the kitchen at the back. She knocked again. Still there was no response. She couldn't see in through the dense net curtains at the front windows so she bent down and peered through the letter box. All was silent within. She couldn't see or hear anything amiss. She just felt a faint breeze, presumably from a downstairs window somewhere at the back of the property. This was odd. Oleg and his minders must be in.

She peered again through the letter box. This time she noticed something lying in the hall just a short way in from the front door. It was a man's shoe. Nothing odd about that, perhaps, except the shoe lace was still tied. It seemed possible that the shoe and its wearer hadn't parted company willingly.

Walking around to the back of the cottage, she noticed a downstairs sash window was wide open. This was strictly against the rules. She pushed at the back door. It gave way easily.

Caution now took hold and she backed out into the farmyard and took out her mobile phone to report in a serious security situation. Annoyingly, however, there was no signal. She walked a little way back up the lane but still she could not get a signal. There hadn't been any public phone boxes on her way there, which was unsurprising, given the safe house's rural location. This situation would arouse anyone's suspicion, but especially that of an experienced officer such as Lorna. She had two options – to try and find the nearest property and ask to use their landline, or to establish as soon as possible whether Oleg was inside. If he wasn't there, then he would have been taken, but he and his abductors might not be too far away. If she could establish how long ago they might have left, she could use landline in the safe house to alert Thames House and arrange a police cordon around the immediate area.

She walked back to the house and crept in noiselessly through the back door. The kitchen was empty but there were signs someone had been making sandwiches. Bread was buttered and placed on plates and she spotted half-cooked rashers of bacon under the grill, but the grill had been switched off and the food left unconsumed. She placed her fingers on the bacon. It was lukewarm. So, too, was the electric kettle.

Moving silently down the passageway, she stepped into the small dining room. The figure of a male sat slumped forward with his head resting on the table. The silence was broken only by the steady drip of blood from the table into a large pool on the linoleum. She stepped forward and placed two fingers on the man's neck. His skin was still warm but there was no pulse. Glancing around the room, she saw another body lying on his back on the floor, his eyes wide open. She saw a single bullet hole in the man's forehead, so she decided there was little point in checking him for a pulse. Given their ages, it was a reasonable assumption that these were the two minders. Clearly, Oleg had been taken, but she would have to check the rest of the house anyway. As she turned around, however, a figure suddenly appeared in front of her, blocking her way.

'You!' Godunov recognised her immediately.

Before she could react, he grabbed her firmly by the throat and slammed her hard against the wall. There was no way Lorna could explain away her presence. What would a Home Office training manager be doing in a Security Service safe house? The best thing she could do was flee. She lashed out at him, clawing at his face, though she could not reach it. She kicked out wildly at him, but it had little effect. There was no escaping the grip of his muscular hand against her windpipe. She struggled and fought as hard as she could but, gradually, she lost consciousness.

Back at Thames House, Harry took the call. As he took in the news, he blanched. He dialled a few numbers but without success. Alarmed, he dashed straight into Adrian's office.

'I've just been told that Oleg's minders failed to call in at lunchtime. I called the safe house myself and tried the minders' mobiles, but there's no answer. It may be that Oleg's been taken.'

'I sent Lorna over there. Have you contacted her?' Adrian asked.

'I tried to but couldn't raise her mobile. Either it's switched off or she's in a place where there's no signal.'

'Maybe she's not arrived there yet,' Adrian tried to reassure him.

Just then, Kirpal joined them.

'Boss, the mobile surveillance team we've put on Godunov just rang. They haven't been able to locate him. They had to ring in from a call box as they couldn't get a signal on their mobiles. It seems one of the major mobile service providers has been hit with a total outage.'

'Christ Almighty!' Adrian barked.

When Lorna came to, she couldn't tell where she was. The place was in semi-darkness and it was cold and damp. She couldn't move. Her hands were bound tightly behind her back and she was tied to a chair. She tried to move her legs but each ankle was bound firmly to a chair leg. The room, if it was a room, seemed semi-derelict. She could hear water trickling down the wall behind her, perhaps from a burst water pipe, and a breeze was blowing in through rotting wooden boards nailed over the windows. The breeze enveloped her chest and waist and caused her to shiver uncontrollably. Glancing down, she saw her blue cotton shirt was torn to ribbons and her bra was missing.

Struggling vainly to free her hands, she felt her fingers come into contact with cotton lace. Clearly, he had used her bra to tie her hands. It seemed likely he had torn strips from her cotton shirt to bind her ankles, too. Godunov was nothing if not resourceful. She tried to work out where she was. Was this a barn or an abandoned warehouse? She could smell something familiar. It was the aroma that hung round Harry's beloved Morgan – engine oil. She guessed this place was most likely a former garage or body shop.

In the gloom, she could now make out walls of grubby white-washed bricks. She recalled having passed a derelict roadside garage on the way to the safe house. It occurred to her that there might be tools lying around that she could use to free herself. Yet she couldn't move a muscle, partly because she was bound so tightly and also because she was cold and cramped. Maybe if she cried out someone would hear her. She suddenly became aware there was more of the cotton fabric stuffed into her mouth. She gagged involuntarily.

Godunov heard and appeared in front of her again. She saw he had an automatic pistol in his hand.

'Good. You're conscious. Now, you're going to tell me why you are here and what you know about me!'

'The hell I am,' she thought.

He smashed her hard across the right side of the head with the butt of the pistol, sending her senses reeling. He tore off the gag then brought the pistol down again against her left temple. She shook her head. She would not speak. She realised that Godunov wouldn't allow her to go free whether she talked or not. She knew who he was and he had guessed who she was. She knew he would have to kill her. So, this was how it would end. There would be no happy ever after for her and Harry. It would end here and now, in this cold, stinking, abandoned place. Alexei Godunov now smashed the pistol straight into her face. She felt the bones and cartilage of her nose and cheeks breaking. She looked up into those cold, grey eyes and steeled herself for what was to come.

Chapter 24

When they told him the news, Harry felt his legs give way beneath him and he collapsed to the floor. He couldn't hear the rest of what they were saying for the loud ringing in his ears. Suddenly, in his head, he was transported back to his old prep school. He was a nine-year-old boy again, being informed, coldly and clinically, by the headmaster that his mother was dead. Back then, it was the school matron who had caught him as he fainted.

'He's in shock,' Carole said, as they helped him up onto a chair.

He wanted to know exactly what had happened. He demanded to see the body. That wouldn't be possible, they explained. The forensics people had to do their bit.

Adrian told Helena, when he broke the news to her, that he hoped Harry would never see Lorna's body. He'd made the identification himself. He couldn't let Harry see her, not like that. Why the bastard had to destroy her face, he said, he couldn't comprehend. He must be some rare sort of misogynist. Adrian confessed he hadn't even realised Harry and Lorna were in a relationship, but, now, it all made sense, of course. They had worked the same duties, requested the same leave. He blamed himself, he told Helena. He shouldn't have sent Lorna alone to the safe house. He couldn't have known the safe house was far from safe, she reassured him, and the minders should not have let Oleg be taken.

How had Oleg been traced to the house, though, she wanted to know? Adrian speculated that, since Oleg had kept his mobile phone with him in anticipation of being contacted and tasked with his mission, then someone, possibly Godunov, had managed somehow to trace him through his phone's signal.

Adrian suggested that, if the phone companies could give that information to the police, they might well have given it to someone who said he was the police.

Harry's first confused thoughts were not for himself but for Lorna's widowed mother. Lorna was her only child. Now she had no-one. Had anyone told her? It ought to come from him, not from a stranger. Then he thought of the poor children who had found Lorna when they'd climbed into the derelict garage to play. They must be traumatised. He couldn't imagine why she had been killed. Had she disturbed Oleg's kidnappers? Couldn't they have just left her at the safe house, bound and gagged? Why did they have to kill her? And why take her to that filthy spot to kill her? He reasoned that she must have recognised her killer. And he must have recognised her. It had to be Godunov. He would have remembered her from her visit to his office. He would have known they'd come to the safe house looking for Oleg and he probably thought no-one would think of checking out the old garage. He had reckoned without the curiosity and adventurous nature of village children.

Carole made him drink the strong coffee.

'I'm driving you home,' she said firmly.

'No, I have to go to Wiltshire, to tell Lorna's mother.'

'Then I'll drive you there.'

Three days into the week's special leave which Adrian had made him take, Harry was pacing the floor in his empty flat. He'd spent the first couple of days in shocked lethargy, lying on the sofa, playing music and just trying to get used to being without her. He had spent his time in a confused fog, simply trying to get his head around the enormity of his loss.

Waking up in the mornings – not that he slept much – was the worst time. That was when the realisation that he was alone would really hit him. Evenings were little better. He didn't bother preparing a meal. He didn't eat much at all. He couldn't. There was a huge boulder in his stomach, or so it felt. By the fourth day, he had tried to pull himself together. He had made himself tidy the flat, tackle the laundry and the ironing and he had even cleaned the windows. He thought it might help if he kept busy. It didn't.

On the Thursday evening, he started to watch a football match on the television, then he realised his heart wasn't in it. He had no interest in the teams that were playing and his concentration kept wandering anyway. It was getting dark when the doorbell rang. To his surprise, it was Carole. She had a cool bag in one hand and a clinking carrier bag in the other.

'I've brought dinner,' she said.

'I'm not really very h...,' he began, but then he saw her determined expression. 'That's very kind of you, Carole. Come in.'

Bustling past him into the kitchen, she unpacked an oven-proof casserole dish and two foil-wrapped potatoes from the cool bag.

'I've made us a boeuf bourguignon and baked potatoes. Bung your oven on and we'll re-heat them. Where do you keep your wine glasses?'

Two bottles of Merlot turned out to be responsible for the clinking of the carrier bag. Harry obediently turned on the oven and set the kitchen table for two.

'That was extremely good,' he said, as they took the remains of the second bottle of wine into the living room and sat down in the comfortable armchairs.

'You shouldn't be on your own, Harry. Not right now. I had a feeling you wouldn't be eating properly. I'll bet you haven't cooked yourself a meal all week, have you?'

'No point cooking for one.'

'Yes, there is. I do it all the time. And the best part is that there's nobody to complain about my cooking.'

'Nobody would have cause to complain about your cooking, Carole,' he replied, truthfully.

Harry knew Carole lived alone, but he'd never thought it proper to ask why. Even at fifty, she was still an attractive woman. All he really knew about her was that she was very good at her job and she was a kind and thoughtful person; a supportive colleague. She had a generous figure and wore the sort of clothes that flattered her shape. The power suits were not her style. She wore less formal attire; colourful blouses and full skirts which went well with her wild hair. He didn't even know if she had ever been married, though sometimes he had wondered. Perhaps now was the time to ask.

'No Mister Murray then?'

Carole laughed, 'No, Lovey. Oh, there was a long-term live-in man once. He wasn't exactly 'Mister Right', though. More of a 'Mister You'll Do for Now'. We had talked briefly about marriage, but then he did a runner with a younger woman. You know the type – all legs, no tits. It didn't last, of course. She was happy to spend his money for him but she drew the line at washing his socks and underpants. And a man needs home comforts. He needed his back massaging more than his ego. Do you know, the arrogant sod was quite shocked when I wouldn't take him back? But I'd realised I actually like my own company. I valued my independence and my job. Didn't particularly want kids, anyway.'

'We did, you know, Lorna and me.'

'It'll hurt for a long time,' Carole said softly, 'and you'll never forget her, but you'll get over your loss eventually. Really, you will. And a man is never too old to have kids.'

Harry thought the brief flicker of disappointment on her face and the ironic inflection in her voice gave the lie to her assertion that she had not wanted to be a mother. In some ways, she was mother to everyone in the office. She was the most maternal woman he knew. She wouldn't have packed *her* little boy off to boarding school at the age of eight, as his own mother had done. They sat for a while in quiet contemplation. Harry realised she was right about him. He wasn't doing too well on his own just now. He was grateful for her company. They soon finished the wine. He wasn't sure whether the warm glow he now felt was from the food and drink or from the company of a good and thoughtful friend. Perhaps it was both.

'What would you say to a large brandy?' he asked at length.

'Oh, I'd say *'hello large brandy. Come to Auntie Carole'*. But I might have to avail myself of your sofa for the night.'

'No need. I actually managed to tackle the laundry today. There's clean linen on the spare bed. And ladies' toiletries in the bathroom – obviously.'

Harry went to the kitchen where he opened the bottle of schnapps he'd intended for Mrs Bayliss. She wouldn't miss it as she hadn't known she was getting it. He would take her something else next Saturday.

'Cheers, my dear,' Carole grinned, as they set about hammering the schnapps.

Chapter 25

Everyone was surprised Harry had come back to work so soon. He assured Adrian he was fine, and that he needed to be there in order to take his mind off things.

Lorna's funeral in the little Wiltshire church was every bit as well attended as the Foreign Secretary's had been, except that the mourners were not hypocritical politicians paying lip service to someone they didn't like. These were shocked colleagues here to show their solidarity and support. These were soft-hearted former school and university chums whose sobs were a genuine mark of respect. These were all the people who had truly loved Lorna. During the service, his mind had kept roaming back to a day at the office when he had told Lorna she was an angel and she had commented that she was just awaiting her wings. Well, now his angel had her wings.

It comforted him to see a tearful Rosie and also Corey Hart amongst the mourners. Carole and Kirpal were there, naturally, also Helena and Adrian with his wife Ellie, and many others, not just from their own section but from other departments at Thames House. There were many tears shed for Lorna, but his own lack of tears surprised his colleagues. Perhaps they didn't understand that it was no longer sorrow that burned in his heart, but something much more conducive to revenge.

The next few weeks would see him apply himself resolutely to investigating Godunov and his contacts. Whenever he couldn't sleep, he would set his mind to planning how he might bring Lorna's killer to justice or, failing that, how he might make him pay. The terms 'justice' and 'natural justice' played around in his head.

Dave Lloyd now acted as a go-between; a tactful interface between the Security Service and the local police force who, nominally at least, were investigating Lorna's murder. All the usual evidential processes had to be observed, and yet not all the detectives' questions could be answered. However, the local detectives trusted Dave implicitly. If DCI Lloyd said something was off limits, then it was off limits.

Adrian hadn't wanted Harry to attend the inquest, but, of course, Harry had insisted. As the list of Lorna's injuries was read out, her mother's cries of anguish echoed around the coroner's court room. Harry slipped an arm around her shoulders. They had never been the best of friends, he and Mrs Bayliss, but now, somehow, he felt responsible for her. He decided he would remain responsible for her, for Lorna's sake.

His red-rimmed, puffy eyes betrayed the fact that he had hardly slept in the weeks following Lorna's death. How could he? Everything in their apartment reminded him of her. The scent of her hair was still upon his pillow. He wouldn't change the pillowcase, not yet awhile. Her shampoo was in the bathroom. He now used it instead of his own, so he could carry her scent with him each morning. He caressed her clothes in the wardrobe. He fell asleep holding her pyjama top to his cheek. He couldn't bear the pain, yet he didn't even have the strength to weep. He felt completely drained. He wouldn't have got out of bed at all, had he not known how much Lorna would have disapproved.

As the detail released at the inquest continued to play upon his mind, gradually, a different clutch of emotions began to grip him. Now he felt a smouldering anger and a fierce determination to avenge Lorna. He had not the slightest doubt that Godunov had killed her. He hadn't made any firm connections between the killing of Lorna and those of Holder and Bowker as yet, other than the fact that the ammunition used in all three incidents had been Russian. But had he glimpsed such murderous capabilities

107

when he had looked into those hard, grey eyes and been gripped by that big insensitive hand? He believed he had. Had Godunov lain that brutish hand on Lorna? Harry had little doubt that he had. As the days passed slowly by, the rage built up inside him like the steam in a pressure cooker. He told himself something had to be done, and soon, to relieve that pressure.

Chapter 26

The next meeting of the entire *Op Skylark* team was held at GCHQ in Cheltenham. The briefing now included Holder's replacement, an earnest young man called Tom Quigley, as well as DCI Dave Lloyd, who was still conducting the investigation into Holder's murder. Following the meeting, Dave suggested he and Harry go for a drink together. He promised he would drop Harry off at the station later, since Kirpal would be driving the office car back to London. Harry was agreeable. The long train ride back to London would mean less time sitting in his empty flat, dwelling on his loneliness.

'I wanted to tell you how sorry I am about Lorna,' Dave said when he placed their beers down on the table. 'It must be devastating for you.'

Harry simply nodded. He had run out of platitudes and ways of thanking people for their expressions of condolence, which expressions all sounded well-meant but didn't ease his sorrow in the slightest.

'I lost my wife three years ago, to cancer.'

Harry looked up suddenly. He could see from the lines on his face and the sadness in his pale, blue eyes, that Dave's pain hadn't gone away. He wondered how long his own would last.

'God, I'm so sorry. That must have been tough.'

'Well, we knew the end was coming. We had time to say all the things we wanted to say to each other. I guess you and Lorna didn't.'

'No, we didn't. Did you have kids?'

'No.'

There was a silence as both men reflected on their individual grief. Harry had liked Dave Lloyd from the start but now he felt there was common ground between them – a tragic bond, a shared pain. Suddenly, though, he didn't want to talk about

Lorna any more. He didn't want his grief to consume him or define him. Time enough to think about her when he got back to his empty flat with all its reminders. He needed to change the subject.

'So, the electronic surveillance on Godunov is proceeding apace. Though I'm not sure it's going to lead us to any other members of the network, not if their identities really have been kept secret from one another.'

'You know what intrigues me most about Godunov?'

Harry did want to know. He knew Lloyd's thoughts would be worth hearing. He nodded as he sipped his beer.

'Him taking over as WOTAK. He didn't need to do that. He didn't do it to persuade anyone that Holder was still alive. He'd know Holder's body would be found when he failed to return to work. And he could've just broken into Holder's flat anytime and taken the computer files. He didn't need to kill Holder to do that.'

'Yes, that makes sense.'

'Even if Holder had seen him at the Minster's house, he wouldn't have known who he was. No, I reckon Godunov killed him just because he could. And he decided to become WOTAK just because he could. He probably realised from reading Holder's drafts of the WOTAK letters, that Holder had got away with the deception but hadn't succeeded in collecting the big ransom. Godunov would have seen it as a challenge. He probably decided he was smarter than Holder. He thought he could get away with it, and he thought he would make millions out of it. That tells me what sort of man he is.'

'A narcissist, you mean?'

'Yes, that's the fancy word for it. Arrogant. Probably has an unswerving belief in his own ability. Big-headed. Well, in my experience, things with big heads often topple over. Arrogant men are often blind to their own shortcomings and weaknesses. They don't think they have any. Their arrogance is often the cause of their downfall. They think they are invincible. Take Napoleon, for instance, and Mussolini and Hitler.'

'And there was that other uber arrogant Nazi, von Ribbentrop,' Harry added. 'From his death cell at Nuremberg, he wrote to people he thought he had cultivated as friends, people he was arrogant enough to expect would help him. People like the Astors and Wallis Simpson. Nobody wanted to know. When someone's that arrogant, in the end, they're on their own.'

'Exactly. Godunov's a loner. A man without family or friends, I would imagine. He doesn't think he needs friends. Maybe that's his weakness – that and his arrogance in deciding to become the new WOTAK.'

Harry nodded. He was impressed with the policeman's estimation of Godunov. Unlike Harry, Lloyd hadn't been to private prep school or university. He was just a very shrewd copper.

'We just need to work out how to exploit that weakness, Dave. Fancy another beer?'

Chapter 27

'He's on the move,' Adrian announced to the *Op Skylark* team.

Adrian explained that another WOTAK letter had been received promising to bankrupt the UK and, this time, the price demanded for not doing so was thirty million pounds. The letter had been posted in central London on Tuesday but Godunov had taken a train to Edinburgh the next day.

'He's staying in a small garden flat which he's rented for a week via an online booking agency and, so far, he hasn't met with anyone or called anyone. The mobile phone he's using is not the one on the Alex Goodenough business card, but the surveillance team are using a digital scanner to intercept calls on any mobiles he does use. The rental doesn't have a land line but we've bugged the place anyway, in case he has visitors.'

'Maybe he's just on holiday?' Carole Murray suggested. 'Even killers need a break.'

'Or maybe he's there as a distraction,' Harry ventured, 'to throw us off the scent of what's really going on. Maybe it's also to give him an alibi for whatever his network is about to do.'

Kirpal nodded in agreement.

'I think it's a distraction. Edinburgh is one of the locations of the LINX IEPs – that is, internet exchange points. He probably wants us to think that's going to be a target but perhaps it isn't.'

'Where are the other IEPs?' Adrian asked.

There are three in London and one each in Manchester, Edinburgh, Cardiff, Leeds and Liverpool. Oh, and one in Brighton.'

Adrian looked concerned, 'So, do we think the sleepers are planning to attack those points?'

'No,' Kirpal reassured him. 'Most unlikely as they're too public. Though he might want us to think that's the plan. There are much better, less populated locations where the internet could be attacked.'

'Care to explain?' Adrian sat down.

'Okay, so, in 2007, an Al-Qaeda plot to destroy a key London IEP was foiled. The Russians will have learned from that. They successfully mounted their own serious cyber-attack on Estonia some years ago, so we know they're capable of doing it. They managed to shut down the Estonian's internet access and it caused major havoc. The financial and banking activity all ground to a halt, individuals and businesses couldn't send e mails, traffic lights failed and ambulances failed to reach the sick. It was Kremlin-sponsored cyber-warfare.'

'Were they trying to start a real war?' Harry asked?

'No, they just wanted to show the world they could cripple any nation which upset or criticised them.'

'What had Estonia done to upset them?' Harry asked.

'Estonia had announced it wanted to join the EU,' Adrian chipped in.

Kirpal continued, 'Yes, and the thing is that, since those incidents, our IEPs are a little better protected, though only a little better, mind. Godunov wouldn't know that, though. After the Estonian incident, he'd expect our IEPs to be really well guarded.'

'Why aren't they?' Adrian asked.

'Well, our government has always been more focused on the idea that a state could deliberately shut down *their own* internet in order to suppress opposition or prevent public disorder – like the Egyptians did to quell the pre-Arab Spring riots, and as the Indians have been doing for some time in in Kashmir. Our government was so impressed with that possibility that they brought in the 2003 Communications Act and the 2004 Civil Contingencies Act.'

'What's the import of that legislation?' Harry asked.

'Well, those statutes granted internet suspension powers to – of all people – our Secretary of State for Digital, Culture, Media and Sport. Those powers are a means of controlling the populace in the event of civil insurrection or a major conflict. The Chinese did it in Hong Kong, last year, and the Iranians have done it, too. See, if people can't access mass communications, it's much harder for them to arrange mass demonstrations.'

'Good God!' Harry immediately grasped the import of this. Kirpal continued:

'You see, our government expected there might be civil unrest here over Brexit – which, of course, there has been – so they stand ready to use that power. If the protest marches and sit-ins get any worse, the government would be happy to shut down the internet for their own purpose. However, they haven't really taken any really firm measures to prevent a shut-down by a hostile foreign state.'

'So, someone within our own government could act against us and shut down the internet. But it's still possible that the Russians, or indeed any other hostile nation, could mount a physical attack on our IEPs,' Adrian surmised.

'Yes, but they don't *need* to attack our IEPs in order to shut down the internet. It'd be much less risky to physically attack our internet at a more vulnerable and less visible point.'

'And where would the more vulnerable points be?' Adrian asked.

Kirpal tapped on his keyboard and suddenly a world map appeared on the briefing room's large screen. The map was criss-crossed with what looked like aircraft routes. He explained what the team was seeing.

'The many coloured lines you see on the map are fibre optic cables. Some are underground but many are undersea. Ninety-seven per cent of all global communications passes along those cables. Ten trillion dollars' worth of financial transactions are facilitated via those cables *each day*. When the Russians annexed the Crimea, the first thing they did was sever the main communications cable to the outside world.'

'I see, and, since we're an island, the UK's communications to the USA and mainland Europe go exclusively by submarine cables,' Adrian added, following Kirpal's train of thought, 'which means that under the sea is where they are most vulnerable.'

'Exactly, and it's why the UK introduced a ban on the sales of our mini submarines to Russia, but that was only as recently as August 2019. By that time, the Russians had already acquired a whole fleet of our mini-subs. Their new super-silent submarines carry them onboard, purely for the purpose of tracking and potentially severing our cables. The stable door was closed but that particular horse had bolted.'

'What would happen if they did cut our cables?' Harry asked. 'How serious would it be?'

'It's probably not a case of if, but when,' Kirpal opined, 'because the Russians don't have a great capability for conventional warfare so cyber-warfare has long been their main tactic. Depending on which cables they sever, we would lose a degree of power, maybe even total loss of power; all public transport would grind to a halt; the stock exchange would collapse; people who've invested in bitcoin or 'digital gold' – including our own treasury – wouldn't be able to access it. Indeed, they'd find it was worthless. And, in terms of communications, we'd be isolated.'

'I wonder why they haven't already gone for the jugular, then?' Harry thought aloud.

'I suspect they're waiting for the right moment,' Adrian sounded grave, 'and that moment could be now. You see, the US President has just announced he's pulling America out of NATO.'

There was a shocked silence.

Chapter 28

'Alexei! *Privet*,' the thick-set man sat down at Alex's table.

'No, Gregory. Speak only English,' Alex hissed at him, 'and for God's sake call me Alex.'

It was only 10am but the café in Jenner's Department Store was already very busy with Edinburgh's shoppers and tourists. Grigori, or Gregory, as Alex insisted on calling him, glanced down at the plate in front of his comrade.

'What's that you're having?'

'It's called an Ecclefechan tart. Very Scottish. Very sweet.'

Grigori rose and went over to the counter to order himself coffee and one of the tarts. He pointed at the confection with the unpronounceable name. He would not annoy Alex any more than necessary by asking him to repeat it. Alex had a temper that was a legend back at GRU headquarters. Placing the freshly-brewed coffee and the tart on a tray, he returned to the table. He took half the tart in one mouthful and nodded appreciatively. With his mouth still full of warm pastry, raisins, walnuts and lemon, he voiced his concerns.

'Is it not too public here? Aren't you worried we'll be seen?'

'That's the point. We want to be seen.'

'Ah.'

Alex sipped his coffee and broke up the tart on his own plate delicately using a pastry fork. It was his second and he had eaten the first one with his fingers before Grigori had arrived, but he now used the pastry fork as he wanted to make the point that he considered the Georgian uncouth.

'Did you get to Cardiff all right? And did you find the place?'

'Yes, and don't worry, I wasn't followed.'

'You oaf! You were *supposed* to have them follow you.'

'Oh, well, they probably did follow me but I didn't see them.'

Alex bristled with contempt.

'If you really are as stupid as you seem, then, of course, they'll have followed you.'

'So, what now?'

'Did you bring all your documentation with you as I asked, passports, driving licence, cash cards, everything?'

'Yes,' the Georgian reached into his inside pocket.

'Wrap it all discreetly in your paper napkin and leave it on the table.'

'Why do you need all my ID documents?'

'In case you get arrested. I'll return them later. You have your cover story?'

'Yes.'

'And you threw away your mobile phone?'

'Not yet. I'll do so as soon as I leave here.'

'Make sure you do. Now, you should kill time until late afternoon. Check out of your accommodation. Then, why not find a nice pub and spend the last of your Expenses on the local whiskies? They're excellent. Then, meet me at Waverley railway station. We'll catch the 16:52 to London Euston. I will buy our tickets. You join me on the platform, but don't approach me or acknowledge me. I'll slip your ticket to you just as the train arrives. We'll sit separately on the train and we'll meet up on the other side of the ticket barrier when we arrive at Euston.'

'As you wish.'

'Now, give me the receipt.'

'What receipt?'

'The receipt for your coffee and cake, you dolt!'

Grigori removed the receipt from his pocket and handed it over. Screwing it up and depositing it on his tray, Alex shook his head in disgust at Grigori's ignorance.

'You leave now and I'll see if anyone follows you.'

'You will tell Colonel Antonov that I did well?'

'Yes, yes. Now go!'

Grigori drained his coffee cup then left the café. A moment later, Alex saw another man also rise from a table at the opposite end of the café and follow Grigori to the exit. Alex smiled to himself then reached across, drew the napkin containing Grigori's documents across the table and slipped them into his pocket. He waited another fifteen minutes, slowly sipping his coffee, before leaving the café himself. He saw his own 'tail' awaiting him outside Jenner's. The mobile surveillance officer followed him all the way down Princes Street. Alex spotted a single taxi with its 'For Hire' sign illuminated and quickly hailed it. He smiled to himself again. He would lead the MSO on a little tour around the city until he lost him.

It was late afternoon when Alex arrived at Waverley station. He checked that the Euston train was due to depart on time and noted that it would be departing from platform nine. He tucked his ticket into his breast pocket and bought himself a newspaper before making his way along to the platform. With a few moments to go before the train arrived, Alex spotted Grigori amongst the crowd. The Georgian was swaying slightly as he stood alongside his holdall near the platform's edge. Clearly, he had indeed sampled the scotch. Grigori also spotted Alex, eventually, but he did as bid and didn't acknowledge him. As the train pulled into the station, Alex slowly crept into position behind Grigori. As before, he timed his move perfectly. This time, there were screams aplenty as the thick-set Georgian fell under the wheels of the Virgin East Coast train.

Picking up Grigori's holdall as well as his own, Alex turned around and mingled with the disembarking passengers. Next, he headed over to platform eight to await the 17:31 London and North Eastern train to King's Cross.

Chapter 29

Adrian Curtis waited patiently outside Helena Fairbrother's office. She had summoned him upstairs urgently but her PA advised she had some important visitors in with her. He sat obediently for the best part of ten minutes until, eventually, her door opened and the visitors emerged. The PA guided them to the lifts to escort them down to reception. Adrian noticed that the visitors appeared to be either Japanese or Chinese. As he watched them go, Helena appeared at her door and beckoned him in.

'Take a seat, Adrian. So sorry to have kept you,' she smiled, and he detected a slight flush of triumph on her cheeks. He was put in mind of the way her cheeks used to flush, for a very different reason, when he and she used to see each other. But that was long ago, almost in another lifetime. That was before her rapid promotion and his marriage to Ellie. He smoothed his tie and placed his palm against his less than trim waistline. Somehow, the few extra pounds he carried nowadays signified the passage of the years since his relationship with Helena had fizzled out. They also reflected the quiet and uncomplicated contentment of his home life these days.

'Now, I have something to share with you,' she said. 'It's some good news for a change, but you must not divulge what I'm about to tell you to another living soul.'

Adrian was intrigued to hear her news. For a second, he wondered if the good news announcement might be something personal. Had she become engaged or even married, perhaps? He realised he knew nothing of her personal life these days. She hadn't changed her name and nor did she wear a wedding ring, for all that signified these days. Since he no longer played a part in her life outside of their professional relationship, he didn't feel entitled to pry.

She continued:

'Two of those gentlemen who just left are brothers who own the Masuda Corporation of Kyoto. They are one of Japan's biggest and most successful electrical manufacturing companies.'

Adrian's mind raced. Had she married one of the Masuda brothers, or were they simply going to get some better lighting at Thames House?

'Oh?'

'The third man was from the Koanchosa-Cho, Japan's Public Security Intelligence Agency. You remember how South Korea and Japan fell out a while back and stopped sharing military intelligence? It was because the South Koreans suddenly started to demand reparations for their nationals having been taken as slave labourers during World War Two. Well, the Japanese refused to pay up and that led to a major rift. Then, America's recent fence-mending with the Chinese over trade issues meant the Japanese were less keen on maintaining close relations with America as well, and, moreover, were ripe for forming new partnerships.'

'Uh, yes.'

'So, the UK stepped up and, for some time now, we've been sharing with them some of our naval and military intel gathered in their region. They're very grateful for that. Of course, the Russians also saw an opportunity and they offered Japan some interesting trade deals, too.'

'Oh, yes?' Adrian still wondered where this was going.

'Well, in return for our intel exchanges with the Japanese, there was a favour to be called in. So, when we learned that the Russians had approached the Masuda Corporation to provide them with four thousand kilometres of fibre optic cables for their Moscow to Finland railway, we saw a way of exploiting the vulnerability of the Russian cables.'

'Ah, now I see,' Adrian nodded.

'It gets even better,' she beamed, 'because the Russians also decided they would install a further three thousand kilometres of cabling along their Arctic coastline. This wasn't to be just *any* fibre optic cabling, though. It was to be a closed internet system for use by their armed forces. It was to be controlled by their Ministry of Defence and it would connect Vladivostok in the east with Murmansk and Severomersk in the West.'

'Severomersk. That's the naval base for the Russians' Northern Fleet.'

'Yes. And, so far, the Russians have been dependent on the World Wide Web, but the new closed internet would not be connected to the web, and, in theory at least, it should be wholly impenetrable. We believe that, ultimately, not just the military network but the entire Russian internet would be isolated from the global networks. The Kremlin's even planning to put together its own version of Wikipedia. *Russipedia*, perhaps. That way, Putin would have control over the truth and total control over his people.'

'So, it would be a great advantage if we could also tap into the Arctic cables, as well?'

'Yes, indeed it would. The cable was also intended to connect a number of abandoned Cold War bases along the Arctic Archipelago, bases which, reliable sources tell us, are being re-activated.'

'And are the Japanese involved in that project, too?'

'No. The Russians knew their sub-Arctic cables would have to be resistant to very low temperatures. They needed the sort of cables used by Canada. So, they asked the Canadians to develop and supply the cables.'

Adrian now saw exactly where this was going.

'So, we asked the Japanese and the Canadians to ... to do what, exactly?'

'The Masuda Corporation and the Canadian Cold River Corporation have added a few ... properties to the cables. These modifications allow the communications carried by the cables to be tapped into by the manufacturers. They even have an in-built obsolescence so that, in the event of, say, war between Russia and the west, the cables could be shut down remotely.'

Adrian was astonished. He could hardly believe what he was hearing. Helena let it sink in for a moment.

'You see what this means, Adrian? WOTAK and the Russians, can do their worst. We have the capability to retaliate in a big way.'

'So, if they severed our cables, we could shut theirs down, too? Or even mount a pre-emptive strike?'

'Better than that, we can covertly intercept their communications for years to come and they'll never know. It'll be like when the Germans cracked the Russian Enigma codes at the end of World War Two and they worked with our people at Bletchley, right into the 'fifties, intercepting Russian military signals – until that American Communist, Aldrich Ames, blew the whistle. Well, once again, we can monitor or block their military signals or even slip disinformation of our own into their systems.'

'Bloody hell!'

'But you must tell no-one. The *Op Skylark Team* must not be let in on this, and nor should Corey Hart or any of your other American connections learn of it. The Canadians apart, we can't let the rest of 'The Five Eyes' in on this, especially since the US has backed out of NATO. Their president is making some strange alliances of his own these days. Apart from the DG at GCHQ, the rest of the JIC members don't even know about it yet.'

Adrian suddenly felt the weight of this enormous secret.

'So, why am *I* being trusted with this?'

'Your section will be on the receiving end of a lot of high value intel from those cables. That intel could generate any number of operations against the Russians. If anyone questions the accuracy of that intel, it'll be your job to tell them that, whilst they cannot know how it is that we know what we know, nevertheless it's come from an A1 absolutely reliable source. But you will never be able to reveal that source.'

'Okay. And when will these cables be laid?'

Helena giggled.

'Three months ago. Sorry, I wasn't authorised to tell you sooner. They're already in place. We're now in position to start playing some little games of our own.'

He saw her cheeks flush again until they were almost as pink as her fuchsia-coloured jacket. It had been years since he had seen her so thrilled at sharing a confidence with him. It was almost an echo of their past intimacy.

Adrian, however, couldn't throw off his astonishment.

'Bloody hell!'

Chapter 30

'Harry Edwards to see DCI Lloyd.'

This was Harry's first visit to Gloucestershire Constabulary. He was soon seated alongside Dave Lloyd in the office of Dave's superior, DCS Martin Harewood.

He was there to explain why Alex Goodenough, who was believed to go by a variety of aliases, was not to be arrested for the murder of Colin Holder. Harry needed to convince the head of Gloucestershire's Major Crime Investigation Team that there was a more serious terrorism aspect to Goodenough's activities. He explained as much as he could about Goodenough's involvement in a major extortion racket and how it was inextricably linked with the murder of the Foreign Secretary, in which investigation SO15 had the lead. He also advised of Goodenough's involvement in some serious cyber-attacks. Harewood nodded. He seemed convinced.

'It's probably fair to say,' Dave chipped in, 'that WOTAK has become a metonym for cyber terrorism.'

Harewood raised an eyebrow. He clearly wasn't sure what a metonym was, but he glanced at Harry, who nodded in agreement.

'Yes, I understand,' the senior detective said, 'and, of course, it's right that the Security Service should have primacy in the Holder case.'

'I appreciate it may seem, initially at least, that justice has not been served, but let me assure you that this cold-blooded killer will be dealt with severely, even if not by Gloucestershire Constabulary,' Harry said.

'I'm fine with that,' the DCS conceded.

'I cannot say how much I value your support, Sir,' Harry added, 'and, if it's not asking too much, I should be eternally grateful to have DCI Lloyd attached to our team – that's if you could possibly spare your best man. He already has a good insight into this Goodenough chap and his motivation, so he would be an invaluable member of our operation.'

Harewood seemed to be wavering. Perhaps this was too much to ask. Harry had another card up his sleeve, however.

'I appreciate you're under great pressure to solve murders. We're all required to show instant results these days, aren't we? But perhaps there's another box your masters are pressing you to tick. The contribution your squad could make to a very high-level, multi-agency operation, would surely impress the Chief Constable more than a mere prosecution in a rather seedy murder case. And when something is finally done about Goodenough, full credit will be given to Gloucestershire's MCIT.'

The DCS wavered no longer. Harry had persuaded him.

'I think we can spare DCI Lloyd for as long as you need him.'

Harry and Dave chatted as they walked to Harry's office car for the drive to London.

'I'm not sure how you did it, but you did it. Cheers, Harry.'

'I suppose I should have asked you first, but it was a spur of the moment thing. I need a right-hand man, especially since Lorna ...'

'I'll give it my best, Harry.'

'You're welcome to stay at my place tonight, and for as long as you need whilst you're working up in town with us. No need to keep commuting back and forth, unless you want to. Our ... my spare room is at your disposal. And I'd be glad of the company, to be honest. How did that Joni Mitchell classic go? 'The bed's too big, the frying pan's too wide'?'

'Yeah, I know, mate. Mine, too. Thanks. Perhaps we can call at my place first then, and I'll collect a few things. I must say, though, that I'm disappointed we're not going up to town in your little Morgan. I've always wanted to ride in one of those.'

'Oh, I sold it. It had too many memories. Besides, I needed the money for something else.'

That evening, Harry and his house guest settled themselves in front of the television with bowls of Harry's home-made chilli and some beers and caught up with the news. One minor news item caught their attention. Seemingly, there had been a major incident on the Russian railway system. The Russians' latest, hugely expensive inter-continental passenger and freight services, which linked some of Russia's major cities with Scandinavia and the Baltic States – the lines which served the Russian Navy's Baltic fleet at Kaliningrad – had suddenly shut down. A statement from the Kremlin blamed the serious incident on copper thieves digging up the railway's fibre optic communication cables. The report added that such thieves had been targeting Russia's many copper mining works ever since the country's economic recession back in 1998 had forced the mines' closure, and now the thieves were after copper cables, too. The head of Russian railway security and the senior executive of *Russkaya Mednaya Kompania*, their state-owned copper company, had been summoned to the Kremlin to explain their failure.

Dave laughed, 'it sounds like something WOTAK might have done – if he were working for us.'

'Doesn't it just?'

Chapter 31

Adrian Curtis ensured he was fully briefed on fibre optic cables before he attended the JIC meeting, since he had been advised this topic was to be the focus of the meeting.

'The first undersea cables were laid more than a century and a half ago, in the 1850s,' he explained, 'and they were owned by private telegraph companies. Even today, the latest hi-tech fibre optic cables are owned by some of the IT giants such as Google and Microsoft. Of course, submarine cables have always been vulnerable to damage, whether accidental or deliberate. For example, as soon as World War One was declared, Britain severed the five undersea communications cables connecting Germany with other locations in Europe and North America, forcing Germany to rely on wireless communications which, naturally, were easily intercepted. Those intercepted communications were decrypted by the Admiralty's famous Room 40.'

'Do the Russians and other hostile nations know where our cables lie?' the JIC chairman asked.

'Oh, yes. Maps of all the world's undersea cables are available to anyone. Ships have to know where they are in order to avoid dropping anchor in a cable corridor. Of course, most damage is accidental – caused by fishing trawlers, earthquakes, land slippage and so on.'

'Damage by shark bites, too, I imagine,' Sir Henry Mortimer, the Cabinet Office man suggested.

'Funnily enough, no, Sir Henry. There's been no instance of sharks attacking cables. Probably they're repelled by the electric field given off by the cables.'

'So, all this activity we read about, Russian ships sailing over our cables, are they tapping into our communications?' Sir

Henry was keen to show he had at least a little knowledge of the subject.

'No, Sir,' Adrian reassured him. 'Although they keep claiming they're tapping into or jamming our cables, in fact, they're not. Anyone trying to cut into a cable, assuming they could get through the cable's armoured sheath, would receive ten thousand volts of direct current. That would be fatal. But they do have some so-called 'cable tapping and general signals intelligence' vessels tracking our cable corridors, and, recently, those vessels have been equipped with titanium-hulled deep-sea vehicles. The vehicles can reach depths of over six thousand metres – lower even than our mini-subs can go. However, they don't yet have the technology to tap into the signals carried via the cables, and they would, in any case, need to decrypt the signals.'

'Are they likely to have that technology some day?' Sir Robert Vanbrugge asked.

It was GCHQ's Director General who answered.

'Not any time soon, Bob. Tapping in by physically attacking the integrity of a cable is not within anyone's capability as yet. The worst the Russians could do would be to sever a cable, perhaps with an explosive device.'

'Then, we cannot tap into their cables, either?' Sir Robert asked.

The GCHQ DG nodded to Adrian. It was time to share the plan with the trusted members of the JIC. Adrian took a deep breath.

'Well, whilst the Russians were using FLAG links for their communications ...'

'I'm sorry,' Sir Robert interrupted, 'FLAG?'

'The Fibre-optic Link Around the Globe – it's a shared cable link,' Adrian explained, 'so, whilst the Russians were using that shared link, thanks to GCHQ's network security agreements with the companies which own the cables, we have been able to intercept their communications. We also had a couple of Russian intelligence officers, recent defectors, who provided us with the codes.'

'Had?' Sir Henry Mortimer frowned from behind his pebble-glass spectacles.

'Yes, unfortunately, one was poisoned and is still in an induced coma, though it's believed he will recover eventually. The other fell, or possibly was pushed under a tube train at Oxford Circus back in August. The Russians changed their encryption codes anyway. However, they've recently established their own secret internet, one which doesn't rely on the World Wide Web or FLAG and which isn't owned by Google or Microsoft. Currently, its use is restricted to the military but, soon, they plan to extend its use and have their own dedicated web.'

'I suppose that will be impossible to tap into, then?' Sir Henry looked despondent.

'Actually, Sir Henry, that isn't the case. In fact, we already have cable probes in place. I can't go into too much detail, for obvious reasons, but suffice it to say that we have been working closely with the cable's manufacturers, who are not Russian, and probes were built into the cables during the manufacturing process. GCHQ are already intercepting their signals and we have our eye on someone who is going to help with the decryption of their military intelligence signals.'

'But, if the Russians know you have another defector on board, won't they simply change their codes again?' Sir Stuart Bridgeman asked.

'No, sir. The man we have in mind isn't a defector,' Adrian assured them, 'he's a GRU assassin.'

Chapter 32

Dave Lloyd put down the phone on the desk he'd been allocated at Thames House. He looked across at Harry.

'That was Peter Webb from SO15.'

'Yeah? Any developments his end?'

'Not sure if it's relevant, but the ethnicity of an unidentified body they've had in the police morgue up in Edinburgh for a while has now been established. He died under a train at Waverley Station.'

Dave referred to the notes he had just scribbled down.

'Tests on the strontium in his tooth enamel suggest he had lived in the Southern Caucasus. And his DNA places him in the Haplogroup for a Georgian. The isotope evidence also showed the deceased had spent the most recent years of his life in Russia.'

'We'll need to let our counter-terrorism section know. They have an interest in suspicious deaths of Russian exiles. Do we have an image of the man's face?'

'They're sending one through right now.'

Within the hour, one of the *Op Skylark* mobile surveillance team had identified the photo as being that of the man who had met Godunov in the café of an Edinburgh department store. In the meantime, Dave Lloyd had obtained more information from the keeper of the evidence store at St Leonard's police station in Edinburgh. Seemingly, the dead man had no documents on him, not even a rail ticket. However, a mobile phone was found a few yards from the body on the rail tracks where he died. Though it might have no connection, the Edinburgh police felt it could have been in the deceased's pocket when he fell in front of the train. Lloyd asked for it to be couriered down to Thames House urgently.

'Godunov may have slipped up,' he told Harry.

Harry sat in Adrian's office with a file open in front of him. It contained the mobile phone in an evidence bag and a printed list of the phone's recently called numbers. Harry explained that forensic examination of the phone had found traces of the deceased Georgian's DNA upon it, in the form of dried saliva and skin cells.

'A significant number of calls made on the dead man's phone were to another mobile, one we know Godunov has been using. Calls to and from Godunov's mobile had been picked up by the surveillance team's scanner.'

'I thought Oleg said the sleeper network didn't know each other's identities?' Adrian said.

'He did, but all of them would have had contact with the head of the network. In all probability the head of the network *is* Godunov.'

'So, Godunov's phone should have a record of calls to the rest of the network. Could we access that without his knowing?'

'We can certainly try. We'd only need a few minutes with his phone to download everything from it. And it's clearly significant that the dead Georgian met his end in the same way as one of the Russian defectors – under the wheels of a train. And it happened the same day he met with Godunov. Presumably, Godunov didn't think we'd be able to identify the dead man and link them both. Dave Lloyd is liaising with British Transport Police and will check out the CCTV footage of both incidents. If Godunov is found to have been present at both incidents, we can assume, and perhaps prove he was responsible.'

'Good. Now, what we need is a plan to fix this WOTAK.'

Carole now poked her head around Adrian's door.

'Sorry to interrupt. Harry, there's a call for you. It's James McLean from CIFAS.'

131

Chapter 33

Two days later, Harry stood in a queue at the bank. He flipped open his pocket diary and removed the slip of paper on which he'd written the account details the CIFAS man had acquired for him. It wasn't long before he reached the head of the queue. He handed the bank clerk the slip of paper and the envelope full of cash.

'I want to deposit the enclosed cash – it's £2,000 – into this account. It's the account of Mr Alexander Goodenough.'

The clerk wearily recited the questions she was supposed to ask these days when people sought to pay large sums to other people. She was obliged to do so, even though it was mainly the elderly or vulnerable people who were being caught up in fraud.

'Do you know the holder of the account personally? You're happy it's not a scam?'

Harry was prepared for the question this time. He hadn't expected it when making the previous deposit the day before, but now he had worked out what to say.

'Oh yes,' Harry assured her, 'I'm buying a second-hand car from a reputable dealer.'

As he walked back to Thames House he wondered, not for the first time, if he were doing the right thing. Seven thousand pounds was a lot of money. Would Lorna have approved of him doing this? He told himself she would. She had never really liked the Morgan anyway.

Carole had been sitting in the French café-patisserie for forty-five minutes and was on her second cup of coffee by the time Alex arrived. He was later than usual today, according to the mobile surveillance team's observation of his daily habits. The café in St Christopher's Place was a good spot for mounting surveillance on his comings and goings, since Alex usually bought his lunch sandwich there. They'd noticed he had a sweet tooth and invariably added a sugar-laden cake or biscuits to his order.

Carole had volunteered for this morning's task. Although she was usually happy enough to be a desk-bound analyst, running her own little domain, she welcomed the occasional opportunity to put other aspects of her training to good use. She liked to get out of the office from time to time and feel that adrenalin rush that came with surveillance duties. Adrian hadn't needed too much persuading that, as a fifty-year-old female, she had the advantage of that cloak of invisibility which age bestows upon middle-aged women.

Alex entered and headed for the counter. She watched him discreetly over the top of her paperback novel. He ordered a sandwich and a flapjack. Whilst he waited for his sandwich to be made, he idly flipped through the messages on his mobile. When his order was ready, he slipped the phone back into his jacket pocket, took out his wallet instead and paid for his order. Turning away, he pocketed his change. Immediately, Carole stowed her book in her bag, got up and headed towards the door marked 'WC', which was located to one side of the counter. As Alex stepped away from the counter with his purchases, Carole collided heavily with him.

'Oh, terribly sorry!' she said.

Alex simply scowled, scraped past her and exited the café. Through the café window, she saw him head towards the adjacent front door of Lurman Corporation.

Once in the tiny toilet cubicle, and with the door firmly locked, she sat down on the toilet seat lid, took the i-pad and cable from her handbag and connected Alex's mobile phone to it. Moments later, she was done. Emerging from the WC, she handed the mobile to the cashier.

'Someone's dropped their phone just here on the floor,' she smiled. 'I'm sure they'll be back for it.'

Chapter 34

The following week, Alex received a summons to meet with Colonel Antonov, the Russian military Attaché. On the way to his meeting, which was to be held in the rather pricey restaurant where Antonov regularly lunched, just around the corner from the Russian Embassy, Alex stopped off at an ATM. He didn't know whether he would be expected to take lunch with the colonel and, if so, who would pay, so he thought he'd better withdraw some cash. He had laid out quite a bit of money lately, particularly with the Edinburgh trip, and he needed to check whether his expenses claim had been processed as yet and the reimbursement paid into his account.

As his bank balance appeared on the screen, he had a surprise. The balance was much greater than he had expected. In fact, it was seven thousand pounds more than he had expected. Perhaps the expenses section had made a rare mistake and entered an extra nought to his payment, he speculated. Well, that was their stupidity. He wouldn't rush to pay it back.

He was deep in thought about the money, wondering if he might get to keep it, as he alighted at Queensway underground station. He did not notice the thirty-something man with the lank blond hair peeping out from under his hat, who also exited the tube station. Protocol dictated Alex should arrive at the restaurant before the Colonel, so he quickened his pace. Fifteen yards behind, on the opposite side of the street, Harry did so, too. He was surprised when Alex did not head towards the embassy but continued on a few blocks. He decided to follow him anyway. He spotted, but managed not to be seen by Thames House's two-man mobile surveillance team which was also following Godunov.

Alex took a seat at the table booked by Antonov's assistant. He chose the seat facing the wall, since he supposed the Colonel would wish to sit behind the table on the comfortable banquette. He ordered a beer for himself and had only taken a single sip when Antonov appeared. He rose to greet the Colonel, who bade him sit.

'Are you eating?' the Attaché asked.

Alex had already seen the menu – and the prices.

'I won't. I'm expected back at work.'

Antonov gave his order to the waiter. As soon as the waiter had walked away, the Colonel came straight to the point.

'So, the railways business, have you found out who was responsible?'

'I don't imagine it was the British. They don't have the capability to tap into our cables, and even if they did, they would have to decrypt the signals. Unless you know of any more traitors from our own military who might be assisting them ...'

'No. No more defectors, at least. The ones in the hospital in West London will not recover. We have people who will see to that. Are you sure the members of *your* network are completely trustworthy?'

'They are now. I dumped the Georgian. His butchery skills were okay but he wasn't bright enough to get the job done successfully. His ignorance was a threat to our success. I can only think someone in our own military intelligence must have been involved in the railways business. I presume you've checked out your staff at the embassy, Colonel?

'Of course, I have. Do you take me for a fool?'

'No, Colonel. I apologise. In the light of the railways incident, do they still want us to continue with our proposed operation?'

'Yes. They want you to do it soon.'

The waiter returned with the Colonel's bottle of wine. He made to pour it but Antonov waved him away. He would pour it himself. Alex took another sip of his beer.

'You've never seen real military action, have you, Alex?'

'That's not the sort of warfare I was trained for, Colonel,' Alex replied. He sensed the Colonel didn't like him very much.

'That's a shame. I became a man in Afghanistan. Wars should not be fought from behind desks. A spell in Syria would make a warrior of you.'

'If you say, so, Colonel.'

Their conversation ceased with the appearance of the waiter with Antonov's meal. Alex took this as a signal to depart.

From the newsagent's window across the street, Harry watched him leave and saw the surveillance officers depart also. Harry realised that Alex hadn't been in the restaurant long enough to have had a meal, so it was more likely to have been a briefing. Having recognised Colonel Antonov when he approached the restaurant – Harry and all his surveillance-trained colleagues made it their business to know every face employed at the Russian embassy – he would not follow Alex any further. His plan was working out better than he had dared hope.

Purchasing a newspaper, he removed an envelope from his pocket, placed it inside the newspaper and headed out across the street. Entering the restaurant, he glanced around looking for a vacant table. He immediately spotted the Russian Military Attaché who was engrossed in his lunch. Passing Antonov's table, Harry bent down by Godunov's now vacated chair and, when he straightened up again, he was clutching the envelope.

'This was on the floor just here. Is it yours?'

Antonov looked up at the blond-haired man then glanced at the envelope. It had Alex Goodenough's name and address on it.

'Oh yes, it belongs to my companion who just left. Thank you. I'll return it to him.'

Antonov took the envelope and Harry took a seat at the opposite side of the restaurant.

The colonel continued to eat his meal but, soon, his curiosity outweighed his appetite and, putting down his knife and fork, he took up the envelope again. It was not sealed, so he removed the contents. It was a bank statement. It was Godunov's bank statement; a list of transactions in relation to his account in the name of Alexander Goodenough. Antonov cast an eye down the column of debits and credits. The colonel's meal began to grow cold as he continued to stare at the figures. At first, he looked puzzled. Then he looked displeased. Summoning the waiter, he paid his bill and left. The waiter collected a menu from the counter and took it to the blond-haired man's table, but that man, too, had left.

Back at his embassy, Antonov fished the indigestion tablets out of his desk drawer and put one in his mouth. Irritated, he snatched up the telephone receiver.

'Dima, I need the personnel file on Alexei Godunov.'

Chapter 35

Dave Lloyd was waiting for Harry when he returned to the office.

'We've had a call from Special Branch. Thames River Police have found a body in the water down near Greenwich. He had a Russian ID card in his inside pocket. He'd been shot in the head and the body's been in the water for quite some time. Could have gone in anywhere. In view of his nationality, they thought we might have an interest. Oh, and they think he might have been tortured. His face was badly smashed in.'

Harry's stomach turned over. He pushed to the back of his mind the image of Lorna's last moments, an image that had invaded his waking hours ever since the inquest. Dave would not have known the exact details of her demise. If he had, he wouldn't have mentioned the injuries to the dead Russian's face. Harry pulled himself together, quickly.

'Did they give you the name on the ID?'

'They've e-mailed through a photocopy. The ID card is intact as it was laminated in plastic, but I can't read the Russian script.'

Dave handed Harry the printout. Harry couldn't make out the name either, as he wasn't familiar with the Cyrillic alphabet, but he did recognise the holder's face. He'd seen it on an urgent internal circular about a missing person. It was the defector whom they had dubbed 'Oleg'. This was the man Lorna had been on her way to see when …

He took the printout straight to Adrian's office.

'They did him over quite badly,' Harry said, 'and his face is unrecognisable. Is that a GRU thing, do you think?'

'Maybe. Well, we won't release any details whatsoever to the press. We don't want to discourage other defections. The Russians do, of course, which is exactly why they left his ID on him. So long as we keep the body under wraps, the Russians can hardly announce his death without incriminating themselves in his kidnap and murder. They might just assume he's been washed out to sea. I don't think we'll be seeing this chap's name on a banner splashed across the embassy's website.'

'The way he was killed – one shot to the head – and his face being smashed in, …'

'You think Godunov killed him, and Lorna, too?'

'I'm positive. If it wasn't Godunov who took Oleg, whoever did would just have left Lorna dead at the safe house with the minders. As soon as Godunov saw her there, though, he would have recognised her. He'd have realised we're on to him and he'd have wanted to know how much we knew about the network. He'd have tried to beat that out of her. Looks like she didn't talk. I'd be surprised if he was alone, though. Lorna wouldn't have gone with him willingly. Even if she was unconscious, he must have had help to get her out of there and down to the place where he killed her. And somebody must have helped him get Oleg away from the safe house. Since we haven't arrested him, he probably assumes we don't know the identities of the whole network. And he's arrogant enough to carry on anyway. It was Godunov who killed Lorna. I'm sure of it.'

'Then I'm not sure you should be on this operation, Harry.'

Harry's face fell. He hadn't expected that reaction.

'Don't do that to me, please Adrian. Don't do that.'

'Okay. I'll leave you on it for the time being, on one condition.'

'Which is?'

'That you agree to undertake a psych-evaluation. I need to know you're okay to continue.'

'You needn't worry about me, Adrian.'

'I'm not. I'm worried about me. Anything happens to you because your mind isn't on it, and they'll come down on me like a ton of bricks. If you get the all-clear, you can see it through to the end, but be careful. When a case gets this personal it's too easy to be blind-sided and to take too many risks. Remember, this is about disruption, not revenge. Now, first make the appointment with the psychologist and then chase up the techies and see how we're going with tracing Godunov's phone contacts.'

Kirpal had just got off the secure phone to NCSC and returned to his desk where Harry awaited him.

'It took Carole just minutes to download all the data from Godunov's mobile,' he explained, 'and now we have details of all his movements – every place he's been with that phone in his pocket. We have every text message he sent and every image he stored; every password, every internet search and every cookie.'

'Brilliant,' Harry enthused.

'That said, however, he's used this phone mostly for voice calls so, although we know which numbers he called, we won't know the content of those calls. But, the analysts at Corsham are carrying out similar checks on all the contacts in his phone's address book and on the holders of every phone he's called using this phone.'

'That sounds like it'll take forever,' Harry said.

'Not at all. The Cyber Centre has programmes to do this instantaneously. We'll have all the information we need before the end of the day. We just need to decide what we want to do with it. Do we move in and arrest them or do we task GCHQ to listen in on all of them?'

'I suppose it depends on how many contacts there are and how big a surveillance op we'd need to mount. If Godunov gets suspicious about having mislaid his phone this morning, he might suddenly decide to dismantle the network and lie low. At the very least, he might get them all to change phones. We should act quickly. How many contacts did he have on the phone?'

'Fifteen.'

'Fifteen? Is that all?'

'Yes, and that includes the switchboard at the Russian Embassy, the Russian Military Attaché's landline and a phone registered to his boss at Lurman, Edmund Gray. But we know he was using several different mobile phones whilst in Edinburgh, so it's possible he has more contacts spread across those phones. Then again, it can't be very convenient to carry around several phones and to try and remember which contacts are on which phone. So, if that is the case, I think he probably keeps all his mobiles in one place – somewhere he spends much of his time.'

Chapter 36

Harry sat in the reception area, wondering what he would say when he went in, and what Adrian would say if, instead of going in, he chickened out and did a runner. Usually, the aroma of coffee relaxed him, but not this morning. This morning, it made him feel queasy. He was just thinking he'd rather walk naked down Regent Street in the rush hour than bare his soul to a total stranger in a private room, when the door opened and that stranger beckoned him in.

'Mr Edwards?' she said.

'Harry,' he rose and took her outstretched hand.

'I'm Amandine Lefevre. Please come in.'

Feeling like a lamb being led to the slaughter, he trotted in behind her meekly and sat in the comfortable looking armchair she indicated he should take. She was younger than he'd expected. He didn't know if that made things easier or harder. He had half expected he would be lying down on something like the old-time psychiatrist's couch, so he was relieved at least to be sitting upright. He felt less vulnerable sitting up. As she took the other armchair, he was also relieved to see she didn't seem to be taking notes.

'You've had a sudden and unexpected bereavement, I understand.'

'Yes, I suppose that's what you'd call it. A bereavement.'

'What would you call it, Harry?' her voice was soft.

He took a deep breath and shrugged.

'I, … it's, … the bottom has fallen out of my world. I've lost the woman I love, the woman I planned to marry. She *was* my world, my soul-mate. We'd been together five years. It was supposed to be for ever. It wasn't an accident or an illness. It was a horrible and deliberate murder. The word bereavement sounds too … I don't have the words.'

Amandine let the silence reign for a few moments to allow Harry to regain his composure and to muster his thoughts.

'How are you sleeping?'

'Sleep? What's that?'

'Would you like something to help you sleep? Your GP could arrange that.'

'No. I have things to do. I'd worry about taking sleeping pills in case they messed with my head.'

'Have you taken any compassionate leave?'

'A few days. I've too much to do.'

'I'm sure you don't need me to tell you that you should take leave. You need time to grieve. It's an essential process. The loss of a loved one is a deep wound. Like all wounds, it takes time to heal. You can't grieve or heal at work.'

'But I don't want to sit alone at home. I can't even make a coffee for one. I find myself taking two mugs off the shelf. It's been years since I cooked for one, shopped for one.'

'Is there anyone who could stay with you, or someone you could stay with?'

'Well, strictly speaking, I'm not alone all the time. A colleague sleeps over at my place during the week. It's just a short-term arrangement. But it does take my mind off things.'

'That's good. What do you do at weekends?'

'My laundry, bit of shopping, have a few beers, watch sport, and I try and keep the place as Lorna would have wanted it.'

Again, Amandine left a silence. He wondered what *she* did at weekends. No wedding ring, he noticed. He supposed she spent her time reading big tomes on psychology. She spoke at last.

'Did they get him?'

'No.'

'How do you feel about that?'

'Oh, we'll get him. I'll get him.'

Amandine simply nodded.

'Make an appointment to see me next week.'

Back at Thames house, Adrian saw him arrive and called him into his office.

'How did it go? With Amandine, I mean?'

'Not as bad as I'd expected.'

'Good. You will keep the appointments, won't you?'

Harry shrugged, 'it's your budget, Boss.'

Chapter 37

Later that night, three figures in dark clothing walked down the alley at the back of the tall Georgian terrace and stopped outside the premises with the large food waste bin outside it. The front of the patisserie on St Christopher's Place was covered by CCTV but there were no such security devices at the rear of the premises. The food bin provided a useful step up as the men silently climbed the back wall and jumped down noiselessly into the yard. Seconds later, they had scaled the drainpipe and were inside the building. They had no difficulty locating the locked office of Alex Goodenough. Two of them had been there before.

Door and desk drawer locks were soon picked and three mobile phones were located in one of the drawers. Kirpal uploaded all the data from the phones whilst his tech colleague attempted, unsuccessfully to access the desktop computer. Harry continued to search the office in case there were more mobiles to be found. The phones were replaced, the drawer locked again and the men left.

At ten o'clock the following morning, confirmation having been received from the surveillance team that Godunov had just appeared at St Christopher's Place, Harry, Kirpal and their tech colleague, now dressed in smart business suits, turned up at the address which his phone traffic had disclosed was Godunov's home. They were half expecting to find some surveillance cameras around the exterior, this being a house rented by the Russian Embassy, but there were none and they had no difficulty gaining entry.

The three-storey, nineteen-sixties' townhouse had an integral garage. The house was reasonably well furnished but devoid of ornaments, photographs or any expressions of personal style. Harry thought it a fairly sterile bachelor pad. There were some books on the shelves, mainly thrillers, and there was plenty of vodka and scotch in the drinks cabinet, but not much in the way of foodstuffs in the small sparsely equipped kitchen. He felt the house reflected its owner – stark and devoid of warmth and personality.

Their thorough search yielded no further mobile phones, and the small safe within the bedroom wardrobe, defied their attempts to open it. A small device was slipped into each of the house's two telephone handsets. With the house left in the same tidy state in which they had found it, the three men departed.

Godunov let himself into his office and switched on his computer. He flipped the plastic lid off the cup of coffee he had picked up at the patisserie and took a bite of the flapjack which would serve as his breakfast. Immediately, his mobile phone rang. It was an automated voicemail from his 'Homeguard' service advising him his silent house alarm had been activated. His concealed camera system would also have been activated. Tapping the appropriate codes into his phone, just seconds later, he was looking, from an observation point on top of the book case, at the three intruders in his living room. His jaw muscles tightened at what he saw. He quickly inserted a cable into his phone and transferred the video recording to one of his large computer screens in order to enlarge the image. He recognised two of the intruders immediately. Yanking opening his desk drawer, he shuffled through the stack of business cards until he found the two from his recent Ministry of Defence visitors. He held them a up to his nose. His eyes glinted with rage.

Chapter 38

GCHQ staff had not been so busy nor worked such long hours since the Gulf War. All leave had been cancelled and unlimited overtime authorised the moment the *Operation Skylark* team had uncovered details of exactly what it was the Russians had been planning. Over at the National Cyber Security Centre, staff had been working around the clock, too. Helena was again summoned to a special crisis meeting of the JIC. She took Adrian with her.

Lt Colonel John Hooper was not present. The Chairman, Sir Stuart Bridgeman, explained that Hooper had been summoned to a COBRA meeting at Downing Street. That high level gathering of the Cabinet Office's Civil Contingencies Committee was sitting to agree what, if any, military response there should be to the recent unwelcome resurgence of terrorist activity in Northern Ireland. The unrest was, the chairman explained, a direct result of the border issues thrown up by Brexit.

'Gentlemen,' Helena began, 'we have uncovered the identities of most of the Russian sleepers and now have a pretty good idea of what their mission was, though, unfortunately, we didn't discover this soon enough to interrupt it. A lot of damage has already been done. Adrian, please fill us in.'

Adrian rose to his feet.

'Gentlemen, some of the sleepers had been placed within IT and telecoms companies. That much we knew early on. But the interception of a significant amount of phone and e mail communications has now led to the identification of a large number of other individuals who have been embedded within a range of different organisations. Their mission is to cause the maximum amount of chaos around the UK, tying up law enforcement and shaking confidence in the government.'

'Which organisations are we looking at?' Sir Stuart asked.

'These include environmental activist groups – a range of groups which are pushing for climate change and those disrupting fracking operations. You'll be aware that, this week, the BBC went off air owing to a large and rather violent occupation of their studios by some of these 'eco-warriors'. Also, some far right groups such as the 'English Supremacy League' and the 'English Identitarian Movement' have been infiltrated by Russian sleepers and have been encouraging and engaging in some of the violent unrest on the streets. The Russians are taking advantage of the general unrest caused by our leaving the safety of the European Union.'

'Have the sleepers been arrested?' Sir Stuart asked.

'Yes, Sir. We rounded up most of them, the ones we know about, that is, though not before Russian money was injected into their operations. Some of that money will pay for their defence lawyers, too. They've already kicked off some very violent demonstrations. Fracking company lorries have been hijacked and burned and their drivers beaten up; airports have been shut down by the environmentalists' drones, and the gangs demonstrating outside Parliament and Buckingham Palace are growing in number and in violence. Gluing themselves to trains is another trick which has delayed the trains' departures and forced commuters to use taxis, which, of course, is more environmentally harmful.'

'You said *most* of the sleepers have been apprehended' Sir Stuart said, 'does that mean there are others still active?'

'Yes, Sir.'

Adrian looked imploringly at Helena. He thought the next bit of bad news ought to come from her. She nodded and took up the story.

'As you may have heard, the violence and disruption has reached such a level that the Secretary of State for Digital, Culture, Media and Sport is currently considering shutting down the UK's access to the internet. He will justify such drastic action by suggesting that this will prevent these dissident groups from rallying their followers. It would also limit press reporting of the many incidents in order to preserve public morale. However, he must be prevented from doing so at all costs. It would play into the hands of the Russians.'

'I don't even know who *is* the SoS for Culture,' Sir Arnold barked.

'It's Mark Tredarran,' Helena informed him.

'The businessman? Chap who owns the Tredarran Corporation?'

'Yes, Sir Arnold,' she nodded gravely, 'he must be made aware – if he doesn't already know – that to shut down the internet would do more harm than good. The UK would be isolated in terms of communications. All our institutions, especially our defence systems, depend on the internet. He must be prevented from taking this course.'

'But, surely, to do so would harm his own business interests, too?' Sir Arnold said.

Adrian glanced across at Helena. He wondered how she would word this particular disclosure.

'Well, he may have other, more overriding interests,' she said.

'Good God! Are you implying he may be working on behalf of the Russians, too?' Sir Robert exclaimed, 'but why?'

'We're not absolutely certain, but what is certain is that Mark Tredarran isn't his real name. Originally it was Marcus Trenda. He was born in Czechoslovakia. He sought asylum here in 1968 just before the Prague Spring. When he arrived, he seemed to have a lot of funds to set himself up pretty quickly. Over the years, he's become a significant donor to the Conservative party and then he stood for election himself. Since his company was a major employer in his local area, even the working-class locals voted for him.'

149

'But how would he actually shut down the internet? I mean, how would he achieve this physically? Is there an off switch or something?' Sir Henry asked.

It was Sir Arnold Mayhew who answered his query.

'I think he would have to ask GCHQ to intervene with the companies, Henry. Minister or no minister, we would refuse. Oh, he could bypass us, but it would be time consuming for him to start directing all the major internet providers to shut down their services. Most would decline and he'd have to take legal measures to enforce them to do so. By the time it all got sorted out, he'd have lost the momentum that a sudden shutdown would cause. Can't we just get him sacked, though? Wouldn't that be possible?'

'Not easily, Sir Arnold,' Helena explained. 'Though the PM could sack him from his cabinet, I'm not sure he'd want to. Tredarran is one of the biggest funders of the Tories. He's a leading member of the Conservative Party himself and, of course, he was one of those MPs who helped arrange for Ivan Thompson to lead the party and to become, initially at least, an unelected PM.'

'Surely, Tredarran would've been vetted before being selected by his party?' Mayhew asked.

'Indeed, he was,' Helena replied, 'but being born overseas and being a successful asylum applicant have never been enough to bar someone from holding elected public office. If you gentlemen will ensure he does not succeed in persuading the government to shut down the internet, the Security Service will deal with Tredarran.'

Chapter 39

Dave Lloyd heard the apartment door slam as Harry left for work. He squinted at the alarm clock on the bedside table. It was eight-thirty. Normally, he would be leaving with Harry. However, they had agreed that Dave would give Peter Webb a call at SO15 and see if he could meet up with him soonest to discuss Edmund Gray and to find out whether SO15 had any knowledge of Gray's links with Godunov's Russian operations. Webb wouldn't be at his desk before nine o'clock, so there was no rush. Another half hour in bed would leave Dave plenty of time for a shower and a bite of breakfast and then he would make the call.

He turned over and snuggled down again under the duvet. He heard Harry's car start up. He could also hear the gentle hum of traffic from the North Circular Road a few blocks away. The sound was soothing and, gradually, he began to sink back into warm, comfortable sleep.

A sudden click roused him back to wakefulness. It sounded like the front door opening, but Harry had left already. Maybe he had come back for something. Surely, though, he'd have heard Harry's key turning in the lock first? A slight creak from down the hallway told him it wasn't Harry. The creak came from a light footstep. Harry wasn't the sort of bloke to creep about, not even to avoid disturbing his house guest. Harry was a slammer of doors and drawers. It was the only thing about Harry that Dave found irritating, that and the fact that he always had the kitchen radio on full blast first thing in the morning. He guessed Harry did it to dispel the loneliness.

Dave slipped silently out of bed and stepped to a position by the bedroom door. Putting his ear to the crack in the door, he could hear someone moving around in the lounge, opening and closing drawers and shuffling about. Clearly, it was an intruder.

A common burglar, maybe? Or could it be something more sinister? Dave was just wondering whether to go and confront the man, when he realised the footsteps were out in the hall again. The intruder was now making his way to the bedrooms. Dave looked around for somewhere to hide, but the small guest bedroom had few places where he might conceal himself. The space beneath the divan bed certainly wasn't big enough to accommodate him. The room didn't have a wardrobe either, just a bed, a single bedside table and a small desk.

The bedroom door knob began to turn. Dave rolled across the bed and threw himself down flat on the floor on the far side of the bed. He heard the stranger enter and begin searching the desk drawers and the bedside cupboard. To his relief, he soon heard the intruder leave the room and step across the hallway towards the flat's master bedroom, leaving the guest room door open as he went. Dave crept back across the bed again and peered through the crack between the open door and the door frame. He saw the shadow of the man moving around in Harry's bedroom. He waited for the intruder to emerge from the bedroom so he might get a good look at him.

It wasn't long before the man appeared in Harry's bedroom doorway and glanced around before turning to head back down the hallway to the kitchen. Through the crack, Dave caught just a brief glimpse of his face, but that glimpse was all that was needed. He had not seen the man before but he had seen his image many times, on file, on databases and on surveillance footage. It was Alexei Godunov.

Dave next heard Godunov give the kitchen in particular a most thorough search. He heard the Russian scraping around in the refrigerator and the freezer. Dave knew those were common hiding places for crooks to keep drugs or stolen jewellery and also, he supposed, for spies to hide weapons or other secret stuff. He risked a quick glance down the hallway and saw the man's back leaving via the front door. He didn't think Godunov had found anything since he appeared to be leaving empty-handed. Perhaps he had just wanted to know more about Harry. Dave hoped Harry would not have left anything lying around which might give a clue to his true employment.

As soon as Godunov had closed the front door behind himself, Dave moved quickly into the living room. Peering out from behind the curtain, he watched Godunov walking to the end of the street and heading off in the direction of the Tube station. Dave stared after him for a moment or two, wondering whether there would be any point in following him. He decided against it, however. Instead, he had a quick look around the apartment himself to get an idea of what, if anything, Godunov might have seen.

He first checked out Harry's bedroom and his attention was drawn immediately to the framed photograph of Harry and Lorna on the bedside cabinet. The photo showed the couple in happy times, arms around each other and broad smiles on their faces. So, now Godunov would link Harry with Lorna and would doubtless link them both with the Security Service. He wondered what Godunov would do with that knowledge.

His thoughts were interrupted by the sound of a vehicle starting up out in the street. From the bedroom window, Dave saw the fairly nondescript car pull out from where it had been parked, some fifty yards or so away. The vehicle cruised very slowly past, allowing Dave to get a good look at the two heavy-set male occupants who, in turn, seemed to be taking a good look at Harry's place. The vehicle then sped up and turned right at the end of the street, heading for the North Circular.

Chapter 40

Harry went along to see Amandine with much less trepidation this time.

'You didn't come last week?' she said.

'Sorry. I had to cancel as things were really busy. I'm here now, though.'

'Have you booked that leave yet?'

'No. Same lame excuse.'

'It would help if you could get away somewhere. A change of scene, some relaxation.'

'A holiday for one? I don't think so.'

'Is your colleague still staying at your place?'

'Yes, he is, and he's good company. He understands about ... bereavement.'

'Sleeping any better?'

'Um, maybe. I'm used to working odd hours, though. I probably don't need as much sleep as the next man.'

'Have you shed any tears as yet?'

'Some. Perhaps not enough to qualify as your definition of grieving. Why, is that what I should be doing?'

'Not everyone grieves in the same way. It's like any essential process in life – you'll know when you're doing it right.'

'Maybe ... maybe I'm an adrenalin junkie. My work brings on the old adrenalin. Maybe that's what I need?'

'Maybe, but don't use your work as a distraction, or as a sticking plaster. You need to face up to your loss, confront your grief. If you don't do so sooner, it'll catch up with you later.'

'I promise, I'll take on board what you say.'

'Good.'

On his return to Thames House, Kirpal had some bad news for him and Dave.

'Godunov's found the bugs. We'll have to go in again and plant some more in less conspicuous places. And I'll have a proper go at his safe.'

'If you find anything to connect him with *Warbler*, that would be most helpful,' Harry said.

'*Warbler*?' Dave asked.

'He's the principal target in another operation,' Harry explained, 'though that op may not necessarily be related to *Skylark*. Need-to-know again, mate.'

In fact, *Warbler* was the code-name which had been assigned to Mark Tredarran, the Culture Minister, and the operation to look into him had been named *Operation Tern*. Given that there wasn't, as yet, a great deal of evidence to connect him with Godunov and his network of sleepers, Adrian Curtis had instructed Harry and Kirpal that their secondee from Gloucestershire Constabulary should not be made aware of the investigation into Tredarran, at least not yet. Investigating a government minister was a fairly contentious move and, in any case, it might come to nothing.

'We'd better do it this morning, then,' Kirpal said, 'and this afternoon, we're putting some cameras in your flat.'

'How the hell did he find out where I live? That's what I'd like to know,' Harry looked angry.

'He's a professional,' Dave opined, 'and he's good at losing his tail. We thought we were following him, but he must have been following you. I'm wondering about those two heavies, though. Who else is following him and why?'

At the Russian Embassy, Colonel Antonov was seated at his desk writing when his assistant knocked and entered.

'Colonel, we've checked out the Chiswick address Godunov visited. It's a terraced house converted into two apartments. We also checked out the owners of the apartments. It's very interesting.'

Antonov put down his pen and sat back in his chair.

'So, interest me, Dima.'

'The ground floor apartment is rented to a retired lady, a former music teacher who rarely goes out. But the upstairs one is owned by a Mr Harry Edwards. This morning, he was followed … to Thames House.'

Antonov looked grave. He picked up the piece of paper he had been writing on, screwed it up angrily and threw it into his wastepaper basket.

Chapter 41

The Thames House surveillance team confirmed that Godunov had arrived at his office and had not been seen to leave, and so, by lunch time, Harry, Kirpal and Dave were in Godunov's town house and were going about their covert business. They had reckoned on having a couple of hours at least to conduct an even more thorough search than previously. Their devices were installed with greater care this time, but Kirpal could not crack the safe. However, he positioned a tiny camera in such a way as it might allow them to see Godunov opening the safe and so get a look at the combination he used.

Kirpal also decided to put another tiny camera. He would insert it into the coving beneath the living room ceiling, so they could monitor any visitors Godunov might have. Glancing around, he decided the corner of the ceiling above the tall book case would be a good spot. He placed a dining chair in front of the book case and, armed with the tiny camera, he climbed up onto the chair.

'Bollocks! I wonder how long this has been here.'

'What?' Harry asked.

'There's already a surveillance camera here and it's not one of ours.'

'Maybe he had it installed after he found our phone bugs?' Harry suggested.

However, Dave looked worried.

'But, if it was here when we came before, he will have seen us. He'll know who we are.'

Just then, Harry's mobile vibrated. He snatched it from his pocket and took the call.

'That was Godunov's surveillance team. It's almost two o'clock and he hasn't been down to the patisserie for his lunch.'

'Maybe he's not hungry?' Kirpal ventured.

'He's a creature of habit,' Harry frowned, 'and he needs his sugar fix. He might have slipped his lead again. Since we're on camera, we'd better get out of here, PDQ.'

The three quickly tidied up, ensuring everything was left as they had found it, and headed downstairs. However, just as they reached the bottom of the stairs, they saw, through the glass of the front door, the outline of a figure coming up the path. Harry yanked open the door leading from the small hallway into the garage.

'Quick, in here!'

They disappeared into the darkness of the garage, closing the door behind them, just as Godunov let himself into the hall. They heard his footsteps – the slight, stealthy footsteps of an assassin – creeping up the stairs. Harry's mind was racing. Had Godunov returned because he had seen them on his surveillance camera? Would he know they were still in the house or would he think they had left already? Should they stay put or make a run for the front door whilst he was upstairs? He had just decided that, since their cover was well and truly blown, they should make a run for it, when the door to the garage was suddenly flung open and the light was switched on.

Godunov stepped into the garage. In the harsh, white fluorescent light, his face looked even harder than Harry remembered it. Harry saw the pistol in Godunov's hand. He stepped forward and waved at the others to say behind him. That way, Godunov could only take them out one at a time, and Harry decided he would be first. If he did go down, maybe Dave or Kirpal could jump Godunov and wrest the gun from him.

'They know where we are,' Kirpal said, nervously, 'and they know who you are. If you kill us, others will come.'

'They'll never find your bodies,' Godunov smiled.

The irony of dying in a garage, just as Lorna had, and probably by the same gun, occurred to Harry. Perhaps it was fitting, he thought. However, thoughts of Lorna suddenly brought the anger and outrage welling up inside him as he found himself face to face with the man who had killed her. Harry's anger instantly translated itself into action and he dived forward with such suddenness that it took the Russian by surprise. Harry, too, was surprised that the gun did not go off. He fully expected Godunov would react instantly and pull the trigger, but, clearly, the Russian hadn't been expecting Harry's move and he fell over backwards.

Harry grabbed at Godunov's gun hand and smashed it against the concrete floor. The gun flew from Godunov's grasp and went clattering clear across the garage floor. In a split second, however, Godunov recovered and headbutted Harry, knocking him off balance. He immediately squirmed out from beneath Harry, leapt to his feet and made off after the gun. Dave and Kirpal rushed forward to tackle the Russian, too, but, suddenly, an almighty deafening noise erupting in the hall stopped them in their tracks.

Through the open door to the hall, Harry saw a shower of glass cascade through the air and heard the splintering of wood as the front door was kicked in. Instinctively, he knew it wasn't the cavalry coming to rescue them. He looked back at Godunov who had not managed to find his gun but had frozen momentarily. As Harry's eyes met Godunov's, he saw an unexpected expression on the assassin's face. It was a look of raw, blind terror.

Godunov flew out of the garage and ran down the hallway towards the back door. He did not make it. Harry, Dave and Kirpal silently spread themselves against the garage wall and stayed put. They could hear three male voices screaming in Russian out in the hallway. Although the words were unintelligible to them, Harry thought he could make out one word being yelled repeatedly. It sounded something like *'predatill'*. Each time that word was shouted, a loud slap, punch or kick followed it. It was obvious that Godunov was taking a

159

fierce beating. There was a sickening crunching of bone and, finally, a single, ear-splitting gunshot. The three steeled themselves for what seemed like inevitable discovery. Soon, however, they heard someone hawk and spit, then there was a crunching of shoe leather on broken glass and, suddenly, all was quiet. Realising that the men had left, Harry, Kirpal and Dave crept out of the garage and into the hallway.

'Jesus!' Dave spluttered as he glanced down at Godunov's lifeless corpse.

The Russian's face was unrecognisable. It had been beaten to a pulp. Harry knew that, somewhere in that bloody mess that had been Godunov's face, there would be a single bullet wound. That seemed to be the Russian way. Resisting an urge to throw up, Dave turned to Harry who, oddly, had a wry smile on his face.

'I bet you wish *you'd* done that to the fucker,' Dave said.

'What makes you think I didn't?'

Dave looked at Harry, uncomprehendingly, but then nausea began to rise in his throat. He swallowed hard.

'I've seen the results of some pretty horrible murders, but this is the first time I've ever witnessed one,' he said.

He fought the urge to retch. It wouldn't do to be sick in front of his new colleagues.

'I'll pop outside and make sure that gunshot hasn't attracted any of the neighbours. If not, we can probably spend a bit more time checking out that safe.'

'Bugger that,' said Kirpal as Dave headed out through the splintered front door. 'Might as well take the safe away with us.'

Kirpal sprinted back up the stairs. As he was about to follow him, Harry spotted Godunov's pistol lying on the floor in the far corner of the garage. He walked across and retrieved it. It was the same type – a Makarov – as that which had been found in Holder's hand. Harry stuffed it into his pocket. He had a feeling it might come in useful.

Chapter 42

Adrian was seated in his office, examining the documents from Godunov's safe. Through the glazed panel of his office door, he grinned at Dave Lloyd and gave him the thumbs up.

'Adrian's pleased with the haul of documents,' Harry assured Dave.

'What'll happen about Godunov – or do we call him WOTAK still?'

'Well, his body has been spirited away. We don't want the Russians making any sort of political capital out of it. He'll be quietly buried in some out of the way spot. A team has already repaired the damaged front door so the neighbours won't notice and call the police. A good result then, eh?'

'Yeah, I suppose so,' Dave looked wistful.

'You don't seem too thrilled?'

'Well, if there's nothing more to investigate, I mean, if we're satisfied Godunov killed Holder, then I imagine my part in it is over. It'll be back to Cheltenham for me, then. I'll really miss working with you guys. It's been quite exciting, if a bit scary.'

Harry hadn't given a thought to the fact that Dave's participation might no longer be needed. He'd had a lot on his mind and he'd been focused on achieving his own goal of bringing down Godunov.

'That'd be a shame, Dave. We'll miss you, too. It's been a real privilege working with you.'

'And you guys have really made me feel part of the team. Kirpal has been great. He's shown me some useful IT tricks and shortcuts. And Carole's an absolute gem.'

'Yeah, you're right. I always say Carole's the glue that cements the team together. Or is that a mixed metaphor? Glue *and* cement.'

Just then, Adrian appeared at his door and called Harry in. Spread out on his desk was a variety of identity documents, all bearing Godunov's photographs but in different identities, mainly British. The mobile phone from the safe was still being interrogated but Adrian's attention was drawn to Godunov's Russian identity documents in particular.

'Bloody shame,' he shook his head.

'It's a good result, surely,' Harry said. 'Godunov's dead but the Russians did it. Our hands are clean.'

'Yes, but I didn't want him dead. I'd hoped to hold the threat of life imprisonment for murder over him and, that way, we might have coerced the latest cipher codes out of him – without alerting the Russians to the fact that we knew he was one of theirs. I was hoping they'd think that we just saw him as a murdering blackmailer. Somehow, though, they found out that we knew he was something more.'

Harry felt a sudden stab of guilt. He hadn't known that was the plan. He'd been too focused on his own plan for Godunov and hadn't given a thought to the bigger picture. His heart sank at the realisation and he felt his cheeks warming. He decided he wouldn't mention the role he had played in Godunov's downfall. Adrian would be furious if he knew. Better that he didn't know.

In that single moment, Harry realised just how much Lorna's death and Godunov's part in it had affected him. He had, effectively, had Godunov killed. That killing had met his own desire for revenge, but it had also spoilt Adrian's plans for Godunov. It had gone against Security Service rules and, indeed, against their goals. Up until now, Harry would never have considered following his own agenda. Had he used his own instincts and thought it through calmly instead of reacting emotively, he might have realised there was more to be gained from using Godunov. However, his hatred for Godunov had blinded him to the main objective – to thwart the Russian sleeper network. He now realised how much Lorna's death had changed him. Regardless of who had actually killed Godunov, Harry knew the assassin's blood was on his own hands. He was responsible for the death of a man, albeit an inhuman beast of a man. Harry realised he, himself, was a changed man, and there was no going back. Adrian must never know what he had done.

'They must have had some doubts about him, though. That's why they followed him to my flat. Maybe they thought he had turned and was working for us. Or, maybe they found out about the extortion racket and they didn't like it. But you speak Russian, don't you?' Harry asked, changing the subject.

'Da.'

'Is there a word that sounds like *'predatill'* or *'predatchil'*?'

'*Predatel*, you mean? Yes, that means 'traitor'.'

'Ah, traitor. His killers used that word.'

Harry nodded to himself and smiled. Adrian might be disappointed at the outcome but Harry absolutely bloody wasn't.

Adrian tucked the documents back into the file and sat back in his chair.

'I meant to ask you, Harry, how has it been working with Dave Lloyd?'

'Yeah, great. He's good.'

'How good?'

'Bloody good. Why?'

'I think we can continue to use him to good advantage. I'll give his Superintendent a ring.'

'Brilliant.'

Dave Lloyd walked along St Christopher's Place and found the patisserie. He rang the bell on the adjacent door of Lurman Corporation. This time he wouldn't have to break in at the back but would be invited in via the front door. Soon, he was being shown into the CEO's plush office suite.

'Detective Chief Inspector Dave Lloyd,' he introduced himself, flashing his warrant just quickly enough so the words *'Gloucestershire Constabulary'* might not be noticed.

'Edmund Gray. Please take a seat,' the CEO said, 'now what can I do for you?'

'It's about one of your employees, Mr Alexander Goodenough.'

'Alex? Oh, I'm sorry but he's not in today. He's taking a bit of leave.'

'Ah, I see. Actually, his neighbours have reported him missing. They hadn't seen him for a while and they'd noticed a few days' worth of milk left curdling on the doorstep and mail piling up in the hall, so they gave us a call.'

'Oh, I expect he simply forgot to cancel them and to tell the neighbours he was going away.'

'Oh, well, if you're happy he's on holiday and hasn't had an accident or anything, then I won't take up any more of your time. Sorry to have bothered you.'

'Oh, that's quite all right. It's good of you to be concerned, but let me assure you that you needn't be. My secretary will show you out,' he offered Dave his hand.

'Oh, just one last question,' Dave said, 'where's he gone on his holiday?'

'I've no idea, I'm afraid. He didn't say.'

Dave took in Gray's smile. He felt it was just a little bit too wide; too wide and too forced.

Gray stood at the window and watched Dave walk back towards Oxford Street. He then turned back to his desk, picked up his phone and dialled. A moment later, he was connected.

'The police were just here … I thought your people were going to make it look like an obvious break-in? Looks like they didn't find the body yet. I had to tell them he was on holiday…. Yes, the policeman accepted that…. Yes, yes, I'll clear his desk.'

Outside, the young man sitting at the patisserie's little pavement table stopped nodding in time to imaginary music, removed his earphones and slipped them into his pocket alongside the small digital scanner. Draining his coffee cup, he took his mobile phone out of his other pocket and reported in.

Edmund Gray left his office and walked downstairs to the office with Alex Goodenough's name on the door. He punched in the four-digit code to unlock the office and went inside, closing the door again behind him. He switched on the desktop computer and spent several minutes trying out different login codes. None of the obvious codes worked.

He stared into space for a moment or two then, on a hunch, he typed in the Word 'Stalin'. It was rejected, so he tried a few other combinations of the name of Goodenough's hero. When he entered 'JStalin' replacing the 'i' with the number one, it worked. He was in. He next began checking and deleting files. It was tedious but it was necessary, and it wasn't something he could ask his PA to do. He scrolled down and hit the 'delete' key repeatedly. One after another, in alphabetical order, the files disappeared. Towards the bottom of the list of documents, Gray spotted a file, the subject of which was unfamiliar to him. He paused for a moment then opened the file marked 'WOTAK'. He began to read the various documents within it. The more he read, the greater was his surprise.

'Well I'll be blowed!' he exclaimed.

Chapter 43

'Should we still go ahead with installing the surveillance cameras at my flat?' Harry asked Adrian.

'Definitely. But I'm moving you out today in any case. I'll arrange for you and Dave to stay in a safe house for the time being. You should both collect whatever you need from your place as soon as possible. Give Kirpal a set of keys and he can go over and get cameras set up.'

'You think they'll come back?'

'Almost certainly. And it won't just be to snoop around. The Russians knew Godunov had visited your flat but they don't know how often he did, or what he might have told you. They can only get that information from you. You'll need to watch your back. Where is Dave, by the way?'

'He's gone over to Richmond to do some more background checks on Edmund Gray. As soon as he gets back, we'll head off to my place.'

'Isn't there somewhere else you need to be this morning?'

'Oh, yes. Almost forgot.'

Half an hour later, he was back in Amandine's office. He didn't know what a psychologist would even call her office. Was it an office, or a surgery, consulting room, therapy room?

'So, how've you been since I saw you last?' she asked.

'Well, I don't know, really. We got him, though.'

'Lorna's killer?'

'Yes.'

'Well, that's good, isn't it? His trial will help bring you some closure.'

'No. There'll be no trial. He's dead.'

Amandine looked surprised. Harry wondered if, perhaps, he was parting with too much information. There were no rules to this therapy lark and he didn't know just how much of his soul he should lay bare.

'Did you kill him?'

'No. Obligingly, his own people did that. Although …'

'Although …?'

'I might have been instrumental in implicating him in something that led to their killing him.'

'So, you took your revenge. And do you feel avenged for Lorna's death?'

'No. I feel nothing. Well, maybe I feel something like … disappointment. Yes, I feel disappointed that I don't feel good about what happened to him. But, then, I don't feel bad about it either. I'd hoped that knowing he was dead would make me feel … better'.

'Your desire for revenge is what's kept you going thus far. It was a sort of emotional crutch. Now that crutch is gone, well, you know what I'm going to say, don't you?'

Yes, Harry did know what she was going to say. If he didn't take time out to grieve properly, he would likely have a breakdown. Harry promised he would take a break, just as soon as his current project was resolved, but he knew he wasn't the type to have a breakdown. In any case, he didn't have time for a breakdown.

Shortly after Harry's return to Thames House, Dave was back, too. Making a beeline for Harry's desk, he triumphantly produced the freshly issued certificates.

'Right. You remember you found Gray's second marriage in the ONS records online?'

'Yes, the marriage at Richmond.'

'Well, I went over there, to York House, to check out that marriage. He married one Irene O'Donnell. That much you'd found out.'

'Yeah.'

167

'Well what isn't on the ONS database but it is in the marriage register is that Irene O'Donnell's previous marriage had been dissolved, too. She was married only a couple of years before, also in the Richmond district, to one Terence O'Donnell, an Irish-born bloke. And see what her name was at the time of her marriage to him.'

Harry quickly scrutinised the two certificates.

'Irina Bobrova. She's Russian?'

'Apparently. I'll check for a Home Office file. If there is one it'll give her place and date of birth. The O'Donnell marriage was probably one of convenience, to enable her to get UK residence as wife of an EU national. Within a very short time, she's divorced O'Donnell and married Gray and they now have kids together. So, Gray is probably, at the very least, a Russian sympathiser. I'm guessing he's more than that, though. But he isn't too good at thinking on his feet. He slipped up when he lied to me about Godunov being on holiday.'

'Yes, and as soon as you'd left his office, he called the Russian Embassy. No, don't sit down, Dave. We've got to catch the tube back to my place and get packed.'

Harry was a little subdued as they loaded up Dave's bag and two of Harry's suitcases into the boot of the second-hand saloon car and headed out of Chiswick. He wasn't happy about leaving his own, comfortable flat, the one he had shared with Lorna. He didn't know how long he would be absent from his home, either.

'Is this an office vehicle?' Dave asked.

'No, it's mine. I bought it to replace the Morgan. At least I won't have to worry about parking a Mazda outside the flat – that is, whenever I'm allowed back there. I could never leave the Morgan out on the street. Too valuable. I own a lock-up garage around the corner.'

'So where is this safe house, then?'

'Fulham.'

'Then, aren't we heading in completely the wrong direction?'
'No, we're going to Beaconsfield first.'
'Beaconsfield? In Buckinghamshire? Why?'
'You gave me an idea – well, it's only a hunch, really. There's someone else whose marriage I think I'll check out.'

The clerk at Beaconsfield Register Office took the fee and told Harry he'd have to call back later for the certificate, so he returned to the car where Dave awaited him.

'I'll have to wait for the certificate, so let's grab a bite here. We can get dinner out in Fulham later.'

'I thought you were trying to save money.'

'Ah, but whilst we're in the safe house, we're on daily subsistence rates. We can have a decent steak dinner this evening. Meanwhile, there's a nice little tea shop just over there that does a first-rate bacon sandwich.'

Harry pointed across at the tea shop but Dave's gaze wandered along the row to the former Victorian court house which now housed Beaconsfield's register office.

'That building looks very familiar, but I'm sure I've never been here before. Why do I know that place?' he asked.

'Midsomer Murders, the TV series,' Harry explained. 'This place is used for Causton Nick.'

'Of course it is. I bloody love that programme!'

Later that afternoon, once they were installed in the safe house at Fulham, Harry settled down in an armchair to examine the certificate he had bought. His hunch was right. He saw a familiar pattern. Mark Tredarran, who, as he already knew, was formerly Markus Trenda, was born in Brno, Moravia, but he had been living in nearby Penn Village, Buckinghamshire at the time of his marriage to one Marina Murphy. The certificate also stated that her previous marriage had been dissolved, and that her father's name was Arkady Bobrov. Bobrov was, he knew, the masculine version of Bobrova. He hadn't really taken notice of the bride's father's name on the Gray's marriage certificate, but he now recalled that Irene Gray's father was also shown as Arkady Bobrov. So, clearly, Edmund Gray and Mark Tredarran had married two Russian sisters, and that made them brothers-in-law. Harry determined to seek Adrian's permission to fill Dave in on *Operation Tern*. He would ask him first thing in the morning.

Chapter 44

Harry and Dave were hard at work when Adrian arrived.

'Good morning,' they chorused.

'It bloody isn't!' Adrian barked as he strode past them and disappeared into his office.

Harry and Dave exchanged puzzled glances.

Moments later, divested of his coat, Adrian reappeared in his doorway. 'My office everyone!' he shouted, 'Carole! Where are you?'

Carole emerged at the double from the section's small kitchen, her mug of instant coffee in hand. She followed Adrian into his office and, sensing his irritation, she offered him her coffee. Absent-mindedly, he took a sip from the mug which had her name emblazoned on it. Grimacing, he fished a small dispenser pack of sweeteners from his desk drawer and droppeded two into the coffee. Harry and Dave piled in and Dave closed the door behind them.

'What's up, boss?' Harry asked.

'Sit down, everyone. Where's Kirpal?'

'Still over at Corsham,' Harry informed him.

Adrian unzipped his document bag and withdrew a plastic evidence type bag containing a document. He handed it to Carole who scrutinised it without taking out of the bag.

'You won't believe this,' he informed them, '*The Times* have received another WOTAK letter.'

'Surely, that's not possible?' Harry said. 'He's dead. Both WOTAKs are dead. Do we have a third WOTAK, or what?'

Adrian shook his head in annoyance.

'We thought we were about to wind down *Op Skylark*, and now this. Your thoughts, Carole?'

'Immediate reaction is that it's very similar to the later letters. Not the same as the early ones, though. Maybe Godunov wasn't

WOTAK. Or, as Harry says, maybe there are, or were, three of them. I'll have to have a closer look at it.'

'Get forensics to check it over first, just in case,' Adrian relaxed visibly. He seemed calmer now that he was with his team, and the coffee helped.

'Where was it posted this time?' Harry asked.

'Central London, day before yesterday. Post box near Marylebone Station.'

'There's very little of central London which isn't covered by CCTV,' Dave said, 'so I'm sure Marylebone must be. I'll check that out. And I'll check out the destinations the trains go to from Marylebone.'

'Thank you, Dave,' Adrian sighed, 'and, by the way, we've lost Rosie Leyton from the operation. She's a fluent Spanish speaker so she's been sent to Gibraltar to report back on the attempted takeover of Gib by the Spaniards. It seems bloody Brexit is eating up everyone's resources. So, Dave, I'll speak to your governor about keeping you on the investigation. Harry, will you update Dave on *Op Tern* and Mark Tredarran?'

They left Adrian sipping at the hot coffee and mentally composing an update for the JIC. Carole headed off to get herself another coffee before examining the latest WOTAK missive, and Harry steered Dave back to his desk and began to explain about Mark Tredarran and his links to Edmund Gray.

Dave began thinking aloud.

'So, has Gray taken over the WOTAK persona, or are Gray and this Tredarran working it together? I hope it is Gray.'

'Why?' Harry asked.

'Because I don't think he's very good. He's no Godunov. He's just a front man and he makes mistakes. He should have had a better response ready when I called on him to ask if Godunov was missing, and he certainly shouldn't have jumped on the blower to call the Russian Embassy before I was even halfway down the street.'

Harry followed Dave's train of thought.

'Yes. He probably also has access to Godunov's office computer now. Perhaps he didn't have that access whilst Godunov was alive, or maybe he didn't need it then. Perhaps Godunov's death has panicked him. The question is, did he know about the WOTAK business *before* Godunov was killed, or has he simply stumbled across it since then? Was Godunov head of the network or was it Gray? Or could it even be this Tredarran character?'

'And, if it is Gray who's taken up the WOTAK mantle, does Tredarran know Gray's doing the extortion stuff on the side. If he doesn't know, and if he should find out about it, I wonder how he'd react?'

Harry thought for a moment then passed Dave the *Operation Tern* file.

'You might want to have a read of the full profile on Tredarran. He's a billionaire, funded, initially at least, by the Russians, and so he probably owes them his loyalty. He doesn't need to get involved in the WOTAK racket, and I can't see him condoning Gray doing that either. I mean, it's quite a canny idea, demanding money by threatening to carry out attacks you're already been ordered by the Russians to carry out. But it could jeopardise their network's activities. And that would really piss off the Russians.'

'You're right. I wonder why that hasn't occurred to Gray. Doesn't he realise they might do to him what they did to Godunov? I mean, I imagine that's *why* the Russians killed Godunov. They wouldn't have been happy about his extortion activities.'

Harry simply nodded. It would suit him if that's what everyone thought. Dave continued:

'And Gray seems pretty well-heeled himself. You'd wonder why he'd risk ending up like Godunov did. I think I'll have another look at his finances. We'll see where he actually gets his money from.'

Adrian emerged from Helena's office deep in thought. He'd been mulling the developments over in his head just as Harry and Dave had, and had shared his thinking with Helena. He made a beeline for Carole's desk.

'Carole have you …, er, why are you drinking out of my mug?'

'Because …, never mind that now, Boss. Look, I've compared the new WOTAK letter with the previous one. They're identical in every way. Same wording, same threats, same demands, same style of typing, envelope address and so on. This isn't a new letter, it's the same one re-printed, even down to the date.'

'That means …'

'That means the lazy sod who sent it probably just accessed the previous letter on WOTAK's word processor and hit 'print'. Didn't even bother to change the date. Sloppy, that. Forensics will probably confirm the paper and ink are the same as the previous one. This is the first time we've had a repeat letter. All the others have been differently worded. Also, I'd have expected him to have referred to the fact that we've ignored all his previous letters, but he hasn't.'

'So, that suggests the new WOTAK may be using the former WOTAK's computer?'

'That's the most obvious scenario.'

'Thanks, Carole. You can hang onto the mug for now.'

Chapter 45

Harry and Dave had found a very pleasant gastropub on the Fulham Road where they served large, juicy steaks and all the trimmings. They selected a cosy booth where they could talk without being overheard. Since it was a weekday, it was gratifyingly quiet anyway. As Harry poured the last of the Côte du Rhône into Dave's glass, Dave related the results of his enquiries.

'Unfortunately, that post box at Marylebone isn't covered by CCTV. But I found out that the Bobrova sisters were born in St Petersburg, according to their Home Office files. More importantly, however, Edmund Gray is skint,' Dave informed Harry. '

'Skint? But what about his big Buckinghamshire house, with the views clear across to Windsor Castle, and the three-car garage and the swimming pool?

'Everything's on credit. He's mortgaged up to the eyeballs and he's fallen behind with the kids' school fees. I'm telling you, he's flat broke. His outgoings exceed his income. He's deeply in debt with loans he can't pay off.'

'You'd wonder how the Chief Exec of a big company could get himself in such a fix.'

'*Cherchez la femme*, I'd say. The young Russian wife seems to have expensive tastes – hair stylist coming to the house, manicurist, too, the tanning salon appointments, beach holidays in the Dominican Republic, not to mention an account at Harrods.'

'Wonder why he doesn't just tell her to tighten her belt a bit?'

'Probably the age-old story. She's younger than him and very attractive. He doesn't want to lose her. He might also be trying to keep up with his in-laws, the Tredarrans. They're right out of his league, though. I can imagine the conversations at home –

'Mark buys my sister diamonds. You never buy me diamonds, you fokkin cheapskate!'

Harry laughed at Dave's passable attempt at a Russian accent. It suddenly occurred to him that it had been a long time since he had felt like laughing at anything. He realised how relaxed he felt in Dave's company.

Just then, the pub door burst open and a group of young women entered and headed for another vacant booth. Their laughter instantly brightened the quiet, oak-beamed interior of the pub.

'Speaking of young and attractive women, …' Dave nodded in the direction of the young women.

Naturally, the arrival of the group brought Harry and Dave's shop talk to an end. Harry saw Dave glance admiringly after the girls.

'Do you think you'll find someone else, one day?' Harry asked.

'Maybe, but not yet. Probably when I'm too old to do anything about it.'

Harry just couldn't imagine himself even contemplating life with someone new. He wondered if he would always be looking for another Lorna, measuring up other women against his memory of her. Dave's expression suggested he sensed the reason for Harry's introspection but he didn't really know what to say. Just then, the pub door opened once again and another couple of young women entered. As the pair reached the booth where Harry and Dave were sitting, Harry looked up.

'Amandine!'

'Hello, Harry.'

'Aren't you going to introduce me, then?' Dave beamed.

Harry's face fell. There was no way he was going to introduce Amandine as his psychotherapist.

'Amandine's …'

'I'm his insurance broker,' she cut in.

176

Harry flashed her a look of gratitude. He suspected Amandine had used that ruse before to avoid embarrassing her clients. Clearly, she was used to diffusing this sort of situation.

'And this is my friend, Sarah,' she indicated the young woman next to her.

'And I'm Harry's older but more handsome friend, Dave. Ladies, Won't you join us for a drink,' Dave urged.

'Thank you, but we're meeting up with some girlfriends,' Amandine demurred, 'nice to meet you, Dave. Have a good evening. Bye, Harry.'

As Amandine and her friend moved further down the pub to join the group who had arrived just before them, Dave looked after them, impressed.

'She's a looker, Harry. Is she French or something? I wish my insurance broker looked like that.'

'I don't really know her that well.'

Dave looked disbelieving.

'I don't, really.' Harry insisted, 'I mean, how often do you take out insurance?'

'Not often enough to be on first name terms with the broker. You sly young dog!'

'No, really. I've only met her a few times, and strictly professionally. It's just … an unusual name – the kind you remember.'

Hoping to deflect Dave, Harry waved his debit card at the waitress who, thankfully, already had their bill ready. To his surprise, however, his card was rejected by the machine, despite several attempts by the waitress to swipe it. Dave produced his own card. Puzzlingly, this, too, was rejected. Between them, however, they managed to scrape together enough cash to settle the bill.

Chapter 46

It was the rain beating against the window that awoke Harry on that grey Saturday morning. Sweeping his arm across the bed, he realised Lorna wasn't there. Lifting his head from the pillow, he glanced around the sparsely-furnished bedroom in which nothing looked familiar. For a second, he couldn't remember where he was. Then, reality kicked in. He was in the safe house. Lorna wasn't there and she never would be. Dave Lloyd had gone home to Cheltenham for the weekend and Harry was alone. Not much point in getting out of bed.

He turned his back on the rain-spattered window and stared at the wall. The floral wallpaper was dismal. The room was dismal. In fact, the entire house was dismal. It was in a nice enough street in a good neighbourhood – the sort of neighbourhood where the arrival of a stranger wearing a hoodie would have residents phoning for the police; the sort of neighbourhood where a foreign assassin would look right out of place. In short, the safe house felt safe enough. Yet he hated it. It wasn't a home. It had all the soullessness and lack of personalisation of that bastard Godunov's house.

The memory of Godunov and what he had done to Lorna caused Harry's eyes to suddenly fill with tears. He took hold of his pillow and curled it around his face. Burying his nose in its softness, he hoped to find the scent of Lorna as he had always found it on the pillows at home. But there was no scent. There was nothing of Lorna in this house.

Suddenly, he didn't want to be here any longer. He didn't want to spend the weekend alone. Never had he felt so alone, at least not since his first night away at boarding school at the tender age of eight. He had felt the same heartache and loneliness again on his last night at that school. That had been just a year later, when he had slept alone in Matron's sick bay until his father had come to collect him the following day to attend his mother's funeral. His father had secured him a place at a local private day school thereafter.

He now began to feel very sorry for himself. The sorrow welled up from the heart of the little boy within him. The tears came fast and hot now as he let himself go and wept into the pillow. Soon, his body was racked with sobs. He couldn't help himself. He didn't ever want to get out of bed again. He didn't want to go on living if it meant living without Lorna. He wanted the pain to stop, but it wouldn't.

He had thought that fixing Godunov would bring him some satisfaction and perhaps ease his pain. But, it hadn't. It felt like a very small victory in a very large war. He blamed himself for Lorna's death and he always would. He should have been able to protect her, he told himself. He should have encouraged her to get out of the game, to become a wife and a mother, to be safe. But he hadn't. He was an abject failure, a miserable excuse for a man. Godunov's death should have made him feel he was in control. But it hadn't. He couldn't even control his own tears. He wondered if this were it – the breakdown Amandine said he would have if he didn't give himself time and space to grieve.

The sudden buzz of his mobile shook him out of his torpor. He turned over and looked at the clock. It was just after ten. After a few moments of calm deliberation, he decided he ought to check his message. The text was from Adrian. It said simply 'check out the news'. He sighed. He saw no point in bothering to shower but threw on a dressing gown. In the kitchen, he automatically took two mugs out of the cupboard, then, remembering, he shook his head and put one of them back and mechanically went about making himself a coffee. Shuffling into the living room, he turned on the television. He had to flip through several channels to find a news bulletin. The red banner headline proclaiming the breaking news made the hair on the back of his neck stand up.

'Seven High Street Banks Hit by Cyber-attack'
It was exactly what WOTAK had threatened in his last two letters. He had promised to disrupt UK banking on an even bigger scale than before. Harry flipped open his laptop and logged on to an online news channel for the full story. There had been simultaneous cyber-attacks on seven UK-based banks which had caused them all to shut down operations. The attack had actually occurred earlier in the week, but details had not been made public until now. The banks hadn't wanted to cause widespread panic or to lose public confidence.

The newsreader said it might be a few days yet before the banks' crippled digital services could be restored. In the meantime, no bank transactions of any kind could be completed, no wages had been paid out on Friday and millions of customers had been unable to use their debit or credit cards. The major retail chains had described the previous day as 'Black Friday' and today would be 'Black Saturday', since sales in all their outlets had dropped to an all-time low. This was a prime weekend when people customarily began their Christmas shopping, and yet they couldn't. Only cash buyers had been able to make purchases, but shoppers had been unable to withdraw cash from ATMs.

Harry realised this was why neither he nor Dave had been able to use their cards to pay for their meals at the pub. He now had no cash left himself, and nor had Dave. He wondered how Dave had managed to buy his rail ticket home to Cheltenham. Perhaps he had blagged his way onto the train with his police warrant. Harry reassured himself he had enough credit left on his own Oyster card to get himself to work on Monday.

Harry didn't understand all the technical detail the BBC's economist was spouting. It was something about DDOS – Distributed Denial of Service attacks. These had flooded and disabled the banks' computer systems with impossibly high volumes of traffic. Harry seemed to recall that the website of at least one of the opposition political parties had been attacked in the same way during the last election. Doubtless, Kirpal would have a better understanding of the mechanics of it all. Not only had banking services slowed down to a halt, but many customers' accounts had been hacked into. The economist explained that the attack, presumed to be by highly organised cyber criminals, had not only cost the UK millions of pounds, but it reflected a threat to our way of life and, indeed, to society as a whole. *'This is warfare!'* the BBC's man declared.

Chapter 47

Dave Lloyd arrived at the office at eleven on Monday morning, having travelled in from Cheltenham on a surprisingly empty train. It was obvious that many commuters, those who didn't hold season tickets, had been affected by the banking crisis. He was surprised to see the normally tidy office in some disarray. Glancing into the office kitchen on his way from the lifts, he observed that the bin was overflowing with used foil take-away containers and the sink was full of unwashed coffee cups. In the main office, he saw that, unlike the coffee cups, Harry and Carole looked washed out and their desks were piled high with files.

'You guys had a sleepover or what?' he joked.

'We've been here all weekend, mate,' Harry informed him.

'You should have called me in, too.'

'No need. One of us at least should be fresh and alert this morning. You got your train okay, then?'

'Yeah. Flashed the warrant.'

Harry had actually been glad to come in over the weekend. It was better than spending a couple of rainy days alone in the safe house with only his grief for company.

'So, all that shenanigans with the banks, then, was that the Russians' doing?' Dave asked.

'Oh yes. And, clearly, WOTAK – whoever he is now – knew it was planned, since he'd alluded to it in his last letter.'

'So, what've we got here?' Dave looked at the mountain of files on Harry's desk.'

'Kirpal's gone over to Corsham with some investigators from the National Crime Agency to try and see what malware was used, but we're concentrating on *Op Tern* and I've been looking at some previous ops to see if I can identify any links or crossovers. Whilst the cyber people are sorting the mess out,

182

maybe we can predict what the Russians are going to do next. Here, have a look at these files.'

Dave quickly became engrossed in the first file Harry passed to him. Of course, he had seen the news reports about the four Russian males who had been arrested in the Netherlands a couple of years back, but the level of detail in the Security Service file was fascinating. The men had been arrested by the Dutch police whilst sitting in a hired car outside the headquarters of an organisation which oversees and enforces the prohibition of chemical weapons. That organisation was in the process of investigating what substance had been used to poison the former GRU man Skripal and his daughter. The organisation had been awaiting the results from a Swiss laboratory of tests on that substance. In the boot of the Russians' hire car, the police had found sophisticated equipment for hacking into WIFI connections, so the men's mission was fairly obvious.

Dave was impressed to note that it wasn't a random arrest. The Dutch had been tipped off by British intelligence in advance of the men's arrival in Amsterdam. He perused stills from CCTV footage which had captured images of the men being met on arrival at Schiphol Airport by a diplomat from the Russian Embassy in the Hague, and saw also images of the equipment found in the car boot, as well as comparison images taken from a security x-ray of similar kit an incoming Russian diplomatic bag which had passed through the airport earlier that week. As a career policeman, he was also impressed at the thoroughness of the Dutch investigation.

One of the arrested Russians had tried, unsuccessfully, to destroy his mobile phone but it had been retrieved and forensically examined. That phone, too, had yielded useful information. It was a newly acquired mobile which had only been switched on once, and that switching on had, of course, been recorded by a mobile phone mast which placed it within the GRU HQ at Moscow's *Komsomolsky Prospekt*.

183

Examination of a laptop in the men's possession had revealed that it had recently logged onto the internet via the WIFI network of a Geneva hotel which was located right next door to a Swiss laboratory. This was the very same laboratory tasked with examining the substance used in the Skripal attack, and which had indeed identified it as a prohibited poison, the Russian-manufactured *Novichok*. Clearly, this team of Russians had been sent to spy on the investigation into the Skripal case.

'What a bunch of amateurs!' Dave declared, as he read further details of the Russians' activities. 'They held brand new, consecutively numbered passports and their air tickets were also consecutively numbered, just like the tickets and passports the Skripals' poisoners had. Don't the Russians learn anything from their past mistakes?'

Harry laughed.

'Amateurs is right. They also held itemised receipts for their taxi fare to Sheremetyevo Airport from the road where GRU HQ is located. Needed them to claim back their expenses, presumably. It's page one stuff from the spies' hand book for boys – never carry receipts.'

Dave stared hard at some of the images which had been downloaded from the arrested Russian's mobile phone. A couple of the photos stored in the phone were of the phone's user, pictured with a blonde female companion. One photo which caught Dave's eye in particular was a selfie the Russian had taken of himself and the young woman, seemingly naked and in bed together. The more he stared at the photo, the more pensive he seemed.

'This woman in the photos. I'm sure I've seen her somewhere,' he said at last.

'Where?' Harry asked.

'Can't remember. Definitely seen that face before, though.'

Less than three miles away, as the drone flies, Colonel Antonov was seated at his desk in his office in the Russian Embassy on Kensington Park Gardens, when his assistant entered, clutching a sheaf of papers and looking anxious.

'What is it?'

'Those military and naval exercises taking place along the northern sea route.'

'What about them?'

'They had to be aborted. It seems that something blocked their access to GPS. None of the ships involved in the exercise was able to navigate. They had to wait until nightfall and plot their way back into Archangelsk navigating by the stars. The Kremlin's furious. They blame Norway and Norway's blaming adverse weather conditions in the Arctic Circle. Moscow aren't buying that. They want to know how anyone had even known about the exercise. It had been planned with meticulous secrecy. They want us to find out if the British were behind this.'

Antonov slowly fumed.

'Dima, get me Mark Tredarran on the phone, immediately.'

Chapter 48

Dave Lloyd was still perusing the files Harry had given him to study when Harry appeared and handed him an envelope.

'What's this?'

'Your subsistence. It's in cash so you won't have to wait until the ATMs are back up and running. I collected mine, too.'

'Oh, cheers,' Dave smiled as he transferred the crisp new notes from the envelope into his wallet, 'oh, and by the way, I've worked out where I'd seen that blonde before, you know, the one in the saucy photos on that GRU man's phone.'

'Where?'

'Harry, you're going to love this …'

Sir Henry Mortimer walked into the lobby of his London club. He glanced around, myopically, searching for his lunch date. Mark Tredarran was waiting for him and rose to greet him.

'Henry, it's been ages. Thank you for agreeing to meet me. Lunch is on me, of course.'

'Well thank you, Mark. This is an unexpected pleasure.'

'Let's go straight in.'

Over the roast beef and the claret, Tredarran hedged around the real reason for his luncheon invitation. It wasn't until they were well into their brandies that he grasped the nettle.

'Have you heard that the Russians are planning to invite private companies to mine for oil and gas in the Arctic?'

'No, I hadn't heard that. But I thought they used the state-owned outfit – *Gazprom* or something, isn't it?'

'Yes. *Gazprom* has had the monopoly on prospecting there, but climate change and the melting of the glaciers is making the oil and gas deposits up there much more accessible. The possibilities are huge, but I don't think the state company is up to the job and Putin doesn't want the Norwegians to steal a march on them. He's putting the contracts out to tender.'

'And you're thinking of going for it?'

'One of my subsidiaries will. The only problem would be if there was something going on up there that might interfere with the project.'

'What sort of something?'

'Look, there's been some sort of hacking of GPS signals up there recently, and then there was that shut-down of the Russian railway networks a while back. I'm guessing we might have been behind that.'

'Might we?'

'Henry, you're on the JIC. If anyone would know about that, you would.'

'Well, actually, I don't. The Cabinet Office doesn't get told everything. There's a need-to-know policy, even at JIC level. You'd have to speak to someone at the Security Service.'

'Oh.'

'But I could perhaps get you an appropriate introduction.'

'Bless you, Henry. That would be great. Another brandy?'

'I wouldn't say no.'

Tredarran left the club with a smug smile on his face. As soon as Sir Henry had drained his brandy glass, he took out his mobile and called up one of his speed-dial numbers.

'Helena? He went for it. When would you like to see him?'

Chapter 49

Helena Fairbrother's PA met Mark Tredarran at the Thames House reception area, signed him in and relieved him of his mobile phone. Locking it in one of the small lockers specifically designated for visitors' phones, she handed him the locker key and escorted him to the lifts. As the lift doors closed on them, Kirpal appeared and went across to the phone lockers. Using a duplicate key, he quickly retrieved Tredarran's phone and headed off with it to the 'Tech' department.

Helena and Adrian were in her office awaiting Tredarran when Helena's PA escorted him in. Helena wore a bold red jacket this morning which Adrian felt gave her a significant advantage – an air of assertiveness. Following the introductions, she offered her visitor coffee, which he readily accepted. Tredarran settled down comfortably in his seat. He wore an expensive suit, Adrian observed. He also wore an expression of extreme confidence and calm anticipation. Adrian didn't expect that expression to last very long.

'Thank you for seeing me, Miss Fairbrother,' he began, 'did Sir Henry tell you why I'm here?'

'Yes, he did. I'm sorry to disappoint you, though. We have no knowledge of anything which might give you a commercial advantage in the Arctic. You'd be better off speaking to the Norwegians, perhaps.'

'But you must have some contacts with your Norwegian counterparts? Couldn't you find out anything from them?'

'I'm not sure our counterparts would be the appropriate people to ask,' Helena smiled. 'The Commercial Attaché at the Norwegian Embassy might be more helpful. Although, presumably, Norwegian firms will be competing for the contracts, too, since their territorial sovereignty also extends into the region. What about the Russian Commercial Attaché?'

This wasn't what Tredarran wanted to hear. His smile did fade, just as Adrian expected. Helena had more to say, however, which he knew would disappoint the Minister even further.

'Since you're here, though, there is another matter I need to raise with you.'

Tredarran's gaze flitted quickly from Helena to Adrian. His expression suggested he was hopeful they were going to disclose details of British Intelligence's operations in the Arctic. Their faces, however, gave nothing away.

'You may recall that incident, some time back, when four Russians were arrested whilst hanging around outside the OPCW in the Netherlands – you know, the Chemical Weapons authority?'

Tredarran shifted in his seat, 'Yes, I read something about it, but what has that got ...?'

'One of them had some interesting photographs on his phone. There were shots of a certain Swiss laboratory where the Novichok used to poison the Skripals was being identified. And, of course, there were some damning photos which one of the Russians had taken whilst travelling around Europe on his covert business, plus, there were some more personal shots.'

'I don't understand what this has to do with me?'

'You might recognise someone in one of those photos.'

Helena nodded to Adrian, who slid a copy of one of the images across the desk to Tredarran. Tredarran picked it up and looked at the selfie of a couple in bed together in what seemed to be a hotel bedroom. His expression turned from one of bafflement through shock to anger.

'I see Mrs Tredarran is acquainted with one of the Russian GRU agents,' Adrian said, 'rather well acquainted, it would seem.'

Tredarran's cheeks began to redden and there was a very pregnant pause as he took in the implications of the image. At length, Helena spoke.

189

'You will, of course, resign your cabinet position. You should also stand down as MP. It would be unfortunate if this were to be made public. That would necessitate your being equally publicly sacked.'

Tredarran thought for a few moments, then slowly and reluctantly, he nodded. However, Helena had another matter to raise with him.

'There is something else I'd like you to see.'

Adrian passed Tredarran a photocopy of the latest WOTAK letter. Tredarran read it slowly and shook his head.

'I don't understand.'

Adrian steeled himself for both a big revelation and also a big lie.

'We've been able to anticipate many of the Kremlin's cyber-attacks and other hostile initiatives.' he explained. 'We were ready for quite a few of them and were able to offset some of the damage. That's because someone who had advanced knowledge of those attacks tried to use that knowledge to demand ransom payments. That someone, who cryptically signs himself 'WOTAK', has unwittingly been tipping us off. That someone is now known to us. He is also known to you.'

Tredarran's expression turned back to one of bafflement. His face was evidence enough to convince Adrian that Tredarran had no idea about the attempts at extortion.

'We know who sent those letters. It was your brother-in-law, Edmund Gray.'

Tredarran's eyes went from wide surprise to narrowing with anger and his lips tightened. He looked again at the letter but did not know what to say.

'We didn't arrest him, because his threats have actually proved quite useful to us in knowing what the Kremlin might do next.'

'Are you going to arrest him now?' Tredarran asked.

'If we do,' Helena said, 'we'll probably have to arrest you, too. Even if you are not involved, either with the Russians or with this pathetic attempt at extortion, the public and the press will assume you are. Awkward questions will be asked.'

'So, what happens next?' Tredarran asked.

'We'll expect your resignation this afternoon,' Helena said, 'and we expect you to deal with Gray. It's been interesting whilst it lasted, but we certainly don't expect to receive any more letters from WOTAK.'

Tredarran nodded meekly. Helena rose to signal the meeting was at an end. The Minister exited her office, with none of the confident swagger with which he had arrived. Helena's PA also rose from her desk and escorted him towards the lifts. Helena closed the office door on her visitor.

'How did we know that was Tredarran's wife in the photo?' she asked.

Adrian smiled.

'Dave Lloyd recognised her from the photo in her Home Office immigration papers. He's pretty smart, that copper.'

Out in the corridor, as a subdued Tredarran waited with Helena's PA for the lift to arrive, Harry appeared.

'I'll escort the Minister downstairs,' he offered.

Whilst the soon-to-be-former Culture Minister retrieved his phone, which Kirpal had replaced in the security locker in reception, Harry opened another of the visitors' lockers and withdrew from it a padded envelope. He escorted the Minister outside the building and, turning his back on the external security camera, he handed him the envelope.

'This might come in useful,' he said.

Tredarran looked a broken man as he sat in the back seat of his official car.

'Everything all right, sir?' his driver queried.

191

'Not really, Andy. Not feeling too good. Would you drive me home, please?'

As the busy city streets gave way to the leafy suburbs of south west London, Tredarran opened the padded envelope. It was heavy and rather bulky, so he hadn't expected it to contain documents. To his surprise, however, he pulled out a Makarov automatic pistol. It was fully loaded.

Chapter 50

Over the course of the next few days, Helena and Adrian scanned the news for word of Tredarran's resignation, but it did not appear. Helena suggested they should give him until the end of the week and then have another word with him. Harry, too, was keeping an eye on the news, though he was expecting to see reports of the fatal shooting, in an affluent Buckinghamshire village, of the debt-ridden CEO of a major software company. He, too, was disappointed.

When Harry and Dave arrived at Thames House on the Thursday morning, there was a message on Dave's desk for him to urgently contact Peter Webb at SO15. Dave went down the corridor to use what he laughingly called 'the bat phone'. When he returned a few minutes later, he pulled Harry to one side.

'There's been a development,' he said.

'Oh yes?'

'Mark Tredarran and his wife have been found shot dead. The death of another cabinet minister means SO15 are looking into it, but they're pretty sure it was a murder-suicide. Seems they both died in their bedroom. On the bed they found the photograph of Mrs Tredarran in a compromising position with that GRU bloke who was arrested in the Netherlands. You know, one of the photos I saw on your file. Looks like they'd been arguing about that and Tredarran must have taken her life and then his own.'

'Christ!' Harry blanched, 'that wasn't meant to happen. That wasn't the plan.'

'What exactly was the plan?'

'He was supposed to resign his post, citing ill health or whatever. Then, I expected … at least I hoped … he'd report Gray to their Russian masters and either Tredarran would be ordered to kill Gray or Tredarran would be spirited off to Russia and the thugs who took out Godunov would be sent to take care of Gray. None of this was supposed to implicate us.'

'Will it implicate us?'

Harry thought for a moment. No-one, not even Dave, knew he had acquired Godunov's Russian-issue Makarov. Even assuming that the Makarov was the gun Tredarran had used to kill himself and his wife, no-one knew Harry had given it to him. He'd deliberately handed it over in a sealed envelope and in a spot outside Thames House which he knew wasn't covered by CCTV. Mark Tredarran wasn't likely to have told anyone about the gun, especially if he had intended using it on his wife. Nevertheless, Harry felt he had made yet another error of judgement. He hadn't meant for the Tredarrans to die. But he decided he wouldn't beat himself up about it. After all, it was highly probable that Tredarran was a part of Godunov's network and perhaps he knew Godunov had killed Lorna. He was probably complicit in Godunov's and Gray's activities.

It was potentially quite a serious and newsworthy incident, however, yet another British minister dead, and his wife, too. It might also emerge that they were killed by Russian-made bullets from a Russian-made pistol. Indeed, this would probably turn out to be the same pistol used to kill Bowker and the defector 'Oleg', not to mention the two Security Service minders found murdered at the safe house, and, of course, Lorna. However, Harry reasoned that detail of the weapon used would likely be withheld from press and public, for reasons of political expediency.

'Maybe it won't implicate us after all,' he told Dave, 'but, please, tell me their kids didn't find them.'

'No, mate. They're away at boarding schools. The cleaner found the bodies. A middle-aged Polish lady. She was more concerned about getting the blood out of the carpet.'

'That's something, at least. Well I'd better go and let Helena know. She might want to impose a 'D notice' on the press and also go for PII.'

'PII?' Dave asked.

'Public interest immunity. That's withholding from the police and the coroner's court anything they don't need to know if it has implications for national security or the wider public interest.'

As Harry walked to his afternoon appointment with Amandine, he felt relieved that Helena and Adrian had taken the news well. They had weighed up the pros and cons of releasing details of the weapon. On the plus side, it would discredit the Russians by implicating them in the deaths of the couple. On the minus side, however, it might deter future defectors and collaborators. They had decided they would ask SO15 to suppress any mention of the weapon and ammunition being Russian, just as they had in the Bowker case. They hoped the Kremlin would think the deaths of the Tredarrans arose out of a simple but tragic domestic row. Tredarran's connections with the Russians and their cyber-attacks would never be made known either. That would certainly shake the nation's confidence in its government. It seemed unlikely, therefore, that the role of Thames House in revealing Mrs Tredarran's infidelity would ever come to light. The upside of the tragedy, Harry persuaded himself, was that another player in the Russian sleeper network was no longer in the game.

What Harry would have liked to know, but did not, was whether Tredarran had had an opportunity of telling his masters that the Security Service knew of his and Gray's Russian connections. It would certainly be helpful if Tredarran had told them of both Gray's assumption of the WOTAK persona and of Adrian's false assertion that this had compromised the Kremlin's hostile operations. However, there was no way of finding this out. Only time would tell. In the meantime, surveillance on Gray would continue and the downloads from Mrs Tredarran's mobile, secured at their home by SO15, would also be scrutinised.

Feeling reassured on that score, and slightly less stressed, Harry walked into Amandine's office and took his customary seat. He thought she looked good today; a business-like pin-striped skirt and high heels teamed with a red rib-knit sweater with a soft roll collar. She looked curvy, soft and feminine, yet, at the same time, confident and professional. He wondered if she had worn that outfit during his previous appointments. He couldn't remember. He'd never noticed previously. They sat for a few moments in silence. She smiled but did not speak. He thought she wanted him to say something first. He would indulge her.

'Thank you for the other night. For not saying anything, in front of my colleague, I mean. I hadn't expected to bump into you and I had no idea what to say.'

'It happens. I didn't know you lived in Fulham.'

'I don't. At least, I'm just staying there temporarily.'

'So how has your week been?'

He had to think for a moment. He was sure he wasn't supposed to tell her everything. He wished there were rules to this therapy lark. Trouble was, she was good at putting people at ease. That made it too easy to talk to her. He wondered how much of his week he could reveal and how much was not relevant to his mental well-being.

'Busy. Very busy. That keeps me going. I did have a bit of an emotional blip last weekend. Finding myself alone and waking up in a strange room. It did get me down a bit. But, from then on, I was busy.'

'Are you sleeping well? No nightmares or anything?'

'Yes, fine. Dave nags me to eat regularly, too. He's been good company. He understands what it's like. He lost his wife, too, you know.'

The silence resumed. He didn't know whether he was supposed to say something or to wait for her next question. Eventually, Amandine spoke.

'A penny for your thoughts.'

'I was just thinking ...'

'Yes?'

'I was just thinking you have really lovely hair.'

He bit his lip. He hadn't meant to say that, but he was so relaxed that it just came out. He hadn't actually been thinking that, at all. Of course, she did have lovely auburn hair, but it was her legs he'd been admiring, though he wasn't going to say so, obviously. He wasn't a *perv*, after all. He felt a sudden stab of guilt for having such thoughts. How could he even look at another woman? He felt it was a crass betrayal of Lorna. Sure, he was still a man, with all the instincts of a man, but it was too soon to heed those instincts. That he should even have thought about another woman in such terms made him feel like a callous scumbag. No, it would be some time – a long time – before he even contemplated embarking on a new relationship. Right now, though, he hoped he hadn't shocked or offended Amandine.

To his relief, she laughed.

'Well that's good. It's good that you see me as a woman and not just as a therapist. Your thoughts are entirely normal and they tell me you're not too preoccupied with your loss, at least not every moment of the day. In fact, you seem so much more relaxed now than during your previous visits. You know, most of your colleagues hate coming here for their psych-evaluation. That's partly because it's not easy opening up, especially for people in your line of work. Mainly, though, it's because they're worried about what I'll have to say about them.'

'If it's okay to ask, what will you say about me?'

'It's fine to ask. I think you're doing really well. We shouldn't need more than another session or two.'

'Good,' he smiled, although he felt himself mildly disappointed at the prospect.

Chapter 51

Kirpal handed Adrian a printed list of contacts, texts and movement data which had been obtained from Tredarran's mobile phone during his visit to Thames House. He also handed copies to Harry, Dave and Carole.

'I don't suppose his phone pinged off a mast anywhere near the Russian Embassy?' Adrian asked.

'Not a chance,' Kirpal replied. 'As a minister, his face is too well known. He wouldn't have risked it. And it's going to be challenging, separating out his legitimate contacts from any dubious ones. Even the legitimate ones, including one or more of his fellow ministers, could turn out to be sleepers, just as he was. There's quite a lot of phone traffic between him and Edmund Gray, but you'd expect that, what with them being brothers-in-law.'

'So, are there any dubious or incriminating contacts we can go on?' Adrian asked.

'Oh yes,' Kirpal reassured him, 'for starters, he's made regular calls to a mobile phone registered to a woman named Lyudmilla Bovda who's based at 55 Savushkina Street, St Petersburg. That address, we know, is a troll factory.'

'Sorry,' Dave interrupted, 'a troll factory?'

'A troll factory,' Kirpal explained, 'is a so-called Internet Research Centre, one of numerous such places we know of in Russia which employ hundreds of people to act as internet trolls or 'influencers'. Each of those employees uses dozens of different identities and they operate in shifts, around the clock, posting on social networks, putting into effect the Kremlin's schemes to de-stabilise other states. For instance, they put out disinformation. You might have seen that ludicrous rumour circulating just after the Brexit referendum that a group of

'Remainers' was planning to assassinate the Prime Minister. That sort of thing.'

'They also claimed that the Novichok used in Salisbury had come from the IRA,' Harry added. 'These are typical tricks in what we call hybrid warfare. It involves such wide-ranging activities as cyber-attacks, assassinations, dirty tricks and propaganda – everything short of rolling out tanks, troops and nuclear weapons.'

Dave rolled his eyes. He'd had no idea of the scale of Russian activity.

'How do you know about these troll factories?'

It was Carole who answered his question.

'As so often happens, it was a defector who told us how it all works. He'd worked there himself and felt the work was driving him mad. Adopting so many different personalities made him feel positively schizophrenic. Now that we know where they are and what they're doing, we can monitor them. Also, the Americans already identified Bovda and around a dozen others at Savushkina Street as trolls who had meddled in the 2016 US presidential elections.'

'How did they manage that?' Dave asked, fascinated now.

Carole was only too pleased to enlighten him.

'Well, for one thing, they obtained and released damning information about the leading opposition candidate, which lost her votes, and then they bigged-up another two of the opposition candidates. That had the effect of splitting the opposition vote between those two candidates, leaving the field clear for their preferred right-wing candidate. They did the same to influence the Brexit referendum, and also the UK's last general election. It's quite simple, really.'

'So, if the Americans knew about the Russians' meddling, why didn't they do something about it?'

'Well, by the time they'd realised what was going on, the Russians' favoured candidate was already elected. After the election, the US Department of Justice revealed details of the interference and also the identities of the Russians involved – Bovda included – and they indicted them for electoral interference. Unfortunately, the US President scuppered the Justice Department's efforts to seek their extradition. He vetoed the issue of US visas to the suspects. So, even if the Russians had agreed to hand them over to face trial, which they never would, no airline would carry them without visas, or they'd face huge fines.'

'So, couldn't we have done something to stop the Russians influencing our electoral process?'

Adrian now chipped in.

'We did our best. Along with the other intel agencies, we drafted a comprehensive report right after the Brexit referendum. It went all the way to the Prime Minister. However, the PM suppressed it.'

Dave was shocked.

'Good Lord! Well, how can we tell these so-called influencers from regular people on social media?'

'We check out suspects' social media profiles,' Harry said. 'They'll look like regular folks, but their profiles will show they have only one friend or contact on that particular site, and that friend will be the page relating to whatever organisation they belong to, whether it's a climate change page or a pro-Brexit group, or a nationalist organisation. No genuine person has just one friend on social media.'

Dave took a deep breath. He could hardly get his head around the extent of the Russians' deviousness.

'So, why would Tredarran have been in touch with this … troll factory?' he asked.

'We might find out if we could access Gray's phones,' Kirpal said.

'Fancy a nice little drive out to leafy Buckinghamshire, chaps?' Harry smiled at Dave and Kirpal.

Chapter 52

They decided to take the red postal van, which was more useful for conducting covert surveillance in the suburbs and villages, where strangers parking up or walking around during the day usually attracted too much attention. The van came with a postman's weatherproof jacket and even stacks of advertising flyers and dummy post which could be posted through doors, adding authenticity to the exercise. The back of the van, however, was equipped with surveillance kit, cameras and digital scanners.

As luck would have it, there was a red post box at the corner of the village street where Edmund Gray's house was located, so it seemed natural to park near the box. Clad in the postman's jacket, Harry strolled from house to house, posting flyers, until he came to Gray's house. It had electronic gates and an external letter box, so Harry was unable to access the driveway and get a look through the windows. He was able, however, to observe a sophisticated alarm system and surveillance cameras. He saw enough to persuade him that covert entry was out of the question. He also noticed that the Grays' letter box was quite full. With some difficulty, he posted a flyer in the box, at the same time sliding out a local weekly newspaper which was protruding from the slot. He checked the date. It was almost a week old.

Returning to the van, he climbed into the driver's seat, took out his mobile phone and dialled the office.

'Carole, it's Harry. Will you give Gray's office a call and discreetly check whether he's there. Only it looks as if he and his family might have gone away. Cheers.'

Sliding open the access grill between the driver's compartment and the rear of the van, he glanced through at Dave and Kirpal.

'Looks like we might have missed them,' he said. 'No-one's picked up their post for quite a few days and, in any case, the house looks pretty much impenetrable. Carole's checking out Gray's office to see if he's there.'

Harry took up his lunchbox and flask and began to consume his sandwich and coffee in conspicuous fashion, so as not to arouse undue interest amongst the neighbours. Soon, Carole called back with some disappointing news.

'His office says Gray's taking a fortnight's family holiday in Canada. Anything else you want me to do?'

'Let Adrian know, would you,' Harry sighed, 'and get the tech boys to see if they can get a trace on his mobile.'

In the back of the van, Kirpal and Dave tucked into their sandwiches, too, whilst they and Harry discussed their next move. Soon, Harry's mobile rang. It was Carole. Harry switched to speakerphone so Dave and Kirpal could hear.

'Okay, so I found the Grays' booking to Canada, but the airline is one of several whose computerised baggage systems went down a couple of days ago and are still down – probably another cyber-attack – so their flight was cancelled. I checked with APIS in case they'd re-booked with another carrier, maybe to go via the US, but they haven't. Oh, their house is up for sale, by the way, with Harveys, the Beaconsfield estate agents.'

'I wonder where the hell they've gone,' Harry sighed, 'and have they gone for good?'

Carole had more information.

'Well now, I called the estate agents on the pretence of wanting to book a viewing. They said an agent would have to show me around as the vendors are away, staying at their holiday cottage in the Cotswolds.'

'I don't suppose they told you the address of the cottage?'

'No, and it would have sounded a bit suspicious if I'd asked. I'll see if I can find out from the council tax and utility companies, but it'll take some time and I'm not hopeful.'

'Okay. Thanks Carole.'

Turning back to the access grill, Harry shrugged.

'Looks like that's that for today,' he said, 'bit disappointing, eh?'

'Maybe not,' Dave said, 'I have an idea. Could you go and fish out some of the Gray's mail from their letterbox. Then let me have your jacket.'

Chapter 53

Clad in the postman's uniform jacket and whistling casually, Dave sauntered into Harveys estate agents. He gave the young woman at the desk his most charming smile.

'Scuse me, Miss. Wonder if you can help me.'

'Morning,' she smiled back.

Dave handed her one of the letters addressed to the Grays.

'I just tried to deliver mail to this address, but they've got one of those continental-style external post boxes and it's jammed full with post and newspapers. I spoke with one of the neighbours who said the family have recently moved to the Cotswolds but she didn't have their address. She said your office is handling the sale of their property and that you might have a contact address for them. If you have, I could re-direct their mail.'

Without a moment's hesitation, the young woman opened her drawer and withdrew one of her files.

'Yes, we have the vendors' contact details. Let me write the address down for you.'

Back at the van, Dave grinned at Harry as he handed over the piece of estate agents' letter-headed notepaper.

'You see, everyone trusts a man in uniform.'

The post office van was soon making its way north along the A6. Harry would have preferred to have changed vehicles, since postmen weren't usually seen making deliveries after six o'clock in the evening and the daylight was fading quickly, but there was no point in heading back to London to change vehicles when they were already some distance west of the capital. He hoped it might be assumed they were working overtime to deal with the extra pre-Christmas post.

He decided they needed to try and track down the Grays as soon as possible. If they weren't at the cottage, he'd have to pass their details immediately to Special Branch in case the family tried to leave the country by sea or via the Channel Tunnel. If they did so, there was a chance they could be intercepted at their point of embarkation. He suspected Gray wouldn't have sufficient funds to rent a private aircraft in order to bypass officials by leaving via a small airfield somewhere.

Arriving at the pretty Cotswold town of Nailsworth, Harry was guided by the GPS along a single-track lane which led up a very steep hill. He realised that parking there discreetly would be difficult, since none of the little nineteenth century former workers' cottages had driveways. Wherever there was a small lay-by or passing place along the lane, there was a car parked in it. The Grays' cottage was at the very top of the hill. He imagined it would normally have a lovely view out over the town, but it was now dark and all he could see of the town below was the street lights. He had to drive half way down the other side of the hill before he found a small spot where he could park the van.

All was quiet as he, Dave and Kirpal walked back up to the top of the hill. Near the house, they spotted a vehicle which they knew from their enquiries was registered to Edmund Gray. Dave placed a hand on the bonnet but found it cold. Another vehicle was parked just beyond it, so Dave walked a little further on and checked out that one also. By comparison, the bonnet of that car was quite warm. Heading back towards the Gray's little front garden, they came to a set of almost vertical stone steps leading up to the front door of the cottage. The cottage itself, however, was in darkness.

It had occurred to Harry that their task might have been easier in daylight, and that they might have been able to effect a clean entry to the cottage whilst the family were out. However, it had also occurred to him that the family might not go out at all, especially as, presumably, they were here with the intention of lying low. If they were lying low inside the cottage, however, it seemed odd that the place was in total darkness.

Harry led the way as they crept up the stone steps. Stumbling slightly half way up, as one of the stone treads was loose and crumbling, he motioned to Dave and Kirpal to be careful. Passing silently around the side of the cottage, they saw that the side door was ajar. This immediately worried Harry, especially since there were no lights on in the house. People who were in hiding surely wouldn't leave the side door open. As he stood by the open door, wondering what to make of it, the silence was suddenly shattered by two loud shots which rang out inside the house. Instinctively, Dave and Kirpal leapt back around to the front of the cottage and crouched down on the path beneath the front window.

'Stay there!' Harry hissed, as he dived sideways into the shrubbery opposite the side door.

All was quiet again and Harry began to wonder if the shots represented yet another murder-suicide. He hoped not, especially as it was likely the Grays had their children with them. He saw Dave and Kirpal peering around the side of the house in his direction. In the low light emanating upwards from a single street lamp on the lane below, he signalled to Dave and Kirpal that he was going in, but that they should stay put. Emerging silently from the shrubbery, he peered in through the side door into the kitchen. He could see and hear nothing. Still keeping low, he crept over the threshold and paused just inside the doorway to listen. The silence was eerie and the darkness within was all enveloping. All Harry could hear was his own heart thumping.

Suddenly, another deafening gunshot rang out in the confined space of the little kitchen. He instantly felt a searing pain in his shoulder as the impact knocked him backwards out through the door and onto his back on the path outside. He now realised that, by remaining crouched in the doorway, he must have been silhouetted against what little light there was. He had made himself a sitting target. He cursed himself for his stupidity.

Dave now took matters into his own hands and, at the top of his voice, he yelled: 'Armed police! You are surrounded. Come out with your hands up!'

Seconds later, two bulky figures swiftly emerged from the darkened interior and, leaping across Harry, they tore off down the path. Harry immediately feared for his colleagues.

'Gunmen!' he shouted, hoping Dave and Kirpal would stay back.

Clutching his shoulder, which burned as if a white-hot poker had been thrust into it, he rose onto his side and, with great difficulty, got to his feet. He staggered after the intruders. He saw Kirpal rush forward and thrust out a leg, tripping up one of the fleeing men who hurtled, head first, down the steep flight of steps, giving a loud scream as he went. The second man was brought to the ground by a rugby tackle from Dave, who immobilised him and gleefully yelled in his ear 'Gloucestershire Constabulary. You're nicked!'

Suddenly feeling faint from the intense pain in his left shoulder, but relieved that the two intruders had not escaped, Harry allowed himself to slowly sink back onto the ground. He tried to support himself on his elbow but could not. He could not even fully raise his head and he reasoned that the bullet must have shattered his collar bone. Just when the waves of pain reached an unbearable high, the garden began to spin and he lapsed into unconsciousness.

A little while later, Harry came to in a haze of flashing blue lights. He was in the back of a stationary ambulance parked out in the lane, and a paramedic was bending over him pressing a dressing to his wound. His pain did not seem so great now and he guessed he had been given a pain-killing injection. Beyond the paramedic, he saw the concerned face of Dave Lloyd.

'The Grays?' Harry rasped.

'The missus and the kids are okay. They'd locked themselves in a bedroom. Lucky we got here when we did or they'd be dead.'

Dave indicated a recumbent figure on the ambulance's other stretcher. 'Edmund's been shot but he's alive. You and he are off to hospital right now. Catch up with you later, mate. Got to contact Adrian.'

Dave's face disappeared. The ambulance door slammed and the vehicle was on the move to the accompaniment of a loud siren.

Chapter 54

The following day, Harry's post-surgery drowsiness was still subsiding as he lay gently napping in his hospital bed. He started slightly as the door suddenly flew open, but was relieved and pleased to see Dave's smiling face appear.

'How's the casualty?'

'Am I in a private room? I hope I'm not paying for this.'

'Don't worry. The office has got it sorted. You're under twenty-four-hour police watch, and so is Edmund Gray. He's in the next room, by the way.'

Dave jerked a thumb in the direction of the half glass-panelled wall which separated Harry's room from the one next door. Both rooms were flooded with winter sunshine which, with the smell of hospital antiseptic, gave the place a safe and calming atmosphere. Dave fetched a chair from beside the door and placed it by Harry's bedside. Sitting down, he reached into the carrier bag he had brought and produced a discreetly wrapped half bottle of Scotch. He placed it alongside the big basket of fruit dominating the bedside locker.

'Alternative painkiller,' he explained, winking.

'Did somebody rob a greengrocer's?' Harry joked.

'They're from everyone at the office. At least you won't need the enema they always give you in these places.'

'So, what's happening?'

'There's lots happening, mate. One of the gunmen is dead. He landed on his head when he tripped down the steps.'

Dave winked again.

'If he wasn't dead, he could have sued them over that loose step. They were Russians, of course. Most recent calls on their mobile phones are from the extension of one Colonel Antonov at the Russian Embassy. The Russian ambassador's being summoned to the Foreign Office to explain himself, for all the good that'll do.'

'And the other gunman?'

'He's being interrogated right now. Gray will be, too, when he's fully recovered. I expect he'll sing like a canary, especially if that means we'll keep him safe from the Russians. We should be able to turn him, and we may even get cipher codes from him. Meanwhile, his family are in the safe house in Fulham.'

'Our safe house? What about my stuff?'

'I've moved it back to your place. Adrian feels it'll be safe enough for you to go home when you're discharged, since we've rounded up all the sleepers that we know about. Corsham are continuing to work on the cyber-attacks as the Russians are still up to their tricks, of course. Here, you'll like this one. Corey Hart tells me one of those troll factories managed to shut down the US President's twitter account. He thought he was well in with the Russians, but it seems they were angry he'd left NATO. They wanted him to stay in NATO and support them. He's hopping mad, though. Twitter is his only way of communicating. He doesn't do whole sentences.'

Harry laughed out loud – until the ache in his shoulder reminded him he shouldn't.

'So, I guess, that's it, eh? No more WOTAK.'

'Yeah, mate. No more WOTAK. No more Dave Lloyd either. I've been recalled. I'm being assigned to lead a multi-agency group on knife crime in Gloucester – police, social services, teachers, youth workers and all that malarkey. Can't say I'm wild about it. It won't be anything like as exciting as it has been working with you guys. I'm going to miss you all'

'I'll be sorry to lose you, Dave. It's been great working with you, too, and you've been great company. Maybe you should consider applying to join us permanently.'

'You know what? Maybe I will. Oh, and, while I remember, I brought in a change of clothes for you, for when they discharge you.'

Dave lifted the carrier bag and placed it in the bedside locker.

'What happened to the clothes I was wearing?'

'Ruined, mate. What wasn't shot through or blood-stained was cut off you by the nurses.'

'Bugger!'

'You should put in a claim. Here, you've got a friend who should be able to arrange that for you.'

'Eh?'

'Your insurance broker.'

'Sod off!'

Dave laughed as he rose and moved the chair back to where it had stood, over by the door.

'Well, I will have to sod off now, as it happens. Got to get back to Cheltenham and do some food shopping. Back to suppers for one, then.'

'Yeah, for me too, Dave, soon as I get out of here.'

Dave shook Harry's hand and grinned.

'So long, Mate. Don't be a stranger.'

'You, too. Whenever you're up in town, there's always a bed at my place.'

'You're on.'

Chapter 55

Later that day, Harry had a visit from one of the hospital surgeons who had Harry's X-rays under his arm.

'You've been told you had a broken clavicle?' Mr Obi asked.

'If that's my collar bone, then, yes, they told me.'

'Well the bad news is that it wasn't a clean break. The bone was shattered. We got the bullet out, but we had to put in some pins to support it whilst it heals.'

'What does that mean?'

'It means it will take longer to heal than a simple break.'

'How long do you think that will be?'

'Minimum six weeks. Though, it could be a couple of months before you have full use of your arm and shoulder. You won't be going back to work for quite a while.'

Harry thanked the doctor, but he was disappointed. He didn't relish the prospect of more time spent alone at home in his empty flat.

Shortly after the medic's departure, a smiling blonde nurse entered. She brought him a fresh carafe of water and straightened his bedding and pillows. Harry tried to help her by lifting himself up the bed but his shoulder hurt like the devil whenever he moved.

'Do you need some pain relief?' she asked.

'No, it's okay,' he told her, 'it only hurts when I laugh.'

'I'll bring you some magazines to read, then'.

'Bless you.'

Harry found it difficult to sleep that night. He could only lie on his right side, which was inconvenient, as he customarily slept on his left. He had done so ever since Lorna had moved in with him. That was because Lorna like to sleep on her left side and he liked to sleep close behind her, with a protective arm around her. He would now have to get used to sleeping on his right side – as well as to sleeping without her. He tried but he just could not get comfortable in the narrow hospital bed. As loath as he was to be a nuisance for the overworked nurses, eventually he rang the bell. It was a male nurse who eventually responded.

'Sorry to bother you, but I really am uncomfortable. I wondered if you'd kindly prop me up on my pillows so I can try to sleep upright.'

'Okay.'

The bulky male nurse stood to one side of Harry, slipped an arm around Harry's shoulders and thrust his hands into Harry's armpits. He had no difficulty lifting Harry's weight and manoeuvring him upright, though it wasn't exactly comfortable for Harry. This chap clearly wasn't as friendly as the blonde nurse from earlier, Harry thought, but he supposed she would have gone off duty. He further supposed night shifts weren't conducive to a cheerful disposition. The night nurse left but returned shortly after with a glass of water and a small paper cup containing two capsules.

'Take these. They'll help you sleep,' he said, thrusting the medication and glass at Harry.

'No thanks,' Harry shook his head. 'I won't need those. Don't like taking sleeping pills.'

'Take them,' the nurse insisted.

Harry didn't much like the man's tone, but he took the tablets and the water and made to place them on the bedside locker.

'Take them now.'

Harry resented the nurse's bedside manner, or lack of it. He tipped the capsules from the paper cup into his mouth and, with his tongue, he pushed them firmly into his cheek, before swallowing a sip of the water.'

The nurse took back the paper cup and the tumbler and, checking the paper cup was empty, he turned to leave.

'Goodnight,' Harry said, but there was no reply.

As the nurse closed the door, Harry spat the capsules out into his hand and lobbed them into the basket of fruit on his bedside cabinet.

As the night wore on, Harry began to wonder if he should, in fact, have taken the medication. He couldn't sleep at all. He reflected that hospitals are never quiet places, not even at night. The corridor lights had been dimmed slightly but were still sufficiently bright to keep him awake. Through the glass panels, he could see the outline of the uniformed constable, who, every half hour or so, paced up and down the corridor outside his and Edmund Gray's rooms. Presumably, he did this mainly to keep himself awake. Occasionally, a young nurse would come tripping down the corridor and would sit chatting with the policeman. Their chatter and occasional laughter also served to keep Harry awake. He watched the luminous hands of the wall clock sweeping the night away agonisingly slowly.

At around one o'clock in the morning, another policeman arrived to relieve the first one. This necessitated more chatter. Harry wished they would have a little consideration for the patients they were guarding. Then the taciturn male nurse came along with a cup of tea for the bored policeman, who tried to make small talk with him as well.

'Good luck with that,' Harry thought.

He felt the urge to toss and turn in the bed but his shoulder hurt whenever he did so. The early hours seemed to pass interminably slowly. When next he glanced across at the glass panel, he could see the figure of the policeman seated alone out in the corridor. The policeman's head was tilted back, resting against the glass. Harry guessed he had nodded off. *'Lucky bastard!'* he thought. He desperately longed for sleep himself but his pain and discomfort continued to deny him this.

By three o'clock, he decided he would give in and take the medication. However, he couldn't quite reach the basket.

Gingerly, he swung his legs over the edge of the bed, placed his feet on the floor and stood up. He still felt the need to hunch over, owing to his damaged collar bone but he began to fumble around in the fruit basket for the capsules. It took some time, but, eventually, he found one of them. One might do, he supposed. However, the nurse hadn't left the tumbler of water. Looking around the room, he saw there was a small washbasin over by the partition wall. He could get water from the cold tap.

As he popped the pill into his mouth, scooped water from the tap and threw his head back to swallow it, a movement on the other side of the glass panel caught his eye. In the adjacent room where Edmund Gray lay recovering from his own surgery, a bulky figure was bending over the bed. Harry guessed it was probably the nurse checking on Gray. However, something didn't feel right. It seemed to him that the nurse was standing by Gray's bed for longer than was necessary to check on a sleeping man. Harry felt uneasy about this. He was also concerned that the policeman supposed to be on guard was clearly asleep. He decided to go and rouse him.

Despite feeling a little unsteady from having spent the past two nights lying down in his hospital bed, Harry shuffled out into the corridor. He placed a hand on the policeman's shoulder to wake him. The policeman did not respond. Harry shook him but, to his surprise, the policeman slipped from his chair and fell to the floor. He was clearly unconscious. Harry remembered the male nurse had taken him a cup of tea a while earlier. He reasoned that the policeman had been given sleeping medication. He could guess why.

Placing a hand on the partition wall to steady his progress, he hurried a few steps down the corridor and flung open the door into Gray's room. The male nurse was still standing by Gray's bed, poised with a syringe in his hand and was clearly about to inject Gray.

'What's that? What are you giving him?' he demanded.

'You go back to bed!' the nurse ordered as he pumped the residual air out of the syringe.

'Not until I see what you're giving him. What's in that syringe?' he asked, stepping across to the bed.

Despite his suspicions about the nurse, Harry was quite unprepared for what happened next. The nurse whirled round and punched him with great force in his shoulder – his wounded shoulder. The immense jolt of pain sent Harry staggering backwards. Suddenly, the nurse was coming after him, brandishing the syringe. Harry knew that, since he had only one functioning arm, whatever he did next had to be effective, otherwise the nurse – or whoever he really was – would probably kill him and Gray.

Reaching out with his good arm, he found himself grabbing a heavy glass object from the bedside locker. It was a water carafe and it was full. Harry lifted the carafe by its neck, swung it in an arc above his head and, with every ounce of strength he could muster, he slammed it into the side of the nurse's head. The carafe smashed, showing the nurse with water and releasing a trickle of blood from his temple. To Harry's great relief, the nurse tottered backwards for a brief second, then fell like a deadweight to the floor.

Breathing in heavily to take his mind off his pain, Harry stepped to the head of the bed and located the emergency call button on the wall. Keeping all his weight leant upon it, he turned to keep an eye on the unconscious nurse.

'Gotcha, you bastard!' he growled.

Within minutes, Gray's room and the corridor outside were full of people and all the lights were fully on. A hospital security guard, a couple of burly hospital porters and another police constable, who had earlier brought an injured drunk into casualty, were all crowded around. Gray was awake in his bed, sitting up, looking both confused and alarmed. The security guard had the male nurse pinned to the floor and one of the porters was sitting on the nurse's legs whilst the constable from casualty handcuffed him. Outside in the corridor, a female casualty nurse was trying to roll the drugged policeman into the recovery position. Harry, meanwhile, stood ignored in a corner, groaning over the now excruciating pain in his shoulder. Staggering back out into the corridor, he eventually diverted the nurse's attention away from the unconscious constable.

'Any chance of some pain relief – for me, that is? And do you have a mobile phone I could use?'

Soon, he had a sleepy Adrian Curtis on the other end of the phone.

'Adrian,' he said.

'Harry, is that you?'

'Adrian, it's not over. We didn't get them all. It isn't over.'

'Harry? Harry?'

The sleeping pill now began to take effect and Harry slid slowly to the floor and, at long last, fell into a deep sleep.

Chapter 56

Harry's journey into work was tricky as he tried to avoid the other passengers bumping into his bad shoulder. He still wore a sling to support his left arm and so his first big challenge of the day had been getting showered and dressed with only one fully working arm.

He received a warm welcome from the team the moment he stepped through the office door. Kirpal and Carole came to greet him. Carole kissed him on both cheeks and Kirpal patted him on his good shoulder.

'How was your Christmas?' Kirpal asked.

'Dull as ditch water, thanks,' Harry grimaced. 'Spent it at a hotel in the Cotswolds with my old man and Lorna's mum. He's as deaf as a post and she's a Fascist. Food was good, though.'

Kirpal steered Harry over to his desk which was cleared of files but festooned with balloons and a 'Welcome Back' banner. Upon the desk there was a large cake. Harry guessed Carole was responsible for both the cake and the decorations. He was touched. He glanced around the office at the smiling faces and was heartened to see that little seemed to have changed in the weeks he had been on sick leave. Christmas aside, he had spent so much time over the past couple of months in his little flat that he was both pleased and relieved to be back at work.

Suddenly, however, his heart almost stopped, as he caught sight of the figure of Lorna seated with her back to him at her former desk. Surely, it must be a ghost? As he froze and stared in astonishment, she looked around and he realised it was not Lorna at all, but a stranger with similar, dark hair. The stranger rose and came across to be introduced.

'This is Cherelle Baptiste, our newest member of staff,' Kirpal explained, tactfully avoiding mention of the fact that she was Lorna's replacement, which, in any case, was evident from the fact that she had been allocated Lorna's desk.

'Cherry,' she said, holding out her hand to Harry.

'Harry Edwards,' he smiled, recovering his composure and shaking her proffered hand.

He could see now that, her dark hair apart she looked nothing like Lorna. Cherry had very dark brown eyes and a flawless coffee-hued complexion. She also had a warm and attractive smile.

'I hear you were shot, Harry. I hope you're much recovered now,' she beamed.

'I'm much better now, thanks. So, when did you join the team?'

'Six weeks ago, now. I transferred from Counter-Terrorism.'

'And is that an American accent I detect?'

'Trinidadian, actually.'

'Well it's very easy on the ear,' Harry said, hoping he didn't sound too effusive.

Cherry pointed towards the door.

'Do you know our other new boy?' she asked.

Harry turned to see who it was who had just come in, coffee in hand. To his surprise, it was Dave Lloyd.

'Dave. You still here?'

'You can't get rid of me, mate. I'm legit now,' Dave said, shaking Harry's hand warmly.

'Meet our new agent handler,' Carole said.

'Really? You've actually joined the firm?' Harry said, surprised but pleased.

'Yeah. Well, I decided I'd given the force my best years, so I took the retirement package and applied to join you lot. I didn't think I'd be successful, but it seems I'm what they call 'an experienced hire'. And Adrian requested me for his section. Feels funny to be called 'a probationer' as well, especially at my age.'

'Where are you staying, then? You know if you need digs you can always stay at my flat.'

'He's lodging with me,' Carole said.

Harry spotted a sudden, almost imperceptible glance passing between Carole and Dave. It suggested to him that maybe, just maybe, Dave was something more than Carole's lodger. The thought pleased him. These were two good people and they both deserved a bit of happiness. Dave had visited Harry several times during Harry's sick leave, as had Carole, and yet neither had mentioned Dave's career change or his move to London. Harry assured himself that Dave's ability to keep secrets would stand him in good stead in his new role. Dave was also a pretty shrewd judge of character, which would be an asset for an agent handler.

'There've been one or two other changes whilst you've been on sick leave,' Carole told him. 'Take a seat and we'll fill you in.'

While Dave went to fetch another cup of coffee for Harry, Carole explained that their Director General, Helena Fairbrother had been shouldered out of her post and replaced by the Prime Minister's chosen candidate. Malcolm Donald, the new head of the service, was, she explained, formerly a special advisor to the PM.

'What's he like, then, this former SPAD?' Harry asked.

'He's a history and politics graduate and a Russophile. He's spent some years in Russia, though no-one's very clear on exactly what it was that he did there. You'll meet him soon enough. He's down here a lot talking to Adrian about Russian issues. He's not a civil servant but he's had several jobs working for different UK politicians and he also runs a technology consultancy company or something like that.'

'Yes, but what's he *like*?'

Tellingly, Carole's lip curled.

'Oh, opinionated, outspoken, rude. Wants to make changes. Fixing things that aren't broken. You know the scenario, a new broom sweeping in changes for change's sake.'

'Well, there's more to that old saying, isn't there?' Harry smiled, 'a new broom sweeps clean, but the old brush knows all the corners. So, where's Helena gone?'

'She's taken some time out to go travelling. She shouldn't have any trouble finding another post, though. No doubt, one of the other intel agencies would snap her up. It's usual also for former DGs to be offered directorships in commerce. Shame, though. Naturally, Adrian's not too happy about it. Did you know they used to be ...'?

'Yes,' Harry nodded, 'I had heard.'

Dave appeared from the office kitchen with a cup of coffee for Harry and some small plates and cake forks.

'Are you going to cut that cake Harry, or what?' he asked.

'I think Carole should do it. She's got two arms. One of mine is still de-commissioned.'

With almost precision timing, Johnston Freeman appeared just as Carole was doling out slices of the coffee-iced sponge cake.

'Mr Harry! You're back. How are you?' Johnston grinned.

'Johnston. How lovely to see you, old chap. Come and have some cake.'

Johnston put down the mail, gratefully accepted the large slice of cake which Carole wrapped up in a paper napkin for him and, wishing Harry well, he left again to continue his rounds.

As they tucked into the cake, Carole, Kirpal and Dave updated Harry on their operations. He learned that *Operation Tern* was still live. Dave, now a fully trained agent handler, had been working with a couple of human resources connected with the operation, one of them being Edmund Gray. As predicted, Gray had been more than willing to disclose everything he knew in return for protection from Colonel Antonov's thugs.

'Whilst you've been away, the investigation has really grown,' Dave said. 'Gray had got involved with Russian criminals through his wife. Those criminals had set him up in business here, but he'd got himself completely out of his depth. He found himself being manipulated by a major Moscow-based cyber-criminal who runs a highly successful, multi-million-dollar crime organisation. What he does is he uses malware, which is developed behind the scenes by the outwardly respectable Lurman Corporation, and he uses it to access the personal and financial data of individuals, companies and organisations. Then he either siphons off their funds or he holds their data to ransom. He also has close links with the Kremlin.'

'Could this criminal be the real brains behind all the cyber-attacks?' Harry asked.

'The theory we're working on is that he's certainly involved in some of them, especially the attacks on financial institutions. This is him.'

Dave handed Harry the file on one Maksim Fyodorovych Yakubov who, Dave explained, had recently been dubbed the world's most wanted cyber-criminal. Dave explained that Yakubov had been identified as the man behind the attacks which had shut down the UK's banks, healthcare computers and transport systems. This cyber warfare was not limited to the UK, Dave emphasised, but was global. Yakubov's organisation had defrauded US companies to the tune of hundreds of millions of dollars. The Americans had recently indicted Yakubov and were offering a bounty of five million dollars for his capture.

'This Yakubov geezer,' Dave explained, 'has squads of workers – a bit like your troll factories – mainly housed in basement offices beneath cafés in Moscow. These workers spend their time e mailing out links which, if any organisation clicks on one, will infect their whole computer network and hold their data to ransom.'

As ever, Kirpal was ready with a technical explanation:

'The software Yakubov uses is what we call ransomware. It was developed by Lurman Corporation and, to be honest, if Colin Holder hadn't started his one-man criminal enterprise as WOTAK, we'd probably never have made a firm connection between Lurman and Yakubov.'

'So why is this Yakubov doing all of this?' Harry asked, delighted to be drawn back into doing what he loved most – investigating.

Dave was pleased to explain.

'For money, of course. Most of the organisations he's attacked have paid up. It would have taken far too long for the crime agencies to identify and remove the ransomware and free up their data, so paying the ransom demanded was the quickest way of getting their businesses going again.'

'It's not just a criminal enterprise, though,' Kirpal added, 'because, although most of the stolen data is accessed for criminal purposes, some of it is gathered on behalf of Russian intelligence. This intelligence product is so useful to Russia's domestic intelligence agency, that the Moscow authorities are under strict orders not to interfere with Yakubov's criminal activities.'

'Yes,' Dave added, 'and Edmund Gray's software company got so tied up with Yakubov's criminal empire that the Kremlin decided to use that connection to put their own man into Lurman as well. That man was Godunov.'

'You got all this from Edmund Gray?' Harry asked.

Dave nodded enthusiastically.

'Yes. He's a frightened man. It was okay whilst he was making good money out of the business but, increasingly, Yakubov was creaming off his profits. Theirs was a parasitical relationship. And Gray wasn't too comfortable with having a GRU thug foisted on him. He felt intimidated by Godunov. When Gray got into financial difficulties, Yakubov gave him a loan or two. The rate of interest was high, though, and Gray couldn't pay him back. Yakubov had him hooked like a fish.'

'So, what exactly do we know about Yakubov?'

'He's a thirty-two-year old; the son of a former government scientist. He's a multi-millionaire and he's untouchable. He's also a petrol head who drives around Moscow in any one of a dozen high performance cars, doing doughnuts around the traffic police and they can't touch him for it.'

'Well, if there's a reward out for him, surely he'll be arrested the moment he steps outside Russia?' Harry said.

'Ah,' Dave grinned, 'but that's the problem. He's not going to set foot outside Russia. Not unless we can tempt him out. We're working closely with the National Crime Agency and the Cyber Security Centre on this one and this is why I'm cultivating a couple of CHISs.'

Harry smiled on hearing Dave using *intelspeak* for a covert human intelligence source. Dave continued.

'Gray and a few others in the network have met Yakubov. They know what makes him tick. We just need to work out what would persuade him to come to England.'

Chapter 57

Although Harry's collar bone was almost fully healed within a couple of weeks and he was able to forego the sling, it was Dave who drove them down to rural Kent. Winter was releasing its grip on the land and the southern counties were witnessing the first flowerings of spring. Meandering over the area of outstanding natural beauty which was known as the Kentish Downs, they spotted the mansion set within its thirty-seven-acre country estate long before they reached it. Dave waved his ID towards the security cameras and the big electronic gates gradually swung open. Dave drove up the expansive driveway and parked outside the huge red-bricked house.

To their surprise, it was the mansion's seventy-four-year old owner himself who answered the door. If Dave was overawed at meeting his long-time hero, Jordan Wilde, singer-songwriter, rock legend and one of Britain's wealthiest men, he tried not to let it show. As Wilde ushered them into the palatial hallway, Harry thought Wilde looked somewhat older in the flesh than he did when in full make-up and flashy costumes on his videos. His hair was an incongruous, light-absorbing shade of black. He wasn't in gold lamé and sequins today, however, but he wore more comfortable looking jeans and a sweatshirt. Three of Wilde's five children – the ones from the most recent of his five marriages, Harry supposed – were playing noisily on the stairs.

'Thank you for agreeing to see us, Mr Wilde,' Harry said.

'Jordan, please. Well, when my secretary told me what you proposed I was intrigued. Come on in, gents. We'll go into the conservatory. We won't be disturbed there.'

Harry and Dave followed him through several elegant examples of costly English interiors.

'Oops, I said 'conservatory' didn't I? My wife tells me it's not a conservatory. It's an orangery.'

'What's the difference?' Dave asked.

'About thirty grand, apparently.'

Eventually, they reached the equally elegant orangery, a huge and sumptuously furnished garden room with tall windows overlooking the lake and grounds. At the rock star's invitation, Harry and Dave seated themselves in the gilded armchairs and introduced themselves. Affably, Wilde offered to make them tea. Guessing how far away the kitchen must be, Harry declined.

'So, you're after Maksim, then,' Jordan smiled, 'I suppose you know that I've met him?'

'No, we didn't know that,' Harry was surprised.

'Oh, yeah. He's a big fan. He arranged my Russia tour a couple of years back and I stayed at his Moscow mansion. He wanted to have photos taken with me and he had this top photographer take them. No cheap selfies for Maksim. We did stylish photos by his pool and in his music room. He's one seriously wealthy dude. He showed me his collection of vintage cars. He hasn't got as many as me, though. I've got twenty-six hot classics at the moment.'

'Actually, Mr ... er, Jordan, that's what we came to speak to you about,' Harry said. 'We understand you're planning to sell some of your cars through Sotheby's next month.'

'That's right. Did you know that the price of vintage cars drops drastically whenever there's an economic recession? I started collecting mine in the eighties when prices were high. They were an enjoyable investment, though, and I do drive them. Then the global economy went wobbly in the nineties' and my nineteen-sixty-one Ferrari Spyder lost half its value. Since Brexit buggered up our economy, my collection has dipped in value yet again. Right now is not a good time to sell, of course, but I want to invest more in my charities for the homeless. God knows, the poor devils need it now more than ever before. Did you know, the UK has more food banks than it has branches of McDonalds?'

227

'That's very commendable. We also understand Maksim Yakubov has approached you numerous times and made you repeated offers for one of your cars but you have refused to sell.'

'Yes, the Aston Martin. It's a nineteen-ninety-seven V8 *Vantage*, hand-built. It does nought to sixty in four point eight seconds. It's one of the last coach-built Aston Martins. Maksim's been pestering me to sell it to him for the last couple of years.'

'But you won't sell?' Dave asked.

'Absolutely not. It's not just one of the world's most desirable cars, it's a part of history – British auto industrial history. It was hand-made in Newport Pagnell. Something as iconic as that shouldn't leave the country. I mean, it's part of our heritage, isn't it? It should be cherished, not thrown around Moscow by a wealthy boy racer.'

'But, still, Maksim is desperate to buy it?' Harry asked.

'Oh, yeah. He even offered me Nikita in part exchange.'

'Who's Nikita?' Dave asked.

'Nikita is his red, nineteen-sixty-one Alpine Sunbeam. Not a great model, but that particular Sunbeam was used in the first Bond film 'Dr No'. Maksim had it imported from the film set in Jamaica all the way to Moscow. Had it restored, nicely, too. See, he doesn't know a lot about cars but he's attracted by a big price tag and by a car's provenance. He doesn't collect cars for their rarity or beauty. Instead, he goes mad for cars that some celebrity has owned. Last year, he paid twelve million dollars for a Maybach Excelero. It was only worth around eight mil, but he bought it from a US rapper. Maksie baby would have paid him whatever he asked. He had his photo taken with the rapper, too. I suppose you'd say he's a celebrity junkie.'

'Why do you think he's so keen to buy your Aston Martin?' Dave asked.

'Ah, because it's a one-off and because it was built especially for another of the Bond films. You might have seen Pierce

Brosnan behind the wheel. I bought it from Pinewood Studios. I think Maksim must be a big Bond fan, too.'

'Who isn't?' Dave grinned.

'So,' Harry smiled, 'if he thought you might sell your Aston Martin to him ahead of the auction, I expect he'd jump at the chance to buy it.'

'You kidding? He'd bite my hand off. He'd be on the next plane into Heathrow. Oh, wait, he can't can he? The Yanks have slapped an arrest warrant on the dude, haven't they? He'd have to send someone to buy it on his behalf.'

'But what if you said you'd *only* sell it to him in person?' Dave asked.

Wilde's tanned and surgically enhanced face crinkled into a broad smile. He wagged a chubby finger at them.

'Ah, ha ha, I see your game.'

The red Alpine Sunbeam rolled off the Eurostar. It had been a smooth and pleasant drive from Paris and Maksim Yakubov was looking forward to a straight run through the Kentish countryside. At the Immigration kiosk, he handed the uniformed border officer the Israeli passport. The officer swiped it into the computer. The name Menachim Fyodor Yakob came up on the screen alongside Yakubov's image. No alarm bells rang. The warnings index registered no warning. Yakubov hadn't expected there to be any problems. After all, the genuine Israeli passport hadn't come cheap. He had invested heavily in return for officially issued documentation. It had got him across Europe successfully and he had every expectation it would get him into the UK.

'How long will you stay in the UK, Mr Yakob?' the officer asked.

'Just a couple of days,' the driver smiled.

'And what's the purpose of your visit?'

'I'm going to the classic car auction at Sotheby's. Hoping to trade in this old jalopy for a better one.'

'It's a lovely motor, Sir. I'd love to own it myself, but I suspect it's well out of my price range. I'll need to see the car's paperwork, though. We have to check it's not stolen.'

Yakubov retrieved the papers from the glove compartment. The officer examined them, nodded and stamped the passport with a six-month tourist endorsement. Yakubov stuffed all the papers back into the glove compartment again. Waving the officer a cheery goodbye, Maksim Fyodorovych Yakubov continued on his way.

Chapter 58

Adrian Curtis glanced around the tastefully furnished lounge as Helena poured their coffee. He admired the neatness of the large, detached house in the leafy Surrey village. The décor was tasteful and feminine. No toys cluttered the lounge, and the absence of framed photographs of anyone other than her parents confirmed his suspicion that she had never married at all. It had been a long time since he had seen her wearing anything other than her business-like sombre separates and her colourful power jackets. Today, she wore casual trousers, a comfortable, baggy sweater and soft ballet pumps.

'Does Malcolm know you're visiting me?' she asked.

'No. He wouldn't be very happy if he knew we were still in contact.'

'And does he know your plans for Yakubov?'

'Good lord, no! I'm keeping him in the dark about that. I don't trust him further than I could throw him. He'll be told about it after we get Yakubov in custody.'

'I'd love to be there when you get him. God, how I miss the firm.'

'We miss you, too. Malcolm Donald's about the most arrogant and difficult man I've ever met, let alone worked with. It's outrageous that, because of his unaccountable time spent in Russia, he failed his security vetting, and yet the PM can put him in charge of national security. He's an absolute liability.'

'Can't you put something in his tea?' Helena jested.

'I'd love to, but he doesn't drink tea, or coffee. And no-one's ever seen him eat.'

'Does he cast a reflection when he passes a mirror?'

Adrian laughed. His face soon grew serious, though.

'I'm uneasy about his years spent in Russia. They've got a record of him at our Moscow embassy. He's on their register of

British businessmen, as some sort of self-employed technology consultant, but no-one there knows anything more about him. He didn't attend any embassy functions, didn't request any introductions to local trade councils, didn't even play golf with Prince Andrew. He's a bit of a mystery.'

'You'll get into trouble if he finds out you're keeping me in the loop.'

'He won't. But I don't care. We may no longer be colleagues, Helena, but we'll always be friends.'

'We will, Adrian, always. Now, are you able to tell me exactly what you've got planned for Yakubov?'

Cherry Baptiste answered the door to the caller at the massive red-bricked mansion.

'Mr Yakubov?' she smiled.

'Yes. Jordan is expecting me.'

'He's down at the garages, Sir. He thought you might like to have some photographs taken with him and some of his car collection. And he has some champagne on ice down there. It's at the opposite end of the estate. It's a bit of a walk, I'm afraid, but I'll take you down there.'

Yakubov smiled broadly at the prospect of appearing in yet more photos with the world-famous Jordan Wilde.

'Oh, well, let's take my car since it's just here.'

They climbed into the Sunbeam and drove around the house and down the long, tree-lined driveway until they came to a clutch of single-storey buildings. Dave Lloyd, resplendent in an authentic vintage chauffeur's uniform, was polishing the bonnet of an even more vintage Bugatti which was parked outside one of the garage blocks. He put down his duster and came forward to greet the guest.

'Good morning, Sir. Mr Wilde is inside awaiting you.'

Grinning like a Cheshire cat, Yakubov, switched off his engine and eagerly clambered out of the Sunbeam. Cherry followed him. Dave removed a remote control from his pocket and pointed it towards the nearest garage block. Slowly the large doors began to rise. Equally slowly, Yakubov's grin faded at the unexpected sight of the police van and half a dozen uniformed officers. There were National Crime Agency staff and plain clothed Special Branch officers in attendance, too. From amongst them, Kirpal stepped forward and took the car keys from Yakubov's trembling hand while a detective came forward to make the arrest and read Yakubov his rights. Also standing there, smiling broadly, was Corey Hart. In his hand were copies of the extradition papers signed by the Home Secretary. Jordan Wilde, however, was nowhere to be seen, and neither was the champagne, the photographer, nor the highly desirable Aston Martin.

As the police van disappeared up the driveway with its millionaire prisoner on board, a delighted Corey shook hands warmly with Dave and Cherry.

'Congratu-fucking-lations!' he exploded. 'Washington's over the moon about this. That sonofabitch took over a hundred million dollars from US companies over the last five years. And not just companies, but lots of regular little folks got ripped off by him. That little red car over there was probably bought with some poor guy's life savings. You Brits just made the arrest of the decade.'

'Not only that,' Dave chuckled, 'I got Jordan Wilde's autograph.'

'Where's Harry, though?' Corey asked. 'I thought he'd want to be in on this?'

'He's moving house this week.' Kirpal explained. 'He sold the flat he'd shared with Lorna. Too many memories. He's had a lot of sorting out and packing to do. It's been a bit of an emotional time for him.'

'Sure. He's had a real tough time of it. Send him my best, won't you? I'll catch up with him soon.'

Still smiling broadly, Corey climbed into his BMW and drove off.

Dave strolled over to check out the Sunbeam. Opening the glove compartment, he found the documents and took them out to examine them. Pocketing the Israeli passport, he put the paperwork relating to the car back into the glove compartment, and stepped back to admire the clean lines of the vehicle and its shiny red paintwork.

'I don't think we can leave this here, Kirpal,' he said.

'You're right. Wilde wouldn't thank us if anyone found out about his role in this. He wouldn't want more Russian criminals coming to his house.'

'We should get it away from here and store it somewhere out of sight till Yakubov gets out of prison.'

Kirpal shook his head.

'Yakubov won't *ever* get out of prison. The Americans will see to that.'

Kirpal took from his pocket another bunch of keys and looked at them for a second.

'You know, Dave, I have an idea.'

Chapter 59

Adrian had expected Malcolm Donald to be put out at not having been informed of Yakubov's arrest before it happened, but he had not anticipated the level of anger that the new Director General now displayed. Adrian found himself as mesmerised by Malcolm Donald's unkempt ginger hair as he had been by the Cabinet Office Secretary's red-veined nose. The DG's fury caused his cheeks to redden and, together with his carrot-hued locks, this gave him the appearance of a clown. Somehow, this image made him seem less formidable in Adrian's eyes, and, indeed, faintly ridiculous. The DG slammed the file down on his desk.

'You should have informed me about this. I should have been fully briefed. Why would you keep me in the dark about such a potentially important arrest? I'm Director General, for God's sake. Who the hell do you think you are?' he stormed.

Adrian remained calm.

'I'm the head of the Russia section, Counter-intelligence, Malcolm. My role is an operational one. Yours isn't. I run the operations. You run the organisation. And in this organisation, we operate on a need-to-know basis.'

'Are you saying you don't trust me?'

'Not at all. But, firstly, you don't have the appropriate security clearance to see some of the material in this case, and, secondly, I've never before been required to bother the DG with operational details. I'm sure you have loftier matters of administration and policy to concern yourself with rather than the everyday workings of my section.'

'The arrest of Russia's biggest cyber-criminal is hardly an everyday issue.'

'And you'll get the credit for it. You'll be the one to tell the PM and the JIC. You'll be announcing it to the press. And I expect you'll be the one who gets a gong in the New Year's honours list. Now, if you'll excuse me, I have to go and personally congratulate my team – *my* team.'

That evening, Adrian's friend and editor of *The Times*, Ronan Rogers, called at Adrian's house. Ronan said he had something important to disclose. Adrian poured them both a scotch.

'Adrian, I've had a visit from three Russian ladies. One of them was Nadia Lukova.'

'The wife of Ivan Lukov? The man who was poisoned with radium a few years back?'

'Yes. It was ten years ago now, but she's still waiting for the promised public enquiry to be held. I hadn't heard of the other two ladies with her, but they claim their husbands were also Russian defectors who, more recently, were assassinated in the UK on direct orders of the Kremlin.'

'What did they want?'

'Justice. They want the government to complete full investigations into their husband's deaths, to identify their killers and to publicly condemn them.'

'That's understandable.'

'Trouble is, Downing Street's press office says there's an embargo on the issue. The say the government is not prepared to release any information or statement as yet.'

'Ronan, you know I can't …'

'Oh, I know, and I wouldn't ask you to divulge anything. But I just wondered what happened to your report on Russian interference in the Brexit referendum. Did it include anything about these killings?'

Adrian sipped at his drink thoughtfully then took a deep breath.

'Well, it wasn't just *my* report. GCHQ and the other agencies all contributed to it. It went to the PM five months ago, but he says the government needs time to read and consider its contents.'

'Five months ago? Just how long is this report?'

'Fifty pages.'

Ronan's jaw dropped.

'Only fifty pages, and they can't manage to read ten pages a month? So, obviously they're supressing it. Any idea why?'

'Even if I had my suspicions, I couldn't say, could I? The main problem is that the report is now the property of the Intelligence and Security Committee of Parliament. However, that committee only exists for the life of a Parliament. When the PM prorogued Parliament in order to hold the election, the committee had to stand down. A new committee will be appointed by the PM, but none has been appointed yet. Until we have an ISC, the report cannot be published. Clearly, the PM's in no hurry to set up a new committee. But what do you intend to do about the Russian widows?'

'Oh, we'll give them their day in the limelight – a double page spread, interviews, photos of them and their children, the usual line, plus a challenge to the government to act. What I can't understand, though, is why the government were happy to acknowledge they'd commissioned your report but now they won't expedite its disclosure.'

'Well, that acknowledgement came from a different Prime Minister, didn't it? That PM resigned and the new boy's taking his own approach, isn't he?'

'So, what's changed since his predecessor's resignation? Why won't anyone come out and publicly condemn the Russians? Who's pulling Ivan Thompson's strings?'

'It's not for me to say, Ronan. The PM must be acting on advice, though – special advice from someone he trusts.'

Ronan looked over the rim of his glass at Adrian. He saw Adrian's mouth curl up slightly at the corner in a faintly mischievous smile.

'Oh, did I tell you our firm's got a new DG?' Adrian remarked casually. 'He used to be the PM's SPAD. He's spent a few years in Russia, though no-one seems to know what he was doing there.'

Ronan smiled. It was the smile of a newsman who sensed there was a good story to be had – one requiring a degree of journalistic investigation.

Adrian smiled, too.

'Are we still on to play golf on Saturday, by the way?'

Chapter 60

Harry watched the removal lorry head off down the road. On board were all his worldly possessions; his furniture, clothes, music collection and all sorts of memorabilia and photograph albums. Much of what remained of Lorna lay in those albums. He had taken most of her possessions to her mother's. He felt Mrs Bayliss had more right to them than he did. She had asked him to donate Lorna's clothes to a charity shop. He had chosen one of the children's charities and it was in that shop that an odd thing had happened. The volunteer, eager to see what was in the black bin liners he had brought, had immediately started pulling out the clothes to examine them.

'Looks like your mum was a well-dressed lady, Love,' she had said, as she spotted a couple of Lorna's smart work jackets. This had struck him as an inappropriate observation, intrusive even, but then it had occurred to him that it was a fair assumption to make that someone of his age would be disposing of the clothes of a dead parent, not those of his partner. He hadn't wanted to get into any explanations or to hang around whilst she expressed her sympathies, so he had simply agreed.

When his own mother had died, he hadn't been there to see the last vestiges of her existence being expunged from his quietly grieving father's life. All trace of her had gone by the time he had arrived home from boarding school for the funeral. He realised that, apart from seeing a few photographs of her, he had no recollection of how she had dressed. He just had a vague memory of the scent she used to wear. He could still envisage the attractive bottle which had sat on her dressing table. It was, he recalled, *Joy* by Patou.

Back in the empty flat, he walked slowly from room to room, remembering. He recalled how much delight they had taken in re-decorating the place to their taste. Lorna had painted the walls and doors and he had laid the laminate flooring and refitted the kitchen. The retired lady in the downstairs flat had come up to introduce herself but also to politely ask them to keep their music down. She had remarked how much nicer the flat would look when they had finished covering all the caramel-coloured walls with the nice white emulsion. They hadn't had the heart to tell her they were actually putting on the caramel-colour to soften the clinical white paint of the previous owner.

He remembered Dave Lloyd's account of how Godunov had entered the flat and snooped around. Harry was glad he hadn't been there at the time. It was an intense violation of his privacy. Of course, it wasn't the only way in which Godunov had spoiled the flat for Harry. Well, no use in thinking about that now. It was time for him to leave. There was little point in remaining and remembering. He needed to move on. Besides, he still had a few bits to clear out of the lock-up garage. He estimated he should be able to squeeze his toolbox and a few other odds and ends into the Mazda, so he locked the flat, drove around to the back of the terrace and parked up near the garage block. He took the bunch of keys out of his pocket. He had already labelled each key for the new owner of the flat and garage.

Bending down, he unlocked the up-and-over door and pulled it open. Surprised, he stood and stared uncomprehendingly at the sight before him. A shiny, red Alpine Sunbeam sat there, its keys in the ignition.

Chapter 61

Harry reached the top of the queue at Mario's and ordered a BLT and a Cappuccino.

'Morning. How's the Signora?' Mario asked.

Harry realised he hadn't been in the sandwich bar in a very long time. It was nice that Mario still recognised him and that he remembered Harry had come here regularly with Lorna, so regularly, that he had assumed Lorna was his wife. However, Mario wouldn't have heard what had happened to her. Once again, Harry didn't want to get into complicated explanations. He knew if he said Lorna was dead that Mario was bound to ask how, when and why, so he simply assured Mario that 'the Signora' was well.

'No bagel for her today?' Mario asked.

'She's dieting, I'm afraid,' Harry lied, realising that, no matter which way he played it, explaining away Lorna's absence would always be difficult. He thought he might not come here again. There were other sandwich bars in the area. It would be a pity, but it was the very least of the many changes Lorna's death had brought about. His whole life had changed. He knew that he, too, had changed.

He was now renting a flat. It was smaller than the one he had shared with Lorna but it was just somewhere to lay his head until he decided whether and where he would buy another property. The décor in the new flat wasn't really to his taste, and it certainly wouldn't have been to Lorna's, but it was different, and, therefore, it held no memories, happy or otherwise. As he strolled towards Thames House, clutching his sandwich and his coffee, he was deep in recollection, absorbed in his misfortune, and he was feeling rather sorry for himself.

A sudden loud bang echoed around the streets, dragging him sharply out of his contemplation. London was a place

241

characterised by sudden loud noises; car horns, car backfires and the slamming of delivery lorry doors, but this loud noise had been none of those. He hastened his pace and very soon heard the urgent wail of emergency sirens. Instinct made him stuff the sandwich into his pocket and break into a run. Passing a waste bin, he ditched the coffee, since the lid had come loose and it was splashing hot coffee over his hand as he ran.

As he turned the corner, he saw the smoke coming out of a ground floor window and the shattered glass spread out widely across the pavement. It was obvious there had been some sort of explosion within Thames House. He stopped short on the opposite side of the road just as staff began pouring out of the building. He looked up and down the street but there was no sign of anything or anyone who might have been responsible for the blast.

A police van was on the scene within minutes and two police officers began ushering people further away from the front of the building. Harry noticed that the police were armed and he reasoned they must be from one of the many tactical firearms teams that, nowadays, patrolled the city. Not long after, a fire engine arrived and firemen rushed into the building.

Harry spotted a worried-looking Adrian amongst the evacuated staff and hurried to his side.

'What happened?' Harry asked.

Adrian pointed to the broken, blackened window.

'A bomb, probably,' he said, 'in the post room.'

'Bloody hell! Was anyone in there?'

'Dunno. I'd better let the DG know. He hasn't arrived yet.'

Adrian punched a few numbers into his mobile phone while Harry watched the fire crew buzzing in and out of the building with various bits of equipment. Moments later, an ambulance arrived on the scene, too. Harry began to regret having ditched his coffee. The cold March wind which gusted up and down Millbank had a bitter edge to it. Soon, Adrian was off the phone.

242

'Islamic terrorists?' Harry asked.

'Unlikely. Postal bombs are not their style. More likely dissident Irish Republicans. The question of a united Ireland is being hotly debated at the moment. Never thought I'd see the return of their bombing campaign on the mainland, though.'

Soon, Dave and Carole arrived on the scene together. They quickly made their way over to Adrian and Harry.

'What happened?' Dave asked.

'Explosion in the mail room. Probably a bomb.' Adrian informed them.

As they stood, helplessly watching the first responders rushing around, they saw, to their extreme dismay, a casualty being stretchered out of the building by two paramedics. Adrian told his colleagues to stay put and he rushed across to the ambulance to try and establish who had been injured. He was back just seconds later.

'It's Johnston Freeman from the post room,' he announced.

'Oh no. Is he badly hurt?' Carole asked, clasping her hands to her cheeks.

'He's dead.'

Nobody spoke for a moment or two. They were all too shocked. Harry recalled how happy Johnston had been when looking forward to his trip to Jamaica; how disappointed he had been when drones over the runway had caused the holiday to be cancelled, and then how elated he had been when eventually, he had returned from that trip. In his mind's ear, he could still hear Johnston singing snatches from 'Jamaica Farewell' as he made his rounds of the offices, distributing the post.

'He has a disabled son,' Harry said at last.

'Bastards!' Carole exclaimed, and her face dissolved into tears.

Dave slipped a comforting arm around Carole's shoulders.

'Isn't all incoming mail screened for explosives?' he asked.

'Yes,' Adrian replied, 'that was Johnston's job.'

Harry had no stomach for attending yet another funeral, but he made himself go. Lorna would have insisted, he told himself. Everyone who knew Johnson was there at the church. It was a very emotional affair, made all the sadder by the presence of the teenage boy in the wheelchair and by all the keening women who stood protectively around him.

The powerful singing of the gospel choir, of which – only now they learned – Johnson had been a member, made the hair on the back of Harry's neck stand up. It was all too raw an experience for Harry. When he eventually reached the top of the queue of people who were waiting to shake the hand of Johnson's widow and to pay their respects, he found himself placing his trembling arms around the lady and hugging her tightly. She saw the tears in his eyes. She felt his pain, too, and she hugged him back.

Chapter 62

In the days that followed, there was much speculation in the press as to who had sent the bomb, but no individual or organisation claimed responsibility. The Security Service's new DG found himself attending his first JIC meeting at Thames House.

Sir Stuart Bridgeman welcomed their new committee member and immediately expressed the committee's condolences to Malcolm Donald on the tragic loss of a member of his staff.

'This is a most unfortunate incident to have occurred so early in your tenure as DG. Have you reached any conclusions as to who's responsible?'

'Not yet, Sir Stuart. But rest assured we are working on it with the greatest of urgency.'

'Have any new procedures been introduced to prevent a recurrence?' the chairman asked.

'I'm informed the procedures in place were considered adequate,' Malcolm reassured him. 'Our mail is scanned first by the local post office and then it goes through our own scanners at Thames House.'

'How was the bomb not detected, then?' Sir Robert Vanbrugge asked.

'It contained mainly plastic explosive in thin sheets and a minimal amount of metal wire, fashioned to look like paper clips when scanned. The forensic specialists are still working on it.'

Sir Arnold Mayhew looked sceptical.

'We at GCHQ have heard that the device used is believed to be Russian. Can you confirm that?'

'Well, I wouldn't like to confirm anything until we're absolutely positive, Sir Arnold.'

'But you are considering this to be a response to the arrest of that Russian cyber-criminal, aren't you?' Sir Arnold persisted.

'We're considering a number of possibilities,' Malcolm replied cagily.

'Well, let me share with you what... possibility ... SIS is considering,' Sir Robert Vanbrugge said, tersely. 'What we know, and I'm sure you do, too, Malcolm, is that Yakubov's father, Fyodor Yakubov, was a government scientist. He was ex-military and he was an explosives expert. Like all of Russia's bomb makers and nuclear scientists, he and his family lived in a smart enclave and he was better paid than many other Russians. That was to prevent the experts from defecting. When the Soviet Union collapsed, however, they lost their elite status and their big salaries, but they still had knowledge and skills they could sell to the highest bidder. So, back in the 'nineties, NATO arranged for them to be brought to England, to de Montfort University, where they were given the best tuition in English and in business and computing skills. They were given financial assistance to re-establish themselves back in Russia as successful internet entrepreneurs, so they could maintain their lavish lifestyles.'

Malcolm did not react or reply to Sir Robert's information, so the SIS DG continued.

'Every bomb maker leaves a signature in the way they construct a bomb. The forensics people at the National Crime Agency have identified the signature of this bomb. It was the same as that of a bomb used to blow up a Russian journalist in Greece a couple of years ago. It also matched that of some devices used recently in the Crimea. That signature is believed to be that of Fyodor Yakubov.'

The Security Service's new DG reddened and his lips tightened.

'Like I said, we're considering *all* possibilities.'

'Come now, Malcolm,' Sir Stuart urged, 'there's no need to be guarded in this room, you know. You can speak freely in this company. We're all signatories of the Official Secrets Act, after all, and, between us, we have decades of experience in intelligence. You can comfortably report all your findings and your suspicions to us. As you see, we can add our knowledge to the pot.'

But Malcolm looked far from comfortable with this suggestion.

'I'll be reporting my findings and suspicions firstly to the PM.'

Sir Henry Mortimer seemed taken aback to hear this. The Cabinet Office PS exchanged a look with Sir Arnold Mayhew before speaking.

'You will bear in mind that the PM is a political appointee, won't you? He isn't a career civil servant or soldier or diplomat. PMs of all political hues come and go. It is our role to act as an interface. We assess the intelligence and, based on our assessment, we give our best advice to the PM of the day.'

'Well, it's interesting that you should raise that point,' Malcolm bristled, 'since, unlike you, Sir Henry, I'm not a career civil servant myself. In fact, it's the PM's intention that a number of posts currently held by civil servants should be filled by outside experts like myself.'

'And who put that foolish notion in his head?' Sir Henry reacted.

'Actually, it was my idea,' Malcolm said.

After the meeting had wound up, Sir Henry drew Sir Robert and Sir Arnold aside.

'Bob, I have my doubts about the new boy. I'd be interested to learn more about his background. What does SIS know about him?'

'I share your doubts, Henry,' Sir Robert agreed. 'Heads of intelligence agencies are meant to be independent of politics. I do know that he was turned down for fast-track entry to the civil service.'

'Do we know why?' Sir Arnold Mayhew asked.

'Yes. Because of the time he spent in Russia, and the fact that we cannot verify what he did during his time there, he could not be security vetted.'

Sir Arnold appeared concerned.

'Gents, this reminds me of the last time it was proposed to put outsiders into civil service posts. Do you remember when they appointed a businessman to be high commissioner at one of the missions in Asia? The chap they chose was a native of that country originally. Quite a decent fellow, by all accounts, but it didn't end well.'

'Why?' Sir Henry asked, 'what happened?'

'The locals shot him.'

'Good God!'

'I remember that case,' Sir Robert added, 'Didn't he recover and they gave him a post as governor of some UK overseas territory?'

'Oh yes. That didn't end too well, either,' Sir Arnold said. 'He was ousted from that post after just a few months.'

'Did they shoot at him there as well?' Sir Henry asked.

Sir Arnold shook his head.

'No, he was recalled over some complaint or other. Not sure what happened.'

'I do remember the circumstances.' Sir Robert added. 'Some rebel Tory backbenchers had forced through an order in council requiring all British overseas tax haven territories to set up public registers of their investors. A lot of the Tory MPs weren't happy about it, mainly because many of them would appear on those registers. Locals in those territories weren't happy either. They feared they'd lose their tax-free status and investors would

248

take their money elsewhere. Their island's economy might suffer. The Governor was stuck between a rock and a hard place – trying to implement government policy whilst maintaining good relations with the local bigwigs. Those local bigwigs, and even some of his own staff, lodged a few complaints about the Governor. That got him withdrawn.'

Sir Arnold was thoughtful.

'You see, there are any number of good reasons why civil service posts should be held by civil servants. Not least of those is our impartiality enforced by the civil service rules which govern us. I must admit, though, that this has given me an idea. Those public registers are open to scrutiny, aren't they? I wonder how Helena is getting on. I must give her a call.'

Chapter 63

Adrian was pleased to find himself back at Helena's house. This time it was for lunch. He had forgotten what a good cook she was. It had been some years since they had shared a kitchen – and much more besides. The fact that she now wore comfortable casual clothes, instead of her usual business jackets, whenever they met, made him feel more relaxed. He did find himself wondering, though, why he had been invited.

After they had eaten and he settled himself into one of the comfortable armchairs in her lounge, Helena handed him a large manilla envelope.

'Have a look at these papers whilst I make us some coffee,' she smiled.

He was puzzled but her face gave away nothing. He opened the envelope and removed the documents it contained. There were bank statements, share certificates, photocopied correspondence, official travel itineraries from Downing Street and transcripts of telephone conversations. It didn't make sense until he recognised the name of the account holder and the locations of the accounts. By the time Helena had returned and poured him a cup of coffee, the significance of the documents was clear to him.

'Bloody hell, Helena! Where did you get these?' he gasped.

'The signals intelligence is from our friends out west, of course. The rest is from Vauxhall Cross. It's marked 'Security Service DG Eyes Only', but, for obvious reasons, those agencies didn't want it to go to Malcolm Donald. You appreciate the significance of this?'

'I certainly do, but I'll need to get my head around it.'

'Take all the time you want. Take the documents away with you. I can't act on them, obviously. In any case, I'm heading off to Canada soon. Now that I've lots of time on my hands, I'm going to take one of their magnificent coast-to-coast rail trips.'

The next morning, Adrian called Harry into his office. As Harry entered, Adrian signalled to him to close the door.

'What is it, boss?'

'I have an unusual task for you – and only for you. You're to mention this to no-one.'

'Oh yes?'

'How are your letter-writing skills?'

'Quite good, I think. Why?'

'I want you to resurrect WOTAK.'

Chapter 64

Sir Henry found himself enjoying yet another free lunch. This time, however, it was at a different, private men's club. With membership fees of £1,500, *The Hereford Club* was one of the more expensive, and therefore more exclusive, clubs. Unsurprisingly, it boasted the Prime Minister, Ivan Thompson, as a member. It also offered small, private dining rooms where sensitive business might be conducted, and it was into one of these small rooms that Henry was ushered. Unlike the late Culture Minister, the Prime Minister could not wait until after they had eaten to seek a favour from Sir Henry.

'Henry, I need your help in your capacity as a member of the JIC. I need information on someone who might be known to MI5.'

'Oh? But, surely, you have your own man inside the Security Service. Can't Malcolm Donald assist you?'

'No. At least, I …, well, I wouldn't want to compromise his position, especially as he hasn't been in the job very long.'

'Well, you put him there. He must owe you.'

'I'm asking *you*, though, Henry. I'm sure that, wearing your other hat, as chief exec of the Civil Service, you'll have an idea of some favours I could do for you in return.'

'I'm sure I could think of a few. Okay, then, what is it?'

The PM put down his napkin, sat back in his chair and drew a deep breath.

'I need you to find out if Thames House have any knowledge of a character who calls himself WOTAK.'

'Oh, I can answer that one myself.'

'Can you?' the PM looked hopeful.

'WOTAK is a Russian. He's an enforcer for the Kremlin. He usually targets people in high places. In some cases, the Kremlin was responsible for them being in those high places in the first place. WOTAK hoovers up the dirt on them and blackmails them. He extorts money for himself and useful information for the Kremlin. He's a really nasty piece of work, an ex-military thug. He's killed quite a few people. He's well versed in the art of torture, too. He even had the audacity to torture and murder one of Thames House's operational intelligence officers – a young woman. He's believed to be a serious psychopath.'

The PM blanched visibly at Sir Henry's words. The Permanent Secretary pressed home his advantage.

'So, Ivan, I take it he's blackmailing you, now. Let's see, would he be threatening to expose you over the personal funding and other favours you get from the Russians, and the promises you've made them in return for getting you elected? Or perhaps he's found out about the means by which you've kept your offshore tax-free investments out of any public registers. Or is it your extra-marital affairs …?'

'How the hell did you …?' the PM interrupted.

He looked quite sick for a moment, but he quickly regained his composure.

'Look, Henry. You can see why I don't want Malcolm Donald in on this. Damnit, the bugger's only been there five minutes but he's already writing his memoirs. I can't trust him. But I believe I can trust you, Henry. I need this WOTAK taken out. Can you arrange that? Will you? Please?'

'I'll do my best. Now, are we having pudding, or should we go straight to the brandy?'

'I'm afraid I've quite lost my appetite.'

'Brandies it is, then. Will you summon the steward?'

The PM leaned over to the wall by the window and pressed the bell-push.

'Now then, Ivan,' Sir Henry smiled, 'we'll stop all this nonsense of putting your people into senior civil service posts, shall we? And you can sack Malcolm Donald and reinstate Helena Fairbrother, too. That'll do for starters. And then, I'm thinking, increasing the powers and the funding of the intelligence agencies would be a good move. What do you think?'

Relieved but noticeably deflated, the PM nodded. Sir Henry sat back, replete and grinning.

'Leave it to me, old boy. You do your bit, and I'll see to it that this WOTAK is hunted down and eliminated – for good.'

ABOUT THE AUTHOR

Retired Civil Servant, Denise Beddows has a background in research, investigation and intelligence analysis. Her career has taken her to work in a number of countries across several continents. She writes – as Denise Beddows – true crime, and – as DJ Kelly – local history and biographical fiction. This is her first spy thriller. A member of the *Society of Authors* and the *Society of Women Writers & Journalists*, she regularly contributes articles to local, national and international press and journals. She reviews books and films for publishers and journals, and is a volunteer researcher for several local history groups. A trained and experienced public speaker, she regularly gives talks on different topics to a variety of community groups and at literary festivals. She is married, with one grown-up daughter. She and her husband live in Buckinghamshire.

Also by this author:

NON-FICTION:

**Bulstrode: Splendour and Scandals
of a Buckinghamshire Mansion**
by DJ Kelly
The beautiful Gerrards Cross estate of Bulstrode, once a hilltop refuge for early man, has been home to medieval Knights Templar; cruel and corrupt judges; blue bloods and blue stockings; a nobleman who twice served as British Prime Minister; ancestors of a US President's wife; the richest woman in England, the most beautiful woman in England; the most scandalous woman in England, and the illegitimate daughter of an early and a gypsy girl who inspired George Bernard Shaw and Hollywood.

'A well-researched and readable look at the often-colourful people connected with Bulstrode over the centuries, with surprising links and tragedy never far away.'
– Michael Rice, President Hedgerley Historical Society

*****

Odd Man Out – A Motiveless Murder?
by Denise Beddows
The true and tragic story of transgendered bus conductress Margaret 'Bill' Allen who, despite desperate campaigning by loving friend Annie, was hanged for the 1948 murder in Rawtenstall, Lancashire, of Nancy Chadwick, an eccentric old woman whom Bill barely knew. Did she do it? If so, why did she do it? If not, who did it? The author uncovers evidence which was suppressed at the time, questions the death sentence and

asks whether society's treatment of Bill would be very much different today.

'... a vivid picture of post-war Rawtenstall and of the difficult lives of three women – a murder victim, her killer and the killer's lover ... an exceptionally well researched account of a true crime and a sensitive exploration of the difficult life and brutal death of this transgendered woman whom history has forgotten.' – Murder Monthly
*****

The Cheetham Hill Murder – A Convenient Killing?
By Denise Beddows
One hot July afternoon in 1933 saw Frances Levin brutally and fatally attacked in her own home in one of Manchester's affluent districts. A recent BBC TV programme revealed that the man hanged for the killing could not have done it. The Author uncovers police corruption, malpractice and suppression of crucial evidence, and reveals a more likely motive and an obvious suspect who was never investigated.

'An old murder case is re-visited in this highly readable book ... a shameful miscarriage of justice is explored and fresh research brings up fresh motives and fresh suspects. The author's conclusions are indeed persuasive' – Bloggs on True Crime
*****

Buckinghamshire Spies and Subversives
by DJ Kelly
Buckinghamshire has a 600-year history of subversion, sedition and espionage. The county has been home to radical plotters, heretic hunters, agents provocateurs and informers. Two world wars brought spies, secret agents and saboteurs to the

county. Many of our stately homes housed wartime code-breakers, eavesdroppers, boffins, intelligence chiefs and even Nazi officers. A surprising number of women spies were incarcerated in the county's gaol and the first use by police of covert surveillance photography was against local women.

'First class and utterly absorbing. Informative, sensitive and revealing. An excellent contribution to the history of British Intelligence and its development through the ages.' – Mark Birdsall, Editor, Eye Spy Magazine.

'A different perspective on a surprisingly large amount of Bucks history ... offers a fascinating insight into people and events our ancestors' lives may have been affected by – whether or not they were aware of it.' – Buckinghamshire Family History Society
*****

The Chalfonts and Gerrards Cross at War
by DJ Kelly
Exploring the ways in which conflict throughout the ages – including two world wars – has affected the people, the way of life and even the landscape of these beautiful villages.

'Especially useful for the family historian ... provides a poignant and insightful exploration of the impact of war on people and places' – Buckinghamshire Family History Society
*****

The Famous and Infamous of the Chalfonts & District
by DJ Kelly

The beautiful villages of the Chalfonts, Gerrards Cross, Denham, Fulmer and Hedgerley have long attracted people to settle. A surprising number of the area's residents have been famous. A few, however, have been downright infamous.

'An exceptionally well researched book and a fascinating read' – Councillor Linda Smith, Chairman, Chalfont St Peter Parish Council

FICTION:

A Wistful Eye – The Tragedy of a Titanic Shipwright
by DJ Kelly
A novel based on the true story of the murder of the author's great grandmother Belle, and of the role played by her great grandfather, William Henry Kelly, in building the iconic liner Titanic.

'A fascinating and thoroughly enjoyable read' – Historical Novel Society
'A mighty fine achievement' – Family Tree Magazine
'Highly recommended' – The Belfast Titanic Society
'A captivating read' – Ulster Tatler Magazine
*****

Running with Crows – The Life and Death of a Black and Tan
by DJ Kelly
A novel based on the true, but hitherto untold, story of William Mitchell, the only member of the British Crown Forces

259

to be executed for murder during the Irish War of Independence. Was this, in fact, a tragic miscarriage of justice?

'An absolutely fascinating read' – Irish Evening Herald
'I heartily recommend this book' – West Wicklow Historical Society
'An excellent and well researched book' – Royal Irish Constabulary forum

All are available from Amazon or from all good book shops

L - #0103 - 120220 - C0 - 210/148/14 - PB - DID2766515